TO THE

CENTER

OF THE

EARTH

GREIG BECK

SEVERED PRESS
HOBART TASMANIA

TO THE CENTER OF THE EARTH

*"Reality provides us with facts so romantic
that imagination itself could add nothing to them"*
— Jules Verne

"I declare the earth is hollow, habitable within, and that it can be reached via deep caverns hidden about the world. I pledge my life to this truth and I am ready to prove my theory true." Arkady Saknussov, philosopher, alchemist, and explorer, Russia, 1485

EPISODE 01

"It is only when you suffer that you really understand"

— Jules Verne

PROLOGUE

1973—Krubera Cave, Western Caucasus, former Soviet Union.

Deep down in the labyrinths, miles below the surface, Lana came to a fork in the cave she had been following. Both tunnels could lead up and out, or only one, or neither.

Please help me, she whimpered.

They were after her, and she knew it. When she had lost her sister, Katya, for one horrible second, she had hoped that they went after her sibling and not her. Now she knew that merciless thought was bouncing back at her, and bad karma was going to bite her—literally.

She chose the tunnel to the left and ran on. Her glow stones were small, grabbed in haste, and so would soon lose their luminescence. Already they were a dull blue now. Lana knew she had only another few hours of light left.

Then what?

She slowed as her tunnel narrowed and the ceiling lowered. In another 10 minutes, it constricted even more and began to feel a little like a throat getting ready to swallow her whole.

Lana sobbed and scurried on, but then in the next few hundred yards, she found she had to get down on her knees and crawl. She scraped her shin on a jagged extrusion but ignored it and kept going.

Her stone was lighting only a few feet around her, and in the next few minutes, what she prayed against happened—her cave ended in a tiny cul-de-sac where the passage had collapsed perhaps thousands of years ago.

She placed her hands against the wall and futilely felt along the ancient stones for any crack or weakness. Finally, she turned and sat with her back to the cold rock.

Could I backtrack? she wondered. *Possibly. Could I do it in the dark when my light fails me?* Unlikely, she knew, especially with the things out there that could see in that terrifying blackness when she couldn't.

Lana's eyes stung and her heart hammered. She was so tired that she felt nauseous. She crawled forward and pulled some of the loose debris from an ancient rockfall into a pile and then set about building a wall over the narrow mouth of her small cul-de-sac. In 10 minutes, she was wedging a last stone in at the top.

Her light was barely illuminating her tiny enclosure now and she sat back, covered it over, and closed her eyes. *Just give me a few minutes rest, please Lord, and then I can think clearly.* Lana's breathing began to slow, and her hammering heart slowed its gallop as her mind drifted.

The secret path to the center of the Earth was supposed to have been a myth, and no one really believed Georgy when he said he could lead them there, to a place of wonders. But it wasn't a myth, it was true, and the things that they found there were more horrifying than she and her lost team could ever have imagined.

The sound of a rock falling out of her wall immediately jolted her to full alert. She reached up to fumble her glow stone back out and held it forward.

From behind the hole made from the falling rock was movement. She smelled and heard the thing before she saw it—pungent, like bad sweat, and shit, and dead meat.

There came snuffling and low grunts, and then she saw the totally white and bulbous eye pressed to the hole. They'd found her.

Lana screamed as her rock wall tumbled inward.

CHAPTER 01

**1972—Krubera Cave, Western Caucasus, former Soviet Union
One Year Earlier**

The five cavers sat around sipping coffee made on their tiny portable kerosene stoves. It had taken them over 100 hours—nearly four days—to reach the 6,250-foot point in the world's deepest cave. And this last day would see them touch bottom, at 7,208 feet.

"Getting warmer," Dmitry Bukin said while staring straight ahead.

Katya Babikov nodded and turned to him. She noticed he looked haunted; they all did. In a world of eternal night, sleep patterns got disrupted, and any sleep that was achieved was never deep but fitful. They'd been descending, squeezing, slithering, and dropping down chutes for sometimes eighteen hours a day, and it felt like they'd been inside the cave for over a month.

"Be thankful we're not in the Sahara Desert or over a geothermal site. Some caves heat up one degree every 100 feet you descend. By now, where we are would be hot enough to cook us alive," Katya said.

"So why is it only getting warmer just now?" Alexi Domnin, their youngest member, and an IT worker by profession, asked. He turned to her. "Geothermal, after all?"

"This area is old, very old—billions of years old, in fact—so the likelihood of geothermal activity is negligible." Georgy Azarov grinned. "Maybe Hell is just around the corner after all."

Katya's sister, Lana, scoffed softly. "For some reason, that thought seems far creepier when you're down in a place like this." She lifted her chin. "You do know the other name for the Krubera Cave is the Devil's doorway, *da?*"

"Yeah, yeah, and there has been devil's doorways, devil's triangles, devil's mountains, and hundreds of other places deemed evil all around the world. The devil must get sick of all the traffic." Georgy drained his coffee. "But today, we ascend to Heaven. Just like the ancient Mayans thought."

"Or at least to a basement sump line." Katya also finished her coffee, wiped out her mug, and packed it and her kerosene stove away. She pulled out her notebook and made some quick notations.

She paused in her writing. "Do you think it is true, Georgy? Already we are deeper than anyone has descended, ever."

"Arkady Saknussov's notes have been true so far. They cost me a fortune, but now I say: well worth it." Georgy half-smiled. "He wrote that this was the way to find the new opening."

Katya smiled as she listened. She loved the way Georgy's eyes lit up when he spoke of the 15th-century explorer, scholar, and alchemist, and knew that a child's enthusiasm burned within him. He had expended decades, plus half his life savings in pursuit of the ancient Russian's notes. And she bet he would do it all again tomorrow.

But then luck had smiled on Georgy only a few years back when he had heard that a certain unique manuscript was appearing at a rare book auction in Moscow. The sellers thought it a work of fiction, but Georgy recognized it as Saknussov's meticulous research into locating a passage to the interior of the Earth.

Georgy had paid a king's ransom to win the book, and Katya had bet he would have gone even higher if need be. None of them really believed Georgy when he had spoken of what he had read. But so far, he had been right. Or rather, Saknussov had.

"He said it was beyond the lake." Georgy got to his feet. "Like I told you, I believe he meant some sort of sump line."

Katya nodded. A sump in caving terms was a passage that was submerged under water. Most times, they were static sink points where water had percolated down over the years. But sometimes they had a through-flow and were connected to underwater streams or sunken passages. And on rare occasions, they drained and refilled without reason— one day they were there, and the next, not.

"Yep, and here's to being the first ones to really cave dive here," Georgy replied with a grin.

Katya shrugged. "Second, actually."

"I said, *really*, dive there." He raised sweat-slicked eyebrows. "Saknussov never planned on diving. Maybe he did, but what diving gear did they have 500 years ago, *hmm*?"

She chuckled. "You're right. I think we've got a shot of finding something really special."

Georgy dusted himself off. "Okay, children of the permanent night, let's press on."

Katya groaned as she came upright. Though she was a committed caver, after so many days in complete darkness, she missed the sunlight. They had at least another 20 hours of work to do—they needed to navigate the last caves as they began to shrink at choke points that then opened out to cathedral-sized vaults and dropped into some chutes that fell away a hundred feet straight down. They couldn't afford to get sloppy for even a second no matter how fatigued they got, as a broken bone at this level could mean a fast death, or the onset of uncontrollable infection, and then a slow death.

In good time, the group finally wriggled through the last snake-hole on their bellies. They pushed their small air tanks ahead of them and dragged their kits behind them tied to their waists with soft rope.

Georgy stood, dropped his gear, and walked to the edge of a pool of water no more than 50 feet across that was so still it could have been a sheet of glass.

"No one has been in here for many centuries." He crouched beside the water and briefly searched a small pack on his waist, pulling free a thermometer. He carefully dropped it in and watched it for a few seconds before removing it. "81 degrees." He turned and grinned. "Anyone for a warm bath?"

"It's so small. Will we all fit?" Lana asked with hands on her slim hips.

Georgy chuckled softly. "It looks it from here. But I bet there will be shelves of stone which the pool extends under, and therefore should be larger beneath the surface." He stared into the pristine cave water. "I think it's only about six feet deep, and as long as we don't stir up the silt, it should remain crystal clear."

Katya opened her pack. "We'll still need the suits in case there's any thermoclines. Swim into one of those, and you'll shock as your muscles cramp when you go from warm to icy water. So let's suit up, people."

It took the group took just 10 minutes to pull on their wetsuits and check their breathing equipment. The group didn't have swim fins, as they didn't expect to be doing all that much swimming, and some things needed to be compromised on for the sake of keeping their caving kits small.

Katya lumped her clothing and pack with everyone else's up against a cave wall and returned with her hand-held lamp. She did a quick check of her diving mask and snorkel and also ensured the watertight seals of her bags were closed tight. All of them would do the same.

As she waited for the others to finish up, her feet and calves tingled. She frowned and looked about. All around them the air became misty, and for a few seconds, she was confused about whether it was just her fatigued eyes playing tricks, or…

Shit.

"Tremor!" she yelled.

The one word said underground that was the equivalent of yelling "shark" when you were swimming in the ocean.

Everyone swung toward her and froze, waiting.

The dust kept on gently raining down, and the vibrations continued to tickle her legs. There was nothing they could do, nowhere they could go, and so they just froze and prayed.

The first real jolt sounded like approaching thunder as it rippled past their cave. Then there came a second sound like cracking ice, deep, but then moving to be all around them.

Katya knew the geology in the area was phenomenally old, and therefore stable. But that didn't mean they never had ground shakes. Above them on the surface the tremors might have been little more than a shimmy. But nearly 7,000 feet down, they could be catastrophic.

Immediately, silence fell, and the movement in the rocks faded away.

"Was that it?" Dmitry whispered as his flashlight beam danced over the cave ceiling.

Alexi snorted. "Maybe the military have decided to ground test their nukes."

"That's a comforting thought," Lana whispered. "Should we extract?"

Georgy turned to her. "Even if we did right now, it'd take us nearly a week to climb out. We're here now so why don't we just see if...?"

The ground jolted to the left, hard, then to the right so violently it threw them all to the ground. Dust and debris rained down, and then huge rocks shaken free crashed somewhere in the cave. All around them, it sounded like mill stones grinding together.

"*Cave in!*" Katya yelled over the top of the maelstrom.

She crouched and held her hands over her head, but there was nowhere to go, and if they were unlucky enough to be under a falling boulder or the entire ceiling fell in, they'd be like squashed bugs, and perhaps just something interesting for future paleontologists to dig up in the millennia ahead.

With another shudder and moan, the ground shake was shut off as quickly as it began. The group stayed down, some keeping their eyes squeezed shut. Katya slowly looked up. The dark air of the cave was filled with dust smoke, and rocks still tumbled, some bouncing away in the darkness.

She spat grit and shone her light upward to ensure the cave roof wasn't hanging just inches above her.

"Is everyone okay?" she asked. She crawled over to find her sister.

Light beams crisscrossed in the darkness.

"Sound off," Georgy demanded.

6

"I'm okay," Dmitry replied.

"I'm good," Katya said. "And Lana is with me and okay as well."

"Alexi?" Georgy asked.

A cough and groan from the dust-filled darkness. "Bit banged up. Got hit. Just need to get this debris off," the young man replied.

"I'm coming." Katya crawled toward his light.

She found him and pushed rocks off his legs. He immediately sat forward to grab one and exhaled through clenched teeth as he pressed the limb, feeling it all over.

"Hurts, but don't think it's broken." He winced. "No high-jump competitions for a while."

"He's fine," Katya said over her shoulder.

"Hey, I *am* a little bit hurt," he insisted.

"Don't be a baby," she said, helping him up.

The young caver hopped for a moment, before gingerly putting his foot down to test it.

"Yeah, okay, not too bad."

"Hey, where's our lake gone?" Georgy scoffed.

The group joined him at where the sump pool was situated. But there was nothing now.

"Holy shit, it drained," Dmitry said.

Georgy carefully walked down into the empty sump basin, shining his light back and forth.

Katya held her light on him from up at the lip. "We should leave now. We were lucky, but if there's another tremor, we might get trapped."

"We might already be trapped, somewhere in those thousands of feet of tunnels, chokes, and chutes above us." Georgy half-turned. "Katya, we're already here now. We've got to make the most of it as we may never be back."

Dmitry had joined him in the emptied basin and had wandered over into the far corner and crouched under a shelf of stone. "Hey hey, I think I've found why the sump drained." He shuffled in further. "There's a new cavern opened up."

The group crowded over, and then crawled in under the lip of stone. Georgy pointed his flashlight into the dark-on-dark void and moved it around.

"Feel it?" He held a hand up flat. "There's a warm breeze blowing up from down there."

Lana added her light. "Look there. Is that writing?"

All the lights swung to where she pointed.

"I don't think so. How could it be?" Georgy looked over his shoulder. "Alexi, give me a clap test."

Alexi squeezed down low and into the new cave. He turned around and put his finger to his lips to quiet them, and then turned back. He clapped once, loudly, and waited.

The speed of sound was around 1,100 feet per second, and given the sound waves needed to strike something and then come back, it was a two-way trip.

Alexi finally heard his echo and turned, grinning. "Six seconds—about 3,000 feet. It's big, and ever-lovin' deep." He grinned. "All virgin passageway."

"Magnificent. And the best thing is it goes down." Georgy smiled, his teeth showing white within the sweat and grime on his face. "Ladies and gentlemen, we are about to set a new depth record, globally."

"Names up in lights," Alexi added.

"Wait, you want to go in?" Katya asked. "Right after an earth tremor?"

"Damned right I do. This is exactly what Arkady Saknussov said we would find." Georgy turned. "Who's with me?"

"Like you said, we're already here." Dmitry nodded. "So, I'm in."

The rest of the group also voted to enter the new cave system. Katya had reservations about the new chamber's stability, but either she went with them or she was going to be the poor sap left behind to mind the gear.

She shrugged and snapped shut her leather notebook. "Fine, let's do it."

Georgy turned to face the new cave. "Into the wild black yonder."

He led them in.

*****

Lana and Katya ran hard, but in opposite directions.

Katya fell to the floor of the cave, skidded for a few feet, and managed to skin her naked knees. Most of her clothing had long torn or rotted away, and she ignored the new wounds as they just added to all the other scar tissue she had accumulated over the weeks, months, or however long she had been down here.

She scrambled to her feet and sprinted again, tears of panic blurring her vision.

Georgy was gone, as well as Dmitry and Alexi, and Lana had simply run blindly off into the darkness.

She held up the phosphorescent stone that glowed blue in her hand and illuminated the stygian darkness ahead of her. She knew if she could just make it back to the opening of the new chamber, she might be okay. Maybe they wouldn't follow her. Maybe.

In another hour, she found the first marks they had made on their way down. Then, in another few hours, she arrived at the hole into the drained sump pool and she began to weep with joy at finding the exit.

Katya clambered up to the piles of gear, now covered in a layer of cave dust. She quickly ripped open bags and stuffed batteries, water bottles, and food sticks into a single pack.

She froze at a noise behind her. *It could be Lana*, she thought. She was the only other one of them who didn't get killed by...

What the hell were they? Her mind screamed the question but refused to even try and form an answer.

Katya dry swallowed. Maybe she should wait for her sister. Maybe she should load up on supplies and go back in after her.

Tears of indecision and frustration blurred her vision and she quickly wiped them with her grimy forearm. Another noise like grunting and then a low moan emanated from the bowels of the dark cave.

I'm so sorry, Lana, she mouthed, and then turned to run. It would take her days to climb out, but she wouldn't stop, wouldn't sleep, until she saw daylight again.

CHAPTER 02

Huntsville Grand Ballroom, Alabama, USA—Today

Jane Baxter clapped politely and squirmed in her seat as she tried to extract a little more comfort from the borrowed dress she wore. She was 30 years old, slim, and with gym-toned muscles. But they seemed no match for dress seams that felt like they were sewn through with iron cable and metal rivets.

But she looked hot, and she drew a lot of admiring glances so she was happy to suffer for her fashion. Jane and her "grotto"—the name given to smaller groups belonging to the National Speleological Society—had a table at the National Winter Ball held this year at the big Huntsville Ballroom in Alabama.

She put her hand over her glass when Andy offered her more champagne, and then she sat back and smiled, feeling good as the green flecks of light from the overhead laser-ball rotated slowly as the speeches were ending and the special announcements were about to commence.

Her friends were all from Charlotte, North Carolina and shared a passion for caving, hence their membership in the society and their gathering here tonight. By day, they were mostly nine-to-fivers, but come weekends and vacation time, they were committed to finding and dropping into the deepest caves they could find.

Jane was a high school biology teacher, and she looked around the table at each of her friends. Next to her on the left was Angela, who owned a sports store and was already rosy-cheeked from too much wine and laughing way too loud. She was always fun to be with and was like a little sister to her.

Next to her was Michael "Mike" Monroe. He ran a successful security firm, was the oldest at 38, athletic, and had high cheekbones undoubtedly inherited from his Russian mother. He listened to the speeches with one side of his mouth quirked up in a permanent ironic smile. He was their unelected grotto leader, maybe only through the force of his personality, intellect, and his sense of humor. When Michael spoke, people listened.

Next was David Sholtzen, here with his wife—he a doctor and she an accountant—and the pair spent most of the evening bickering, as always, like a pair of lovebirds constantly pecking and talking over the top of each other.

Ronald "Ronnie" Schwartz, the lawyer, who was giving his mobile phone his full attention, and next to him was Andy and his date. The guy was a great caver, only 23, and as for work, he was "between engagements," as he called it. But coming from a wealthy family, he probably didn't have to make his mind up too soon on a life's career. He said his date was 21, although she didn't look old enough to order a drink, but she laughed at everything Andy said and seemed happy to just be in his company.

The event was packed with a good crowd of 400 members that night, and as the MC rounded off the first tranche of speeches, backslapping at tales of new caves found and new frontiers achieved, he got to the final piece of news—the competition. He walked forward and cleared his throat.

"Bring it on." Andy sat forward and Jane turned to see Michael flick his eyebrows up at her.

One of their wealthy members had donated a cash prize of $1,000,000 for the deepest cave descent before the end of the year. It was called, "The Hollow Earth Challenge," a joke about the old belief that the world had a hollow center, or alternatively, all deep caves led to Hell.

Michael, who always had his ear to the ground, had heard about the competition long before anyone else and had worked to arrange passports and travel information to his desired target.

She had never seen him so electrified. Maybe because he had a personal interest in that he was a true believer in the Hollow Earth concept. He would talk at great length about the seismic waves passing through the planet and what their distortion really tells us.

Jane had often wondered whether it was just his quirky sense of humor working, but she had seen him frustrate too many geologists with his facts and theories to know it was not just his imagination at work. He really believed it.

Michael had done his homework and knew that there was a cave in the former Soviet Union, called the Krubera Cave, that was said to be the world's deepest. No one was allowed near it anymore, as it has been closed to the public for decades for reasons unknown.

But Michael said he knew why and had contacts and a lead. If the competition was confirmed, they were locked and loaded and ready to leave the next day.

The group listened intently and Andy held up his hands with fingers crossed on both. His girlfriend giggled and grabbed his arm.

The competition would be fierce and the bragging rights alone were attractive. Plus, the money would be more than just icing on the cake.

The MC said the words: *One. Million. Dollars*, and David finally stopped bickering with his wife to fist pump the air. "*Yes*." He grinned, and his wife kissed his cheek, proving that the quarreling was probably just part of their usual evening ritual.

A fellow caver wandered over to their table and leaned over Angela, placing his hand on her shoulder.

Angela looked up and gave the man a flat smile. "Harry."

Jane groaned. Harry Wenton was the dashing English hero of the caving scene. He was from an incredibly wealthy family who had an estate in Bristol, and though he really did have an impressive list of spelunking drops to his credit, his main notoriety was that of a local Don Juan who tried to date every single—and some not so single—women he could get close to.

Though a professional in most senses of the word, he was not popular because of his overuse of explosives to widen caves. It meant he had been responsible for finding numerous deep caves but had also collapsed many existing caves. He knew how to use dynamite; he just wasn't very good at it.

Plus, he was the only caver to take a handgun with him—a small and compact 9mm Beretta Storm. The reason was he had once emerged from a cave in the Indonesian wilds to discover a band of pirates waiting for them. They'd robbed everyone of everything from their equipment to their boots, plus knocked the teeth from the mouth of one of Harry's friends. Ever since then, Harry had wanted to be ready for anything. Now he was.

He and Angela had dated for a few weeks until Harry had simply dropped her for the next pretty young thing that caught his eye. He had once tried to date Jane, but she treated him with the disdain he deserved, and Harry had simply sniffed with indifference and moved on.

"Taking up the challenge, Michael?" Harry Wenton's eyebrows rose.

Michael half-shrugged. "Maybe. Not a great time of year to organize a trip to the caving areas. Still snow in the Appalachians."

Harry grinned. "Oh, I agree." He sipped his champagne, a smirk in his eye. "If you're only referring to the local ones, right? But to even qualify as being serious about the challenge, you've got to get below 5,000 feet." He tapped his chin. "Let me see, where would *I* go? Hmm, there's the Reseau Jean Bernard system, as well as the Gouffre Mirolda caves in France that'll get you there, as both are over 5,200 feet deep."

Harry seemed to think for a moment more. "Mustn't forget the

Lamprechtsofen Vogelschacht Weg Schact in Austria at 5,354 feet, and then there's the Illyuzia-Meshonnogo-Snezhnaya in Georgia that's 5,751 feet deep."

He went to turn away, but then paused. "Oh yeah, Georgia. That's right, there's also that other one in Georgia whose name escapes my mind that's around a whopping 7,200 feet deep." He lifted his chin. "Any ideas?"

Michael kept his poker face and shook his head slowly.

"Doesn't matter. Anyway, ladies and gentlemen, may the best team win." Harry winked, gave Angela's shoulder a parting squeeze, and moved to the next table.

Angela stuck her tongue out. "Creep."

"Do you think he knows? About the Krubera Cave?" David asked.

"About the cave? Yes. About our trip? Unlikely," Michael said, and then, "but who cares if he does? Even if he makes it all the way to the bottom, I know of someone who found a way to get deeper."

Andy frowned. "Deeper than 7,200 feet? But that's the absolute basement, isn't it?"

"Only the known one." Michael smiled confidently.

"That'd be cool if true. Even if it's just to see the look on Harry Wenton's face when he loses." Jane turned to him. "So what now?"

"Tomorrow, we meet for a planning session. I have something to show you that will blow your minds. Plus bag us that million dollars."

"I'm in." Andy rubbed his hands together, and his girlfriend leaned into him, hugging his chest like a limpet.

Everyone agreed, and Jane beamed. "Then Denny's it is for coffee and pie at 9 sharp."

*****

Next morning, Jane, David, and Ronnie bustled into the back booth at their local coffee shop. Michael and Andy were already there and the young caver had an enormous plate of scrambled eggs, crispy bacon, and doorstop-thick wedges of toast that he was shoveling into his mouth like he had just been rescued from a desert island.

Jane laughed. "Burn a few calories last night, did you?"

He winked. "I've never had any complaints."

Jane elbowed him. "At least not to your face."

They ordered coffees as the bell over the door tinkled and Angela waved and headed their way. They skidded along the booth seat to make room for her.

"One hundred and sixty-six thousand, six hundred and sixty-six dollars, and sixty-six cents," Andy said through a mouthful of egg and bacon. "That's how much we get each if we win."

"Nice." David ordered a donut to go with his coffee. "That'll sort out my home renovations."

"New car for me," Ronnie added.

"Wow, you guys have already got it spent, *huh*?" Jane grinned. "But yeah, new car, holiday, and some new clothes would be pretty cool."

"Michael, what's on your wish list?" Angela asked.

He raised his brows. "You know, I hadn't thought about it. I'm not really focused on the money. It's the adventure that'll be invaluable to me."

"Yeah, right. Me too." Angela winked.

"I'll have his share," Andy chuckled.

"So, Michael, who is this person who knows of a secret cave somewhere in the depths of the Krubera Cave? Can we meet him or her?" Jane rested her elbows on the tabletop.

Michael smiled. "Sure, if we can develop a time machine and travel back to 1485."

Andy lowered his fork. "Oh great, yeah, that million bucks suddenly sounds a lo-*ooong* way away." He snorted and continued eating.

Michael reached into his pocket and pulled out some folded papers. He spread them out on the tabletop and everyone leaned forward.

They were newspaper articles that he had obviously pulled off the Internet. But they were slightly tattered, as if he'd had them for a while.

"Is that Cyrillic? It's in Russian," David groaned.

"Well, it's lucky you have someone whose Russian mother taught them how to read and speak it then." Michael lifted the first page. "This is an article from October 1973 and tells of a woman who emerged from the Krubera Cave—one of the first ever to descend into it. Unfortunately, it doesn't give her name. She was apparently the only survivor of a team of five members."

"In '73? You said she was one of the first—I thought no one went into the Krubera until the mid '80s." David whistled. "Even now, it's classed as one of the most dangerous for cliffs, narrow choke points, and waterways, even with modern equipment. What happened? Cave-in?"

Michael smiled. "The team followed a path described by an ancient Russian alchemist named Arkady Saknussov. They apparently descended to 7,300 feet and there, at the very basement, she claims the alchemist's notes led them to another hidden passage, and that took them deeper than any human being has ever traveled before." He looked up, his gaze level. "All the way to the center of the Earth."

There was silence around the table for several moments before Ronnie burst out laughing. "April fools, everyone." He slapped the table. "She sounds level-headed. But seriously, I shouldn't laugh. The trauma of losing her friends probably gave her post-traumatic stress."

"There's more." Michael's expression was deadpan. "She says the world they found down there was teeming with strange life, light, and there was also an ocean." His lips curved up on one side.

Jane sat back. "Seriously? *This* is your secret lead?"

Michael nodded slowly, his gaze level as he stared back into her eyes.

"Where is she now?" Angela asked.

He shrugged. "Well, that's where we run into a problem. She is or *was* in an asylum for a while. But a little Russian birdie told me she's being cared for and living a solitary life somewhere down in southern Russia."

"In an asylum? *Sheesh*. You can sure pick 'em." Jane's eyelids drooped. "And you know where that is?"

He bobbed his head from side to side. "Sort of. Somewhere in Krasnodar. Maybe." He sat back. "Older city, population around 1 million, and over 28 square miles of urban sprawl."

"28 square miles, and a million people? So, she's somewhere in a place that has about the same population as San Francisco? Doesn't sound like a long shot at all." David toasted Michael with his coffee cup.

"Down there, beyond the deepest caves, below the crust and the mantle, there's another world. I know it." Michael stared into the eyes of each of them. "Come with me. We can do it."

Jane held his gaze. "Just how long have you been working on this?"

"Three years," he replied automatically. "It's all ready to go. Say the word and I'll confirm tickets, accommodation, and transport—all my treat."

"Confirm?" Jane asked.

"They're already reserved." Michael grinned and sat back.

"Adventure? Yep, I'm in." Andy pushed his plate away.

David bobbed his head. "What have we got to lose? I second that."

"Nothing to lose and a million bucks to gain. Plus, I've already booked my holiday leave." Angela raised her hand. "I third that."

They all agreed, and Jane folded her arms. "So what now?" she asked.

"Now?" Michael smiled broadly. "Now we head to a small Russian suburb on the outskirts of Krasnodar to ask about a crazy woman who was rumored to have journeyed to the center of the Earth." His eyes twinkled, and he leaned closer. "They say what she saw drove her insane."

"Then she sounds just perfect for you." Jane reached for her coffee.

CHAPTER 03

Krasnodar, Russia, 92 miles northeast of the Black Sea

It took them forty hours of traveling to arrive in the bleak Russian city, and then a further two days moving from government offices, to street cafés, and also town squares, enquiring everywhere, and all receiving nothing but blank stares or a shake of the head from the people they asked.

"Remind me, that little Russian birdie that said this woman was in Krasnodar, wasn't just a real talking bird, was it?" Andy chuckled.

"Very funny. She's here somewhere. I can feel we're close," Michael replied. "We just haven't looked in the right places yet."

At just about the point of rebellion, in one smoky bar, an ancient-looking local man with the palest eyes Jane had ever seen said he remembered the woman.

"This one a very sad case," he said. "I knew her as little girl. Always smart and strong." His mouth turned down and his nose crinkled. "But when she come back from hole in ground..." He shrugged. "...then she not well." He made a circle around his ear with a finger.

Jane threw Michael an *I told you so look*, but he ignored her.

"Does she live close by?" Michael asked.

"She lived here all her life." He looked up with rheumy eyes. "But no one sees her now. She in mental house."

"An asylum?" Michael asked. "She's still in there?"

"I think. I don't know." The old man looked away, losing interest.

Michael waved the barman over and ordered him another drink. He also left the change, about 1,100 rubles, and slid the notes to the man.

"Where can I find her?"

The old man looked at the money for a moment, and then slid it back to Michael.

"When you see her, she may need this more than me. Try hospital records." He gave them an address and directions, and then lifted his drink, toasted the pair, and turned to vanish back into the smoke-filled barroom.

*****

Jane, Michael, and their small team unloaded from their rented van outside the gates of the cold, gray edifice.

The imposing building was desolate, with peeling paint. Many of the trees still hadn't put on spring growth and most of the hospital grounds looked scrabby, more frozen mud than garden, and just downright depressing.

The main building they were in front of needed repairs to most parts of the structure, from new tiles on the roof, broken stairs, shutters missing, and some of the windows were cracked and stuck over with old newspaper.

"Wow, mental health has come a long way in Mother Russia." David pulled his jacket collar up.

"They're expecting us?" Angela asked.

Michael grunted. "Sort of. I sent word ahead that we were a group of visiting psychiatric health professionals and interested in the effects of caving trauma and resulting psychosis. They agreed to see us when I told them we were happy to pay a consulting fee."

David scoffed. "Is there any law about pretending to be a doctor around here?"

"You're a real doctor, so my statement was partially true." Michael winked.

"You said this woman's entire cave party all died in the cave, right?" Ronnie asked.

"Yep, and the story given out by the local media was that it was due to a cave-in." Michael zipped his jacket. "But if it was just a cave-in, then why did the government not ever make public the results of its rescue attempt, and instead closed the caves to the public?"

Michael pulled his collar tighter. "Then there's the rumors that the sole survivor, this woman, was down in the caves for nearly a year."

Angela scoffed. "Yeah, right. I mean, how do you survive for that long in a cave over 7,000 feet deep? There's nothing down there but maybe some blind spiders and pond scum."

Andy sniffed from the cold air. "I agree. I call bullshit."

"And it would be unless you found another food and water source. Like the one she said they found at the center of the Earth," Michael replied.

"More like they closed the caves because they're unsafe." Jane turned. "This area is usually known for its stable geology. But is there a cave-in risk we need to know about, Michael?"

"Of course there is." He faced her. "There's cave-in risk in nearly every cave we enter. That's part of the thrill, isn't it?" Michael's eyes gleamed.

"My money is on the Russian government using the caves to store radioactive waste," David pronounced. "I read that they do that if they're deep enough in stable areas. Means they don't have to dig storage pits."

"And we're planning on breaking into that?" Jane scowled.

Michael put his arm around Andy's shoulders. "In the words of my young friend here: *bullshit*." He grinned. "Come on, Jane, we've got to meet a lady about a deep, dark hole in the ground. And remember..." He pointed at each of them. "We're *all* health professionals."

Michael walked the team up the rutted driveway and toward the steps. Up on the front landing, he turned. "You guys wait here. We don't want to overwhelm them or scare her—she's probably in her 70s now. Jane and David, you're with me."

Michael straightened his clothing, cleared his throat, and rapped on the door. The sound echoed inside and then there was silence. After a moment, Michael raised his hand to knock again, but paused and turned his head to listen, as there was a soft creak from behind the door.

"*Da kto tam?*" the female voice was firm.

Michael leaned forward. "*Ah, Zdravstvuyte, gospozha Babikova. Eto Frensis Doktir Monroe. My razgovarivali po telefonu.*"

Jane didn't understand a word, but she guessed he was introducing himself and reminding her that they had sent word that they were coming.

"Yes, yes, I remember. You are the American psychiatrist," she said in heavily accented English. "One moment, please."

The door creaked inward, and a draft of cabbage and onions, plus cleaning fluid, wafted out before a stern-looking woman revealed herself.

Michael bowed slightly. "Sister Olga?"

The woman nodded, her eyes darting from Michael to Jane and then David. Michael touched his chest. "I am Doctor Monroe from the Alabama Center of Health Excellence." He turned and motioned to Jane first. "These are Doctors Baxter and Sholtzen."

The pair nodded, and the woman turned back to Michael. He reached into his jacket pocket and pulled out an envelope.

"We appreciate you assisting us in our research project."

He handed her the envelope and she peeked inside before making it disappear under her tunic. She looked past Michael to the others waiting on the front landing.

"You three only. The patients are easily frightened." Olga stood aside and ushered them inside.

She closed the door behind them, and Michael glanced at Jane who turned her mouth down and grimaced back at him. He knew what she meant; the smell was horrible, and the *hospital* was probably more a holding tank than any sort of medical care facility.

"This way." Olga turned and led them along a dark corridor with only a few light bulbs working.

A few other severe-looking nursing sisters poked their heads out to stare as they passed by. There were also some of the patients, he guessed, in wrinkled white pajamas that had vacant, heavily medicated expressions with some simply standing in the darker alcoves and seeming oblivious to the world around them.

"How is she?" Michael asked.

"Ms. Babikov is at peace now." Olga came to a door and knocked, listened for a moment, and then began to unlock it. "Her door doesn't need to be locked, but she likes it that way. And we are never allowed to turn her lights out. She said she must always be in the light."

Olga pushed open the door. "Katya, some people to see you. Come say hello."

A tiny woman materialized in front of them.

Jane was a little shocked and worked hard not to show it. Though she was only supposed to be mid 70s, the woman looked much older, and Jane had to remind herself that this woman's life had probably been much harder than theirs had ever been. But it was the tumors all over her forehead, nose, and ears that startled her.

Katya pulled the shawl tighter around her shoulders and Michael bowed. "Good morning, Ms. Babikov. I am Doctor Monroe, and these are my colleagues, Doctor Jane Baxter, and Doctor David Sholtzen. We've come to talk to you for a while. Is that alright with you?"

The woman's eyes were distrustful and moved across their faces. Jane smiled broadly and held out her hand.

"Hello, Ms. Babikov."

The woman took Jane's outstretched hand and just held it. "You can call me Katya."

"May we come in?" Michael asked.

The old woman nodded and stood aside.

Jane and David followed Michael who walked into the center of the brilliantly lit room. There were a couch and two armchairs, several lamps, and a globe on a low-hanging cord overhead. Jane noticed that there was also kerosene lamps scattered about. *Maybe for emergency lighting*, she thought.

Katya excused herself to freshen up in a small toilet room, giving the trio a chance to look around.

Jane's first impression was that the old woman had done her best to personalise her small room with faded pictures on the wall, plus some sewn tapestries with words embroidered in Russian she couldn't understand.

On a table was a photograph in a wooden frame and she approached it, squinting at the faces. She reached out to lift it closer.

"Hey, look at this."

She turned it around. It was a picture of five smiling young people all dressed in overalls, with headlamps strapped to their foreheads and belts dangling with old-style climbing gear.

Michael looked down over her shoulder. "I bet that was her caving team."

Katya returned, holding a tray that had a teapot covered in a knitted cosy, three teacups, all of differing china, plus a small plate of broken biscuits. As she laid it down on a side table, Jane quickly placed the picture frame back on the tabletop. But not quick enough.

"My friends, you found them." Katya's eyes twinkled. "I knew you would." She went and retrieved the frame and held it close to her breast for a moment.

"Was that your team that went into the Krubera? All the way to the bottom?" Michael asked.

Katya sat down and motioned for them to sit as well—the choices were a threadbare armchair, a stool, or the bed. "Help yourself, please." She pointed to the pot.

Michael poured them all tea and placed a biscuit shard beside each cup. He perched carefully on the small stool.

"All the way to the bottom? Yes. Did you know we were the first? Well, except for Saknussov." Katya stared at the picture. "The handsome one on the left is Dmitry." She sighed. "He was always laughing, very funny man. Next to him is my sister, Lana." She bobbed her head for a moment. "We always argued over little things like clothing."

Katya's eyes glistened as she traced the image with one withered finger. Once again, Jane thought how ravaged the woman looked for her age. *Did her experiences do that to her, or the cancers?* she wondered.

Katya continued. "Then in the middle is Georgy, our leader; a good, decent man, strong. I loved him." She smiled ruefully. "Then I am next. I was pretty then. And without fear." She turned the picture around to Michael momentarily. "Before the cancers came for me."

He nodded, and she went on.

"Finally, there is young Alexi. He was little more than a boy." She looked up. "He was the first...to be taken."

Taken? Jane wondered at the term. *Did she mean he fell, got caught in a cave-in, or got lost? Is that what she meant?*

Michael put his teacup down. "Katya, I want to thank you for seeing us. Your memories are important to us." He sat forward. "You were the last member of a fateful team. I wanted to see you to get an understanding about what a caver can expect in the Krubera Cave. To avoid dangers."

Her eyes narrowed and she stared into Michael's face for a few seconds before shaking her head. "No one goes in there. No one is allowed. And that is how it should be."

She stared again, and then her eyes shifted to Jane. She reached over, grabbed her hand, and traced the palm with fingertips as she studied it.

"It is as I thought when you greeted me. These are not the hands of a doctor or bureaucrat. These are the hands of a caver." She dropped the hand and smiled sadly. "I am not well, but I am not stupid."

Katya sighed and then turned the picture of her friends around to them once more. "This is you. Do you see?" She tapped the picture more forcefully. "This group is you. Because *we* were you—brave, strong, confident." She snorted. "Overconfident. Naïve. Stupid. We went caving everywhere, but only in the deepest, most dangerous ones. We liked to take big risks and we always won. But then one day, you roll dice and you lose. And you lose everything."

The old woman reached out for her tea and Jane saw her hand was shaking.

"When you went into the Krubera Caves, was there a cave-in?" Jane asked. "Was that what took Alexi and the others?" She put her cup down.

"Krubera." She looked up, and her eyes shone. "Do you know that cave has many names? Verona, Crow Cave, and also it is called the Devil's Doorway?"

Michael shook his head.

"My poor friends. We knew it was called that but didn't know why. Then we did, and it was too late." She slumped, and her teacup slid.

Michael reached out to take it from her. "Is that why it is off-limits? Because it's so dangerous?"

"You will not go into the caves," Katya intoned.

"Is the cave's geomorphic structure unstable? The geology is quite old here and should be solid," David asked.

"It is stable, but there was a tremor when we were deep in the caves. We were at the basement, 7,200 feet." She snorted derisively. "Not the true basement."

David whistled.

"We wanted to dive in the sump pool, look for sunken passages. But the tremor stopped us. Only from diving," Katya said.

"What happened?" Jane gently pressed. "Think back. What happened down there?"

"I don't need to think back. The memories never leave me." Katya's eyes became flint hard. "There's a world within a world." She looked up at them. "Do you know who Arkady Saknussov is?"

"Yes, I do," Michael replied. "He was the 15th century Russian scholar and alchemist who believed the world was hollow." He smiled sympathetically. "There are many, like me, who believe in that wild theory. That hundreds of millions of years ago the Earth's molten core began to cool and shrink, and then pulled away from the mantle. It created a space...a space for an entire new world. An untouched paradise."

"Yes, exactly what Georgy believed." Katya stared now.

Michael felt Jane's eyes on him. He went on. "In 1864, a French author by the name of Jules Verne was said to have adapted Saknussov's theory into a story, called 'Voyage au Center de la Terre,' or A Voyage to the Interior of the Earth." He smiled. "I mean, Arkady Saknussov was obviously the model for Jules Verne's Arne Saknussem."

"I think so too." Katya reached out to take back her now tepid cup of tea. "I studied more of Saknussov's theory when I returned. I spent years seeking out his notes, his research, and his theories. But when I try and talk about it, warn people, they put me in here." She waved an arm around.

"Saknussov was said to have vanished without a trace. Do you think he found his way down...to the interior?" Michael felt his heart hammering.

Jane made a noise in her throat, but he ignored her.

"*Do you?*" Michael urged.

"Yes." Katya looked up. "*Yes.* I *know* he did. But his theory was wrong in one regard—it is no paradise down there."

Suddenly, the old woman's eyes blazed. "Why are young people so stupid?" she spat.

Then Katya's jaw set. "I will report you if you go there. I would see you in prison, and alive, then ever let anyone go down into that hell again."

Michael held up his hands. "No, no, we are not going there, we promise. Besides, no one is going down into the Krubera anymore, as it's all still sealed up, I hear." He shot Jane a glance. "We plan on going to the Illyuzia-Meshonnogo-Snezhnaya system. It's around 5,751 feet deep."

"Good." Katya mumbled something and made a sign over her face like a circle with a cross inside it. "That cave is better for you. I know it is a good cave. It will test your skills, but it is...safe."

They sipped tea in silence for a moment more, and Michael sensed the woman was pulling away and taking her memories with her. He had come a long way and needed to know more. *This opportunity would never present again*, he thought. He put his cup down.

"Katya... Katya..." Michael waited until she half-turned to him. "Just a little more of your generous time. Please tell us what happened...when you got to the pool? You said the tremor stopped you from diving. How did it do that?"

"It was gone, the pool." She spoke as if in a trance, her eyes unfocused.

"Gone? You mean drained away?" He sat forward.

She nodded. "One minute, it was there, and the next, it was all gone. Like pulling the plug on a bath." She nodded as she remembered. "The tremor swallowed it and also opened a new chamber. And stupidly, we went in."

Michael looked quickly at Jane and she lifted her eyebrows slightly. He poured Katya some more tea and also gave her his piece of biscuit. "How big was it? How deep did it go?"

"Just like the old alchemist said—all the way." She smiled dreamily and held up three fingers, scraping them in the air. "We followed the three marks of Saknussov, all the way down to the center."

Michael swallowed. "And that's why you were down there so long. I heard it was nearly a year before you came out."

She shook her head. "No, I never came out. I'm still there now. I'm trapped." She mumbled something in Russian and Jane took her hand.

"You're safe now, Katya. You're home." Jane patted her small hand.

"No, everything I loved is down deep in those caves—my friends, my lover, my youth, and my mind." She drew in a huge breath and then let it out in a deep, shuddering exhalation.

David finally sat forward, concern creasing his forehead. "Katya, do you hear their voices, in your head?"

"Their voices, and their screams. Always screaming." Her face crumpled. "My poor sister, Lana. She wants me to help her. I can't." Tears welled in her eyes.

"Can you hear them now?" David pressed.

Katya ignored him. "Down there were wonders—an entire ocean under eternal daytime with a strange blood-red light. There were mushrooms as big as trees, and crystals the size of buildings. But there were also monsters." Her face crumpled. "And worse." Tears welled in her eyes, and Jane continued to hold her hand.

"Help me understand. Even a year isn't enough time to travel all the way to the center of the Earth." David tried to look into her face, but Katya kept her head down. "It's not possible."

"By the gravity wells," she said softly. "That's what Georgy called them. He said they were places where the planet's magnetic pull was distorted and allowed us to travel through the mantle." She smiled. "It was fun then—we could fly."

Jane turned to Michael, and perhaps she was expecting to see him look skeptical but instead he was enthralled. He had many theories about how one could get down and return so quickly. This was something he hadn't expected.

"They said they didn't believe me, that I made it all up or suffered from some type of stress sickness. Or maybe I hit my head." Her tears now ran freely. "But if they thought I was making it all up, then why did they seal the cave? And why did they lock me away in here?"

She gripped Jane's hand, hard. "Why, why?" Her eyes were fearful and wide. "I tell you why—to keep the *things* trapped down there."

*****

As they were leaving, they stopped at the door and Michael turned and took the small, frail woman's hand in his. "Thank you."

She lifted her eyes to him. "I know you are lying. I know you are going. Because young people have no fear of death or of dying." Her lips lifted into a rueful smile. "And they are stupid."

"I have one last question," Michael said softly, and the woman looked deep into his eyes, waiting. "Would you not like to be proved sane? That someone could prove it was all true, and maybe, just maybe, quieten the screaming?"

She stared for a moment more, and as Jane came closer to hear more, they both switched to Russian. After a moment, Katya motioned for him to follow and he turned to hold up a finger to Jane and David, indicating he'd be just a moment.

After a few minutes, Jane was about to follow when Michael returned, stuffing something into his breast pocket. Unexpectedly, he reached down to hug Katya, and she hugged him back.

"Tell my sister I'm sorry." Katya pulled her shawl tighter around her shoulders. "I will pray for you," she whispered, and then was gone.

*****

"So, insane, *huh*?" Andy grinned.

David drove the van back to their hotel and gripped the wheel until his knuckles were white as they wended along slippery, snow-covered roads. He spoke over his shoulder.

"I think so. I'm a general physician and not a psychologist, but I can tell you that Ms. Katya Babikov exhibited all the textbook signs of severe psychosis—hearing voices, depression, feeling trapped by and within past events."

Jane shook her head. "I don't think so. She was certainly troubled. And whatever happened to her certainly shook her up. She's suffering loss, but she's not insane."

David spoke over his shoulder again. "By the way, did you guys see those facial tumors? That's radiation necrosis. I told you the Russians

24

probably stored radioactive waste in caves."

"*Whoa*, seriously? I thought that was a myth." Ronnie sat forward. "Is there something we need to know, Michael?"

Michael stared straight ahead.

"You told us she actually said she saw an underground ocean, mushroom trees, and monsters? Yeah, I think I'd say *very* troubled," Angela said through a smile. "Like off the freaking chart troubled."

Jane noticed Michael hadn't said a word since they left. "What do you think, Michael?"

He sat like stone for a moment more, and then he spoke without turning. "I believe her."

CHAPTER 04

Town of Gagra, Abkhazia, the foot of the Caucasus Mountains

The group sat in the small smoky bar and drank the potent, gritty local beer. The team was all still hopped up on enthusiasm and the promise of adventure, which was expected, as everyone who did caving as a hobby, pastime, or full-time job, was in some way addicted to adrenaline.

The next morning, they were due to load up on supplies, and then make for the cave by midday, and Michael felt both exhilarated and scared half out of his wits.

He had spent the first hour allaying the group's fears about Russian radioactive waste dumps, and in the end, he had flat-out lied and told them that when he had spoken to Katya by himself she had told him she had the tumors before she went into the cave.

He didn't think for a second there would be radioactive waste and had another theory about that. Time would tell if he was right.

Now, his mind worked overtime as he replayed all the woman had told him and he worked it in among all he had learned over the years. He knew with every fiber of his being they were on the verge of discovering something of unparalleled importance. Maybe even world-changing.

Jane bumped his elbow, breaking his reverie.

"Already there?"

He chuckled and nodded. "Yeah, I guess."

"So, what do you think we'll find down there? I mean, really find?" She sipped her beer but kept her eyes on him. Everyone at the table stopped talking to listen.

"Answers," he said. He looked at each of his friend's faces. "Answers to questions we've been asking for centuries."

"Michael, there was something you said to us before we left that keeps playing in my head. You said that you had been planning this for a long time. How long exactly?" David asked.

He smiled. "Years. And years." He sipped his beer. "And it took me years before that until I even learned that the woman might still be alive. I just didn't know where she was. All records of her seemed to have been conveniently lost. But I'm a pretty good detective."

"Helps if you speak Russian," Jane replied.

"That's true. You tell someone from a Russian government department you're an American, and only speak English, they hang up on you." He chuckled.

"Let's cut to the chase, Mr. Monroe—you really think there's something down there besides a deep cave, don't you?" Angela rested her elbows on the table and leaned forward.

He nodded. "Saknussov was alive in the 15th century, and his theory of a hollow Earth has been kicking around ever since then. The entry to the inner world was said to be only via extinct volcanoes, or the deepest caves, and these places were also rumored to have been at the North and South poles, the north of Canada, Hangchow in China, and even somewhere in the Amazon Rainforest. But I knew there had to be more."

"Come on, man." Ronnie Schwartz's brows were creased together. "This is all science fiction."

"Once, the idea of going to the moon was just science fiction. Or of walking on the bottom of the ocean, or flying, or traveling faster than the speed of sound." Michael turned to Ronnie. "The only proof we have of a solid core, wrapped in a liquid outer core with a thick mantle, was given to us only a few short years ago by seismologists. And it's still only a theory today. Or maybe science fiction."

"I thought the Earth's solid core gave us all our gravity. It has to be there," Andy said.

"Wrong. The Earth's mass gives it most of its gravity." Michael held his hands up, fingers open as though holding a ball. "When an earthquake happens, it sends waves—shock waves—through the planet. Seismologists hear and record these vibrations. It's like we tap one side of a giant bell with our knuckle, and someone listens on the other side for the noise."

He moved his finger around the imaginary ball. "So, depending on which way those vibrations travel, they pass through different areas of the Earth. And those different areas affect what they sound like at the other end.

"Seismologists found that some vibrations were going missing as they traveled through the planet. They called them 'S-waves,' and something was making them vanish inside the Earth. They believed that the reason for this was simple—S-waves can only move through solid material and can't make it through liquid.

"So, they decided those waves must have come up against something

27

liquid—molten liquid they hypothesized—like in the center of the Earth."

"And?" Jane asked. "That's the accepted science."

Michael held up a finger. "But the S-waves won't pass through something else as well." He smiled and leaned forward. "Air." He saw them hanging on his words.

"I've spoken to many geologists who all agree that the inner core truly is a solid, probably wrapped in the liquid core." He made a fist and wrapped his hand around it, indicating one core over the other.

"But here's the thing. Many, though not publicly, say that the molten core is cooling and has been shrinking over billions of years. It is sticking around the solid core and actually pulling away from the upper mantle, leaving a void that had been filled with air, water, and…perhaps even, life."

"You said that to the old woman. Which just affirmed her neurosis." David shook her head. "Just how could anything survive being so close to the molten core?"

Michael leaned his forearms on the table. "Remember Katya mentioned the red light? I believe there is a sheet of solidified volcanic glass, perhaps hundreds or thousands of feet thick, providing insulation. And one more thing that proves it for me." He craned forward. "Katya Babikov and her friends went there and saw it themselves. And she returned."

"Yeah, just her." David drained his beer. "Look, Michael, I love you, buddy, but it's going to take us about four days to descend to around 7,000 feet—around one and a half miles. But the mantle alone is 6,000 *miles* thick. Doing the math, at that descent speed, we would need…" he looked up, calculating for a moment, before snorting. "Over 50,000 years to make the drop. That might be a little more time than I can afford to be away from my job."

Michael threw his head back and laughed. "Yeah, yeah, and it always perplexed me about how this was possible, until Katya gave us the key." He turned to Jane. "When she mentioned the gravity wells."

"Gravity what?" Andy frowned. "What does that mean? I've never heard of that term, ever."

"It's actually more of a physics term. But at this point, I don't have all the answers. But I do know that Earth's, or any large celestial body's, gravity is a function of its mass, core, and its rotation. As you descend below the surface, then the careful balance of these forces is disrupted. It is possible, that deep down there could be some sort of sinkholes that run for hundreds or thousands of miles that might be nearly gravity free."

"Like in space?" Andy's brows shot up.

"Maybe. Katya said they could fly in them. That's how they traveled so quickly."

David sat back. "Excuse me, but I think my head is about to explode."

"What are we getting ourselves into?" Ronnie asked. "This is more than a few weeks caving to reach and return from 7,000 feet, isn't it?"

"What are we getting into? Possibly the biggest thing since Christopher Columbus discovered the New World. This is Nobel Prize material." Michael held his hands out. "The adventure alone will be mind-blowing, but just imagine what we might discover there."

"We won't make it back in time for the competition," Andy complained.

"Who cares?" Michael slapped his shoulder. "The advance on your book deal will be a king's ransom."

"*Phew.*" David grimaced. "Wish I could tell Jenny."

"We can't tell anyone just yet. Not even your wife." Michael pushed his chair back. "One more drink for the table, and then we better hit the hay. Big day tomorrow."

"I'll help you carry them." Jane also stood to follow him.

*****

At the bar, Michael ordered the drinks, and Jane looked up at his face. She knew he was still holding things back.

"I don't think I can go." Resignation clouded her features. "You heard Katya Babikov—she was gone for around a year. I can't vanish for that long." She motioned toward their group. "And you haven't told them that either."

"No." Michael inhaled deeply through his nose, his nostrils flaring. "Because you're right, they might say no. And I need them. All of them." He looked down at her and placed one of his large hands over hers. "And more than anything, I need you."

She continued to stare up at him, trying to read him, and she felt him squeeze her hand.

"I need your strength, your counsel, and I need your friendship. Please come, Jane." He stared, and his blue-eyed gaze pierced hers.

He looked like he meant it. And he looked like he hadn't contemplated her not being at his side. She kinda liked that.

Jane stared up into his handsome face. "When we left, what did she give you? The old woman?"

A small smile spread across his lips, and he reached into his breast pocket. He drew out a leather book, only 8 inches by 6 inches, and he placed it on the countertop.

"Her notebook."

She looked down at the book and saw it was crammed with loose papers and even news clippings. She undid the string holding it and eased the leather boards open.

"Is this Arkady Saknussov's manuscript?" She felt her frustration rise as she flipped a few of the pages. "It's all in damn Russian."

"What did you expect? It's written by a Russian citizen." Michael smiled. "And no, not Saknussov's work, but Katya's. She has some of the ancient Russian's notes in there that's she's copied, but primarily, it's her experiences from her expedition."

She snapped the book shut and slid it back to him. "What does it say?"

"Everything we need to know, I think," he replied. "I'll finish reading it tonight. But know this—it means we're not going in blind. The shortcuts Katya and her team found we can adopt, and the mistakes they made, we can avoid."

"To the center of the Earth." The thought dumbfounded her. "It seems so…impossible."

"No, it's very possible. And it gets even better. It seems Arkady Saknussov left them a trail of breadcrumbs." He placed the book back in his pocket. "And those breadcrumbs are still waiting down there for us to follow."

*****

Michael lay on his bed in a room surrounded by climbing gear. They had the technical side of the equipment, such as the ropes, pins, carabiners, climbing anchors, and dozens of pill-sized lithium batteries. Plus, the supply side, being dried food, vitamin pills, and water-purifying tablets. This was rarely a concern, as there was always water in caves.

He read from Katya's diary notes, and each page both startled and captivated him. It had been an obsession of his ever since as a boy he had read Jules Verne's *Journey to the Center of the Earth*. And then soon after, he read the 1818 theories of John Cleves Symmes, an American Army officer, trader, and lecturer who was convinced there were passages to the world's interior.

But then this was followed by the first whisper of a real hollow Earth that had been mentioned to him in a geological forum. The thought that someone had already traveled there, perhaps for the first time over 500 years ago, was astounding.

He would go there, and dangers be damned, he thought. He turned a page of Katya's notebook and sat forward. He read the passages again and then let his eyes slide to his special equipment on his desk table—several knives and a bolt gun. The gun was used to fire metal pins into cave walls.

He hoped the old woman had been exaggerating. But his gut told him it was true. He suddenly wished the bolt gun were a real weapon.

CHAPTER 05

The next morning, they'd hired a truck to drop them off as high as they could drive into the Caucasus Mountains, and then followed a trail by foot up the steep hills.

The climb was wending, the hillside steep, and in some areas the track following the contours of the geography was little more than a few worn areas on the tough Caucasus' grasses.

"The world famous Krubera Cave, *huh*?" Andy said between puffs.

Michael chuckled. "You expected it to be more like Times Square?"

But the kid was right; there was nobody around, and the only living thing they'd seen so far was a few goats staring suspiciously from rocky outcrops and a handful of large and shiny, gimlet-eyed crows watching them pass by.

"There are fresh tracks in the mud," Jane said over her shoulder.

Michael sped up a little, passing David. "Maybe a few of the goat herders."

"Only if they wore modern climbing boots," she replied.

Damn, he thought. Between the goats and the weather, tracks shouldn't remain for very long, a day or so at most.

He also spotted the tracks then—made by modern boots, some large and a few small. Whoever they were, there was a mix of men and boys or perhaps men and women.

"Could there be another team out here?" Ronnie asked.

Michael frowned as he looked at the tread styles. He had a sinking feeling in his stomach that was exactly what it was. And he bet he knew who it was: Harry Wenton.

It took them another hour to reach the entrance to the cave. None of them had ever been to this site before, but they knew to keep a sharp eye for a small rip in the earth, of no more than 8 feet by 3 feet. It almost seemed a secret entrance, and probably the reason it remained undiscovered until recently.

Anyone who visited the place for the first time expected the deepest cave in the world to be a jaw-dropping spectacle, a little like what cavers referred to as a Hollywood entrance—a massive opening in a towering cliff wall a little like King Kong's lair on Skull Island.

Michael had studied many pictures of the site and used his GPS to locate where it should be, but as they came over the rise, what he saw was unexpected.

"What the hell? They built a well over it?" Angela asked.

"No, they built a front door and locked it, remember?" Jane replied.

There was a round structure of bricked-in cement that looked exactly like an old well. Except across the top was a heavy iron door.

Michael felt a flare of anger as he lifted the padlock and chain. "Already cut." He examined the severed links and saw it was still shining and fresh where the bolt cutters had been used. He sighed. "Maybe less than a day ago."

"One guess," Angela said.

Jane nodded. "Yep, gotta be Harry Wenton, and by the look of the tracks, he came with his own posse." She backed up a bit and looked around at the ground. "I'm thinking he's got a team of four, including himself."

"Sonofabitch." Michael slammed down the chain.

"Do we proceed?" Andy asked.

"Damn right we do." Michael gripped the handle and with a scream of unoiled hinges, he pulled back the slab of hammered iron. "We know where we are going, they don't."

"What does that say?" Ron asked.

On the inside of the steel door was Cyrillic lettering scratched into the heavy gauge steel.

Michael read it, frowning. "It's nothing."

"Come on, Michael, you can read it. Tell us." Jane rubbed a thumb on the writing. "It's old. Probably done when the steel door was made."

"It's a joke." He snorted.

"Good, I could use a laugh," Ronnie said.

"*Abandon all hope all ye who enter here.*" Michael shrugged. "A joke."

"What the hell?" David frowned.

"Hell is right," Jane said. "That's from Dante's Inferno about traveling to the underworld."

"The cave is deep. Like I said, it's someone's idea of a joke. Don't worry about it." Michael looked down into the cave depths.

"Interesting that Dante wrote that in the 14th century. The same time period that your Russian friend, Arkady Saknussov, disappeared into that same underworld." David cocked an eyebrow.

"Yeah, interesting." Michael stared down into the darkness, inhaling the smells of ancient, dry earth. "There's over 8 miles of known cave down there, and just remember, it'll take them and us four days to get to the sump pool level." He straightened. "And we've got the better team."

"Damn right we do," Andy said. "Let's do this."

"Equipment check, and then we drop," Jane said.

The team set about the last check on their gear, placing their headband lights on sleek helmets that molded to the shape of their heads. They had equipment belts on which hung carabiners, pins, eyehooks, and other equipment. Also, each had a small holster with a bolt gun—that fired a metal, self-anchoring expansion bolt into solid rock that an eye-nut could be attached to for threading rope through. Michael had insisted they all take one with them, and also spare cartridges.

Everything else was placed in slim packs—one on their back and one on their chest.

Lastly, they stepped into their climbing harnesses—contraptions that fit over each thigh and went around their waist. At the front was a set of rings that they could use to thread rope through and also to make dangling a lot more comfortable.

Jane was last to slide her pack back over her shoulder and the smaller one on her chest. She fastened the tough material down hard.

Michael turned her around, checking her over. "Looking good, nice and tight."

"You're talking about my pack, right?" She grinned up at him.

"Yeah, that too." Michael grinned as he tugged a strap a little tighter on her.

Jane rotated her shoulders, feeling loose and limber. She knew that everything they took needed to be light and thin, as some of the squeeze points were little more than a single foot wide, so anything bulky just wasn't going to make it with them.

"Andy, you're up." Michael peered into the hole. "Right there." He took one of his loops of rope from his shoulder and reached down. But then paused. "Even better, it's already roped up for us."

Jane and the group watched as Michael checked the rope and the hanging ring attached to a bolt sunk into the rock. "All good. Looks like it's been replaced recently."

Many cavers left equipment—some good, some just rubbish—but strong and secure hooks were always appreciated.

Andy threaded the rope through the carabiner and the ring at the front of his harness. He then wrapped it around his hand and let one end dangle down into the darkness.

"*Banzai!*" he yelled as he dropped fast.

There was the sound of the rope zizzing through the drop equipment. His helmet light got smaller, and then he stopped to hang about 100 feet down.

"More ropes down here, and they look just fine." There was the sound of jangling equipment. "Gonna rig up on the new ones and drop some more, so rope is free for the next one of you guys."

"I'll go." Jane threw a leg over the small brick wall.

In seconds, she had rigged up and looked up at Michael. "See ya on the dark side."

She stepped back and then let the rope slide through the rings and her hand. The Valtek rope they had obtained was a dream; it had slight elasticity so if you had to pull up suddenly you didn't get bruised from the stop. Plus, it was strong enough to basically lift a baby elephant.

She quickly came to where Andy had crossed to the next set of rings and did the same. In another few minutes, she came to the first pitch, or landing site, about 200 feet down.

Andy was waiting for her. He pointed.

"They went thatta way."

She nodded. "Could you hear anything?"

He shook his head. "Nothing. It means they've got to be at least 6 to 10 hours ahead of us."

"Crap. Michael's gonna be pissed." She knew how focused the guy could get, and she didn't want him trying to move at breakneck speed to run Harry Wenton down. Though she had never been to the Krubera Cave, she'd heard plenty of stories of people having accidents in here, and the consensus was that it was for expert-level speleologists only.

One after the other, the team dropped to the pitch and assembled.

"Only about 7,000 feet more to go." Michael grinned and looked around. He inhaled, smelling the rich scent of ancient stone and mystery. "Where we are going wasn't known until the '70s. At the time Katya and her team finally made it to the bottom, they were the first." He turned. "Or second, if we count Arkady Saknussov."

Angela shone a small flashlight on her wrist around the cave floor, and then upward. "I read that it was littered with bones when it was first found."

"It was." Michael watched her lightbeam for a moment. "Lots of animals fell in here: dire wolves, small antelope, and even some early humans. But even if the fall didn't kill them, there was no way out."

Andy was also looking up. "Hey, question."

"Shoot," Jane said.

"What happens if the authorities come back and decide to fix the lock and chain?" He slowly lowered his gaze to Jane.

"Oh my God, I didn't think of that." Angela chuckled a little nervously.

"Could that actually happen?"

"Welcome to our new home." David grinned. "Don't sweat it—we'll just have to evolve into mole people."

Michael continued to look up toward the light high above them. "I doubt they'll be back any time soon. But even if they did lock us in, have you ever seen what a bolt gun can do to a brick wall? Don't worry about it."

Michael did a last check on his GPS, and then pointed to the darkness beyond them. "Ronnie, you're our best point man. Take us in."

*****

Krubera Cave's small and almost invisible opening on the surface was why it was only recently discovered, but Michael could now also see why the caves were never penetrated very far until by professional cavers only a few decades ago.

The going was tough, and not at all like how caves were portrayed in movies where people walked through wide tunnels with flat floors, over natural bridges, and entered caverns with high roofs and magnificent stalagmites rising like snow-covered trees from the cave floor or stalactites hanging from the ceiling like giant dagger teeth.

The Krubera was more rift tear, where the mighty plates of the Earth had been torn asunder. Maybe that was why it was so deep. But the hard and sharp stone passages made for tough going.

Some walls pressed in close with little more than a foot of width to wriggle through for hundreds of feet. Then there were the squeeze points— holes in the ground, wall, or ceiling that needed to be inched through while pushing or pulling your equipment along behind you.

The best way to enter the tiny holes was feet first. If, for whatever reason, you got stuck, it was easier to backtrack if you didn't have to do that in reverse.

The group had been traveling for an hour on a vertical plane before they came out of a narrow cleft and stood on a ledge. Ronnie held up a hand and then put a finger to his lips. The group quietened and even held their breath as they listened.

After another moment, Michael heard it: the soft clang of a steel carabiner against stone, and perhaps also the sound of scraping. It was faint, and a long way away, but it was there.

"They've a good lead on us, but we're not out of the game just yet." Michael walked to the end of the ledge and shone his light down and then along the rift walls. Where they had gathered was on the edge of a cliff face that was a giant tear in the rock.

His light could never hope to extend all the way to the next pitch, which he understood was some 500 feet straight down. He leaned out and found the bolt and hanger waiting for them, plus existing ropes. "Okay, over we go."

Ronnie led them down, and from a caving perspective, this was the easy stuff, as straight drops meant no obstacles.

It took them less than 20 minutes to be gathered at the bottom. Now at about 1,000 feet down, the cave smelled of dry, ancient dust and the sharp odor of cold rock.

To one side of them were the remains of an ancient fire, where earlier cavers had decided to heat their coffee or simply take a break with more illumination. There were also small piles of white powder and exploded metal jackets.

"Carbide batteries." Michael saw the small note written beside it in Russian. He grinned and translated. "We do not shit in your house, so please do not shit in our cave." He turned. "Can't argue with that."

These days, most professional cavers were pretty responsible and brought piss bottles, and even plastic bags to take a dump in, so they could take it all back out with them. But many cavers lived on high-protein, low-fiber food before entering a cave and while down below on an extended adventure, some of them could even hold it for a week. That meant the first thing they did when making it back to civilization was run to the crapper and drop a log the size of a loaf of bread.

"Let's go. And we keep it as quiet as possible." Michael held out an arm. "Ronnie, lead us in."

For the next few thousand feet, Michael and his team made good time. So far, they were simply following ropes, chimneys, and known squeeze points, but he knew that the first teams in to explore had to explore, test, and then backtrack out of a lot of dead ends. It might have taken them days to travel a few hundred feet in the right direction.

After 12 hours of descending where they needed to squeeze through slits in the solid rock and crawl on their bellies, Michael finally decided he would call a halt for the day. There was rougher terrain ahead, and fatigued cavers, no matter how experienced, made mistakes. And mistakes a few thousand feet below ground could be deadly.

They came into a chamber roughly 40 feet around that had some natural shelving for them to stretch out. They lit small propane stoves to make some coffee and had a meal of applesauce and dried beef.

The spirits of the group were high, and enthusiasm still burned in all their eyes. *Good*, Michael thought, as where he hoped they were going was going to test every one of them 10 times over.

Jane had her mat laid out next to his, and their packs would be their pillows. If possible, they'd try and snatch a good six hours sleep.

As they lay there, Angela and Andy had popped earphones in, but their differing tastes in music still leaked out to permeate the tomb-like silence of the cave.

Jane lay on her stomach and rested her chin on her hands. "Hey."

Michael lifted his head. "Yeah, what's up?"

"I was thinking."

"Oh no." He grinned.

She flicked some gravel at him. "Seriously."

"Okay." He straightened his face. "What's on your mind?"

"You remember what Katya told us about where she had been? Did you believe all of it? Really?" Her gaze was direct.

Michael turned on his side and rested his head on one hand. "I don't exactly know what was real and what was brought about by some sort of psychosis from lack of food and water...and also the terror of being lost for a year below ground. Plus, a hundred other things she might have experienced down there."

"She said, 'Down there were wonders—an entire ocean under eternal day with strange red light. Mushrooms as big as trees, and crystals the size of buildings.' And then she said, 'But there were also monsters.'"

He nodded, waiting.

"That's crazy." She snorted softly. "You said yourself before we met her that they thought she was insane."

"She was certainly damaged by the experience," he said. "But let me put something to you." He rolled over and edged a little closer so he could lower his voice.

"The Earth is over 4.5 billion years old. And over those billions of years, it has been struck numerous times by significant asteroid strikes. Some so big, that one of them blasted enough material from our planet to create the moon. Another wiped out all the dinosaurs. Imagine that one was so significant that it cracked the planet's mantle and the ocean poured in. By then, the magma core was shrinking and water stayed there. Above it, the cracks in the planet healed over from the heat of the blast, cauterized and fused shut like a wound."

"Sounds a little like a science fiction movie from the 1950s." She smiled.

He continued. "Now, say that the magma core is sheathed in thousands of feet of volcanic glass, holding it from the ocean and the land that exists on the inside of the mantle—the sky at the core is down, and the land up. The glass also shields the world down there from much of the heat." He smiled. "Tell me, Miss Biologist, what color would the sky be if it was magma behind glass?"

She grinned and her eyes crinkled at the corners. "Gold, orange...*red*."

"Correct. And now consider that the primordial life that entered with the ocean water now found a new warm environment to evolve and grow in." He smiled, as she looked skeptical. "Come on, Jane, you're basically a scientist. Never say never."

"Okay, we know concurrent evolution can occur. So I'll concede it is possible, if everything happened like you said. But the odds of that are millions or billions to one."

"Many evolutionary biologists say the odds of life springing up on Earth were said to be billions to one." Michael smiled and lay back down. "And yet, here we all are."

*****

Just five hours later, Michael opened his eyes. He was mentally alert, but the muscles in his thighs and shoulders screamed from all the physical strain. A day of caving delivered the same physical exertion as running a full marathon. After another day, he'd get used to it, but for now, he just had to deal with the pain.

It was always disorientating waking up in complete darkness, and in a cave, you lost night, day, and all time orientation. They would need to remember to take Vitamin D to ensure their muscles stayed in shape.

He checked his watch—it was 4pm in the afternoon—but it didn't matter anymore. They had several more days of descent before they arrived at the sump pool. Or where Katya said the pool had drained away. Unfortunately, he didn't think he'd be there before Harry Wenton and his team.

While he urinated into a bottle, he tried to think who it was that would have accompanied him—the guy certainly had a wide circle of friends, supporters, and assorted hangers on. Most rich people did.

After another moment, he gave up; he had suspects, but way too many. He'd find out soon enough. And then what? What exactly would or could he do? He alone had Katya's notebook and the keys to finding his way down.

He doubted Wenton even knew about the drained sump and might have only been racing to the bottom of the Krubera Cave to claim the million bucks and the bragging rights. Michael hoped so. He'd happily let him have it, and then wave him goodbye as Wenton and his team headed back up.

But what if they found the extra cave? Michael finished pissing, zipped up, and screwed the cap back on the bottle. He couldn't stop the guy from doing what he enjoyed doing. And for that matter, what would happen if Wenton tried to tag along with them?

He sat back down next to his pack. If Wenton wanted to tag along, then in that case it'd be clear-cut: Mr. Harry Wenton would be joining the

Monroe expedition, and not vice versa.

Beside him, Jane made a little snuffling sound in her sleep, and he looked across at her, making sure his light didn't shine directly on her face. He was glad she came because out of all of them, he trusted her the most. And he had to admit—he liked her, a lot.

She opened her eyes a crack and rubbed her face.

"Good afternoon, sleepyhead." He reached across for her water bottle that had rolled a few feet from her and handed it to her.

"Afternoon? Oh yeah, right." She took the water and pushed herself upright. She grimaced and looked around. "Times like this, I wish I had a dick."

Jane rummaged in her pack for her piss bottle and special cup that allowed her to wee into it.

"Back in a minute." She rose and walked a few feet away from the group, becoming invisible in the darkness.

In a few more minutes, the others began to rise, small lanterns came on, and coffee was prepared.

Michael would give them a minute or two to gather themselves and then he'd call them in for a cave meeting. It was his responsibility, even this early in the expedition, to check on the physical and psychological well-being of the group. If need be, he could cancel or task one of them to assist an ill caver back to the surface if they were mobile enough.

Even though Michael's muscles ached, and his throat and eyes were gritty and dry, inside he burned with curiosity and excitement. If he could run all the way down, he'd do it in a blink.

Michael turned his flashlight to where they'd proceed next. The cavern they were in shrunk to a choke point no more than 16 inches or so wide. Running wasn't exactly an option, and probably wouldn't be until they resurfaced into the light. And for now, Michael had no idea when that would be.

CHAPTER 06

Harry Wenton was first into the sump chamber and pushed his helmet back on his forehead to wipe his slick brow.

Almost immediately, his team came out of the narrow rift opening and spread to either side of him.

"Maggie." Wenton walked forward.

"Yo." The young woman eased up close to him.

"We're at the bottom, right?" he asked.

The group gathered around him.

"Yep." She checked her stratigraphic plotter. "Registering a depth of 7,221 feet, and 11 inches exactly." She flicked her eyebrows up. "This is it, alright."

"Well?" He pointed at the empty basin. "What's wrong with this picture?"

Maggie Harper looked past him and then frowned.

Wenton turned to her. "Those expensive maps you had me buy said that this is where the sump pool is supposed to be."

She walked a few paces forward. "What the hell?" She turned. "Jamison."

The gangly youth put his hands on his hips. "This is it. We came the right way. No question."

"Well, work it out." Wenton sat on a pile of broken rock and took out a pack of cigarettes. From a caving perspective, smoking in a deep pristine cave was one of the cardinal sins of speleology. But then again, he was pissed off. And also, rules were for other people.

He'd just descended over 7,000 feet into a damn deep hole in the ground and now it may look like they took a wrong turn. A picture of the sump pool was supposed to be their proof of a successful arrival.

He lit one, inhaled deeply, and then blew a cloud of smoke into the beam of his headlamp.

He looked at his young team. Maggie Harper, his current girlfriend, was 32 and an athletic golden girl. She had desperately wanted to come on this cave drop, and said she'd do anything to be picked. And she did. He grinned and drew in more smoke, looking again at the outline of her figure in the near shapeless overalls.

The other three cavers he'd brought were Jamison Williams, an Ivy League enthusiast who was capable, as well as being a tech genius. He'd brought along a few toys to help them map their cave and place markers. Then there was Marcus "Jazz" Lawrence, a track and field champion in his school days, and totally fearless.

Rounding his team off was Bruno Markowitz, Russian ex-military, who had been involved with caving rescue teams for many years. Wenton had worked with Bruno before and the guy was strong as an ox, loyal, and sometimes a little brutal, which was a hangover from his military days. On this trip, his language skills had proved invaluable.

Wenton sighed and leaned back on an elbow. All he thought he needed to do was get to the absolute lowest point he could manage, take a reading, and then head back. He had expected to be sipping champagne and then collecting a check for a million dollars by Christmas. Plus rubbing a few noses in it come acceptance speech time.

Maybe the sump pool being gone was a blessing, he thought. Meant he could get down an extra few feet and claim another record.

Wenton sprang forward. "Come on, people, please tell me we're in the goddamn right cave." He stubbed his cigarette out on the rock beside him and stood.

"This is it, I'm sure of it. We came the right way, and that pool was here. I can still see the mineral water-level line." Jamison read from the pulser he aimed into the basin. He turned slowly. "That's weird."

Wenton groaned. *Here it comes*, he thought.

Jamison held the device out toward a shelf of stone at the far side of the empty sump pool. "I'm getting another reading—a deeper reading."

"How much deeper? We only need a few more feet to set a new world record," Maggie announced.

"No, no, I mean *deep, deep*." He looked up, and then began to walk forward. He got to the edge of the former sump pool line and eased down. "The readings are off the chart."

Wenton followed him in.

"Holy crap." Jamison turned but Wenton was already behind him, with Maggie and Bruno crowding in as well. "There's another cave under here."

"This isn't on the maps," Maggie said excitedly. "This must be newly opened."

"Let's go for it," Marcus enthused.

"Wait a minute. What are the readings?" Wenton asked.

Jamison shook his head. "Plotter can't get a proper fix." He turned and grinned. "It's too deep to allocate a measurement."

Wenton backed up from under the lip. "We're not just going to set a record...we're going to make history." He felt his fatigue fall away like scales. "Rig up, everyone—we're going in."

"Harry, we're not really provisioned for a lot more caving." Maggie blew out her cheeks as she looked toward the new cave. "How far will we go?"

Just a couple of feet more than Michael Monroe will go, he thought. He smiled back at her. "Don't worry, we'll just check it out."

Harry Wenton then turned to the caves they had just come from and walked toward the opening. "Everyone quiet so I can check where our competition is up to."

The group stopped and waited for a moment. Wenton listened but couldn't hear them but knew that Michael Monroe would be coming fast. As he was about to turn away, he heard something—soft, like a scraping of nails on stone.

Wenton turned his head about. *Odd*, he thought and turned slowly. *That seemed to come from the new cave.*

CHAPTER 07

Jane watched Michael as he moved like a machine through the caves. He had let his team catch a little more sleep when they were about six hours out from the sump pool. But now in the final stretch he had worked them hard, leading from the front to try and catch Harry Wenton.

Michael entered into the sump pool cavern breathing heavily, and like the rest of them, greasy with perspiration that had collected cave dust to be like a paste on their skin. Jane rolled her shoulders, feeling the uncomfortable slickness on her back.

She followed Michael as he first consulted Katya's notes, and then jumped down into the empty basin and moved to the shelf of stone at the rear.

"*Yes.*" He turned. "It's here, just like she said it would be."

"Holy shit," Ronnie said. "So she wasn't just pulling it out of her wild imagination."

"We go in," Michael pronounced.

"Not so quick," Jane threw back. "We need to have a quick planning meet, grab a coffee, and fuel ourselves up first." She saw Michael's expression harden. "Come on, Michael. This is a group effort, and we need to load up on energy. Down there is all unknown territory. We don't know what to expect."

"Yeah, we do." His mouth curved a little.

Jane put her hands on her hips. "I wouldn't believe *everything* Katya wrote…or told you."

He shrugged. "She was right about this." He bobbed his head. "But okay, I agree. Let's take some rest before we head in."

"Michael." Andy was peering at something toward the rear side of the cave.

43

"What have you got?" Michael asked.

"Some dirty bastard stubbing out his smokes." He pointed.

Michael leaped out of the basin and crossed to Andy. He crouched, lifted the butt to his nose, and then rolled it between his thumb and forefinger.

"Fresh." He stood and turned back toward the sump pool. "That bastard Wenton has gone in."

CHAPTER 08

Maggie Harper lifted a hand to stop them. "Got a fork in the road."

Wenton joined her, looking at the three cave mouths before them. "Interesting." He turned. "Jamison, give us a depth check."

Jamison pointed his pulser into each, storing the results and then moving to the next. After a few moments, he turned, reading from the small screen on the device. "No help. They're all telling me they continue on until the pulse waves dissipate." He looked up. "All deep, no blockages."

"That's a big help." Wenton walked to the mouth of the first cave and fished in his pocket. He retrieved his cigarette lighter, flicked it, and held it up. The small orange flame rose like a tiny luminous tongue. It was unmoved.

Wenton moved to the next. In front of this one, the flame bent back toward him. He moved to the third and once again the flame was unbent.

"Got a breeze coming at us from door number two. That's our path forward." He half-turned. "Maggie, do us the honors."

*****

Michael felt a little guilty about only giving the group 20 minutes to catch their breath, but he knew this was too important.

He had hoped when Katya had told him about the opening in the sump pool that it might not have been so easy to find. But he guessed having to descend over 7,000 feet below the earth was enough of a deterrent for most people. Even most professional cavers.

He knew Harry Wenton was a pro, and he would have chosen a team who were just as competent. The glimmer of hope he had was that Wenton wouldn't know what the new cavern actually meant. And that might mean he'd be satisfied with traveling a few hundred or so feet just to satisfy his curiosity and some sort of record, and then he'd turn back.

Whereas Michael had plans to go all the way. He hadn't really thought just how long he was prepared to give this expedition, and also how long the team would stick with him.

He remembered an old caver telling him once that you never conquered deep caves—you outlasted them, endured them, and suffered them. And, in turn, the caves would try and grind you down, and get you to make a mistake. The deeper the cave, the more chance you'd make that mistake, and the cave would win.

But if you did stick with it, sometimes it would reward you by showing you something that no one else on Earth had ever seen. And that was what drove him. Michael took a deep breath; he'd worry about those bridges when it came to cross them.

"Let's roll." He walked them toward the end of the sump pool and crouched under the lip of stone. Everyone waited behind him as he hung there for a moment, staring in. His light only extended for a few dozen feet and beyond that there was darkness and silence. The only thing he experienced was a warm, slightly earthy-smelling breeze blowing into his face.

Hot air rose, and unless there was water somewhere below, then the smells should have only been of rock dust, age-old mustiness, and little else. Michael felt it was a good sign.

"Going in," he said and stepped through the tumbled-down hole in the cave wall.

Inside, the cave opened up a little and walking just a few steps forward, Michael found himself on a ledge that had a gentle curve along a towering cliff face and on the other a drop off that fell away into impenetrable darkness.

"It's a ledge and looks good. Come on in," he said over his shoulder.

Andy was first in and went to the edge to point his pulser downward, waited a few seconds, and then read the numbers.

He whistled. "Vertical drop for around 8,000 feet." He turned and shook his head. "That's a mile and a half, straight down, and deeper than the entire Krubera."

Michael nodded. "Think of it as us climbing Mount Everest, but upside down."

"Into the belly of the beast," Ronnie whispered as he stared down over the edge.

"A beast?" Michael snorted softly. "I remember reading a book by James Tabor called Blind Descent. He likened caves to living organisms, whereby they had bloodstreams and respiratory systems, they got infections, infestations, and could even be corrupted." He turned to Ronnie.

"And they sometimes took in organic matter, digested it, and then usually flushed it out slowly through their river systems."

Michael turned away. *But sometimes the caves swallowed down that organic matter and kept it in their belly forever*, he thought, as he remembered Katya's notes.

"Let's stay sharp." Michael waved them on.

They continued downward, the rock shelf they were traveling on wide enough to allow a good pace. Michael looked up and found it hard to ignore the feeling of weight as miles of rocks was pressing down on you from above. One shimmy and movement of the earth, and they could all end up nothing more than an interesting line of color between sedimentary rock layers.

To this cave, tens or perhaps even hundreds of millions of years old, they were like motes of dust; insignificant specks that lived and died in the blink of eye.

Michael only slowed to examine interesting formations that loomed out of the blackness. He'd had a love of caving and the deep earth ever since he was a boy when he had ventured alone into a disused mine on his grandfather's property.

Most people were afraid of the dark, as it contained things that couldn't be seen and a world that hid from the light—mysteries, oddities, and danger. But cavers reveled in those things. Because around the next corner, over the next cliff, or through the next squeeze hole, you might encounter something truly wonderful.

As Michael passed underneath a shawl of stone, he stopped dead. "Whoa." He grinned and waved Jane over. "Come check this out."

"Holy shit." David lifted his light. "Writing. It's Russian, right?"

"Yeah, but old-style Russian." Michael translated. "*We few venture into the unknown, for the greater knowledge of all mankind.*" He turned. "*A.S.*"

"A.S.—Arkady Saknussov," Jane finished.

"Hole-*eeey* shit." Ronnie grinned, open-mouthed.

"We're on the right track," Angela said. "I cannot get my head around this guy Saknussov came all this way over 500 years ago. I don't know how."

"Because it was more than just a hobby or passion for him," Michael said. "It was his life's work. He was determined to prove his theory true, and nothing was going to stop him."

"He was going to get his answers or die trying," Jane said. "And he never came back, did he?"

Michael shook his head. "Because maybe he found his Shangri-La."

"More tracks—recent ones." Andy looked back at them. "Wenton?"

"Yeah, they're still ahead of us," Michael said. "Let's keep moving."

The descent was easier than in the upper caves as the rift in the earth had dragged the huge crustal plates apart just enough for the tiny human beings to travel easily.

After another hour, they stopped for a protein break. The fact was, they expended huge amounts of energy caving and needed to continually replenish their stocks. As it was, all of them would lose considerable weight underground. The loss of weight only became an issue when there was an accompanying loss of muscle mass—and that would only happen if they stopped eating.

In 10 minutes, Michael had them moving again. But their ledge had begun to narrow to be only 18 inches wide, so it had to be traversed with their face to the wall.

It was then they came to the three cave mouths, and Andy quickly found track evidence that Wenton's team had taken the middle cave.

Michael's grin split his face from ear to ear.

"What?" Jane said, also smiling.

Michael pointed. "Wenton took the middle cave."

"So, do we follow?" Angela asked.

"No, he went the wrong way." Michael fist-pumped. "At last, we get our first break." He reached into his pocket for Katya's notebook, undid the string, and then quickly paged through it.

"Which one?" David asked. "They all look deep."

Michael read. "We ventured into all the caves, traveling for several hours to check which was the best chance to take us to the Earth's interior. All continued deeper, but the cave on the left reached an almighty chasm that would have exhausted our rope and our appetite for adventure. The cave in the center delivered the first of the horrors of our journey. But the cave on the right is the pathway where we found the marks of Saknussov."

He snapped the book shut. "So, now we begin to follow the true path of Saknussov, instead of trailing behind Harry Wenton."

"I don't like it," Angela said.

"What? What's not to like? We get the lead," Michael asked.

"Well, for a start, what exactly does the '*center cave delivered the first of our horrors*' mean?" Angela scowled. "If there's something dangerous in there, then we need to warn Harry."

Jane exhaled and groaned. "She's right. The guy is an ass, but we can't let a fellow caver walk right into danger."

"Oh right, so five minutes ago, we're all not believing anything that Katya Babikov has said, and now, we do need to worry about what she said?" Michael held up a hand; he had no time for this. "Listen, Harry and his team are way too far ahead for us to do anything about it unless we run, and we're not going to do that. I'm sure that by the time we caught up, if we even could, Harry would have found out what it is he needs to be mindful of."

Jane paced away for a moment but then came back. "Dammit, he's right, Angela. Harry had half a day's start on us. It's not worth it."

Angela's lips pressed flat for a moment but eventually she gave an almost imperceptible nod. She walked to the mouth of the middle cave and leaned into it.

"Harry! *Harry Wenton!*"

The name bounced away into the cave, and she stood with her head cocked for a moment. But there was no reply.

"David, leave a cave note for him," Michael said. "Tell him that there are dangers down here, and we'll see him on the surface."

David Sholtzen nodded and then removed a small board with laminated sheets on it, plus a marker pen. He looked up, pen poised. "Should I tell him we've gone into the right…"

"*No,*" Michael shot back. "No, David. Best they head up and we'll meet them top side."

"Okay dokey." He wrote the message, and then rock-tacked it to the wall at the cave mouth. David peered into the darkness for a few more moments. "Good luck, Harry."

Michael smiled as he readjusted his pack. "Onward."

He led them into the right-side cave.

*****

The caves got bigger, and drier, and the added exertion meant they used up more water in their bodies—perspired it and exhaled it—at a greater rate than they dared gulp it down.

So Angela's words brought them to a sudden stop.

"There's water."

She crossed to a slime-covered wall with a pool at its base, crouched, and shone her light into it.

"Hang on, smells a little weird, and there's something crusting the edges that could be a mineral build-up, or some sort of primitive cave fungus."

"Is it clear?" David asked.

"*Hmm,* a little cloudy," Angela replied.

"Good enough for me as I'm nearly out, and I have one hellova dehydration headache." Ronnie took his canteen from his belt pouch at his back and shook it—there sounded like only a few drops left.

"I dunno. Looks a bit off." Angela looked up. "Michael, Jane, what do you think?"

Ronnie knelt by the pool. "Shouldn't be a problem. We'll just use a purifying tablet for any bugs."

Michael shrugged. "Might be okay. Caves are fairly pristine environments. But then again, no one has ever tested water from this depth. I'll pass."

"He's right. Small pools of stagnant water are always high risk," Jane added. "Just remember, aside from bacteria, there's a lot of crappy fungus that lives in caves."

David looked into the water. "She's right, Ronnie. You could get brain rot from Pseudogymnoascus destructans, or if you inhale Histoplasma capsulatum, it'll collapse your entire respiratory system."

"*Pfft*, they're all spread by bats, and none of those little suckers are way down here." Ronnie shook his head. "Pussies." He drained the last of his canteen and then dipped it into the water to fill it up. He finished by dropping a small pill inside and shaking it. "Give it five minutes for that to dissolve and guess which one of us won't be thirsty anymore?"

Andy also looked into the water, and Ronnie nodded. "Go ahead, it'll be fine."

The young caver looked to Angela who almost imperceptibly shook her head.

"Nah, I'll wait. Besides, you can be a guinea pig." He turned. "Michael, what do you think?"

"I'm thinking if he ends up with diarrhea, I can't wait to see him try and get it all in his poop bag." He chuckled. "Okay, everyone, let's keep moving."

In another half-hour, they found themselves passing through a huge cavern. Their spirits were still high as only a while back they had passed a simple carving in the cave wall of "AS" and an arrow, indicating the Russian alchemist had passed this way and wanted them to know it.

Ronnie was already drinking from his canteen and grinning. "Tastes like...*heaven*. Anyone wants a sip, feel free." He farted loudly and then sipped again. He lifted the canteen in either an offering or a toast.

"Wow, really going for it, *huh*, buddy?" David raised his eyebrows.

"Yeah, it's unbelievably moreish," Ronnie replied and swigged again. Jane sniffed. "What's that smell?"

Michael snorted. "Probably Ronnie. But you tell me, you're the biology teacher."

David also sniffed. "Sour lemons. Like citric acid. Have you guys ever smelt stink bugs on lemon trees?"

"Yeah, they stink, alright," Angela piped up.

David nodded to her. "They suck the sap of the new shoots on citrus trees and sometimes on the lemons themselves. They ingest it, but also use some of the concentrated citric acid as a defense mechanism—they can squirt it into an approaching predator's eyes. They've blinded lots of curious dogs and cats."

"They sound nice," Michael said. "Remind me never to own a lemon tree."

"The humidity is off the charts in here," Jane said.

"So?" Ronnie asked. "We already know there's water in here."

"Yes, but it shouldn't be suspended in the air like this." Her feet began to squelch. "Mud now?"

Brittle crunching under their feet followed this, and Jane shone her wrist light down at the cave floor. "What is this?" She crouched. "Hold up, everyone."

Michael shone his light around and then turned to her. "Is it some sort of branching crystal?"

Jane lifted up a long stick-like thing. "No, no, this is a bone."

"Here? We're at about three miles down. Nothing lives this deep," Michael announced.

Jane looked up. "How do we know that? Have you been down three miles before? Has any of us?" She held it out. "This is an animal leg bone, small femur." She looked it up and down. "But damned if I know what from."

"Maybe something crawled in here long ago and died." Ronnie came closer. "Happens a lot. There's this cave in the Australian outback that is a treasure trove of mega fauna, because they fell…"

"Ronnie, you remember some of those drops we came down? How's an animal going to get down here?" Michael scoffed.

"Do you think it's indigenous to the caves?" Andy asked. "There are thousands of animal species that live in caves—troglobite, I think they call them." He wandered a few paces out from the group, looking down at the cave floor. "There are lots of bones. All over." He turned back. "And some of them don't look that old."

"Troglobite, that's right. Cavernicolous species." Jane examined the bone under her light. "But they're tiny, and usually insectoid. But this thing looks mammalian." She peered at it intensely. "Weird, looks a bit…dissolved."

"Maybe that odor in the air is because the atmosphere has a high sulfur content. That'd break down things pretty quickly," David said.

Angela sniffed. "We better not hang around if that's true—it'll corrode our equipment."

Jane slowly stood, still turning the bone over in her hands. "I don't know if that's it."

"Hey." Andy, still a few dozen feet from the group, held up his arm with something glistening on it. "Rain." He touched some of the drops and a viscous string stretched from it. "Sticky rain."

More drops of the liquid pelted down around them.

"Holy shit." Where the drops had landed on Andy's arm, small wisps of smoke curled into the air. "What the hell is this?"

"What's going on?" Angela held a hand up over her face, as some of the drops began to fall among the others.

"I don't like it." Michael pointed. "Andy, get back in here."

As the group watched Andy, something shot out of the darkness from the cave ceiling, and like an elastic piece of rope, stuck to the young caver's helmet. Like magic, it stretched tight, pulling his helmet upward. He immediately reached up, choking for a moment, before his helmet strap was ripped free and the helmet disappeared up into the darkness above him.

"What the fu…?" he yelled, holding his abraded neck.

Everyone turned to point lights toward the ceiling but the cavern roof was well out of reach of the strength of the beams. In another few seconds, Andy's slime-covered helmet clattered back to the floor.

The group stared at it for a moment as it rocked back and forth. The slime coating glistened in the light like a rainbow.

"What the hell just happened?' Andy jogged out a little further to retrieve it.

Jane backed toward the group. "Andy, can you come back over here with us, please?" She turned to Michael who was facing the cave ceiling. "Michael, get us out of here."

The elastic shot down again and this time glued itself to Andy's shoulder. It tightened and Andy was yanked backward. He spun his arms wildly, and with a tearing of the tough cloth of his suit, he was free.

"Everyone, get to the wall!" Michael yelled.

The group ran to the wall as the fleshy rope-like things continued to shoot down at them. In seconds, they were at the wall with their backs pressed to it.

More of the tendrils shot down, some only just missing them by inches.

"There's more than one." David held his knife out, slashing at the things.

"We're too exposed here." Jane pointed. "That small shelf."

Just 50 feet from them was a shelf of stone about 10 feet above the ground, forming an ideal shelter from above.

"Go!" Jane yelled.

The group ran for it, but the small herd of humans on the move proved irresistible to whatever was tracking them from above.

Another tendril flew down and scored a direct hit on David. It immediately tightened and then began to draw back in. David screamed and started to be dragged for a moment.

"*Ach...help!*"

Then to everyone's horror, he began to get lifted off the ground.

Michael and Andy ran at their struggling friend and grabbed him, tugging down and managing to get the guy's feet back on the cave floor. But then another rope shot down to stick to Andy's shoulder. He screamed as he was tugged up as well.

"What the hell is going on?" Angela backed away.

"No, stay together!" Jane yelled and then turned. "*Michael.*"

Michael could see nothing in the darkness above him, but whatever had hold of his team must have been of significant size to be able to lift grown men from the ground.

He reached for the holster-like pouch on his belt, drew forth his bolt gun, and quickly placed a cartridge of bolts into its feed. He aimed upward where he thought the strings were ending, and then fired.

The bolt shot away, and he heard it clang against rock—a miss. So he fired once, twice, three times more.

There came squeals from hundreds of feet in the air, and then out of the darkness something like a giant bag came sailing down to thump to the cave floor in the middle of them.

David and Andy were released, as there came a sound like shuffling from above them. But a long, fleshy appendage still trailed to David's back.

"Holy crap. David, stay still." Andy whipped out his blade and began to saw through it.

David slapped at his back. "It stings. Get it off, get it off."

"Stay still." Jane came and used her own knife to pick the thing from his clothing.

They gathered around the fallen body. "Jane, please tell me what the hell I am looking at here." Michael kept his bolt gun ready, but they could see the fist-sized hole the bolt had punched right through a furred and protruding abdomen. A dark, jelly-like substance oozed from the wound.

"Is that a spider?" Ronnie asked with a tremor in his voice. "Hey, isn't there a giant prehistoric one that used to live on Earth?"

"Yes, but this isn't it." Jane had her knife in her hand and held up the thing she had cut from David's back. It looked a little like a meaty bear trap or one of those carnivorous Venus flytrap plants, in that it was oval with spikes around the outside and suckers on the inside. It was attached to a long and elastic boneless limb that now leaked dark blood.

"This is from no spider I know of. Or anyone knows of." She carefully crouched beside the thing. "It's almost colorless and blind. A true cave-dwelling troglobite. This thing evolved down here."

"With no eyes, how did it see us, or find us, I mean?" Angela had a hand on a still jittery David's shoulder.

"Look here." Jane pointed to the head and upper body. "Those are sensory hairs. It—they—detected our movements as vibrations in the air. Then when it does sense movement, it shoots down these things to snare its prey and haul it back in."

"It shouldn't exist," Andy said. "I know there are tons of insects that have evolved to live in caves—mites, spiders, scorpions, all sorts of weird things. But they're tiny. What could it possibly feed on down here?"

Michael grunted. "The bones you found. Big predators need big prey animals. Or lots of small ones."

"It's huge, and it certainly had no fear of taking on something the size of us." David got unsteadily to his feet.

Jane used her knife to prod at the body. "Things in caves evolve quickly, but no human has ever been this deep. Well, not since Katya and her team. We have no idea what it really is or what it lives on. But you're right, it shouldn't be down here."

"Down here?" Michael turned to her. "Or *up* here?"

The group looked from Michael back to the strange corpse—it was segmented like a stretched spider with multiple legs, but on the end of each instead of the sharp-tipped leg like an arachnid was a claw for gripping rock. The upper body and eyeless head bristled with hairs, some fine like silk, and some like spikes.

"We should head back," David said softly. "I think we've come far enough."

"No," Michael said. "This is amazing, and nothing like this has been seen before. Every step we take will be dangerous, but caving always is— you all know that. But every step we take, we may find something stupendous. It is an opportunity only a few privileged individuals on this weary and cynical world will ever get the chance to take."

Michael looked to each of them. "This is our time. We are more than cavers this day. We are Marco Polo, Christopher Columbus, and Neil Armstrong, all rolled into one. I say, *seize the day*."

The group stood looking from one person to the other for a few moments before Andy shrugged.

"I'm a little scared shitless," Andy said and looked up. "But I vote we go on."

"And I'm dumb enough to second that." Ronnie half-smiled.

"Jane, what do you say?" Angela asked.

She looked from Angela to the group. "I say we go back. Get some better kit, and only *then* come back." She pointed at the horrifying creature. "We're not ready for this. I mean, what else could we run into? Michael, I loved your carpe diem speech, but you've got to lead us out."

"I know we're scared. I'm scared. The unknown is scary. And I won't for a second keep anyone here who wants to go back topside." Michael held her gaze. "But Jane, c'mon, you know as well as I do that it would take us months, years maybe, to be ready for another drop expedition." He smiled flatly. "Or we may never come back at all. And all the while assholes like Harry Wenton will be touring the world, being celebrated as a great explorer, ground-breaker, and champion for simply sticking it out a little longer than we did." He lifted his chin.

"I don't care about any celebrations. I just don't want anyone to get hurt, or worse," Jane replied evenly.

"My life would feel forever unfulfilled if I backed out now. It's our time to win, and that time is now." Michael lifted his hand. "I vote we go on."

Angela looked back at the dead creature. "I don't think it can get any worse than this." She shrugged. "We're all the way down here, and I have to admit, I'm curious as hell. Maybe a bit further wouldn't hurt."

Michael swung to Jane, waiting.

She threw her hands up. "Okay, okay." Jane looked back down at the creature. "But by the way, we have no idea of whether this is truly as bad as it gets. And if it does get worse, then we leave, deal?"

They agreed.

She snorted softly. "And we better sleep with one eye open from now on."

Ronnie stared at the creature and wrinkled his nose. He scratched his head, and then lifted his chin momentarily to also rub at his neck.

He grimaced. "A shower would be nice. I feel like I rolled in poison ivy."

"Hey." David had his head tilted. "Does anyone else...?"

"Yeah, I feel it too. *Tremor*," Michael whispered.

CHAPTER 09

"What do you think?" Harry Wenton asked.

Maggie stared at the stone bridge and bobbed her head. "Looks solid enough."

He walked to the edge beside the bridge and stared down into a chasm of impossible depths for a few moments. Then he lifted his eyes to the other side. For some reason, he had a nagging feeling they were going in the wrong direction.

"Okay, we'll check it out but just for a while. Let's drop our excess packs to lighten the load."

They dropped their kit in a pile and took just their basic caving equipment. Jamison held up the boom box—the pack of dynamite, consisting of eight full sticks, and half-dozen quarters.

"Bring this?" he asked.

Wenton looked at the box for a moment, and then nodded. "Yes, make space in your kit."

Harry Wenton was first across, but Jamison paused on the bridge to drop a glow stick over the edge and they watched it fall. They had been able to track it for a few moments before it fell from sight, with no sound of it striking anything.

He pulled out the pulser and aimed it downward and after a moment shut it off. "No reading." He looked up. "It can't find a floor or obstacle to bounce back from."

Maggie shone her light down into the rift and on the opposite rock wall, and then upward. "All those striations in the stone, probably dating all the way back to the Silurian period. This rift is damn old, hundreds of millions of years at least."

Jamison looked down into the darkness. "Like a continental rift—an

56

old sliding plate, maybe even from Pangaea, supercontinent," he said. "This could drop for miles."

Marcus was out in front. "One thing's for sure—we've just set a new depth record." He turned, arms outstretched. "And every step we take is another record." He cupped his mouth. "*Yehaaa!*"

"Keep it down, fool." Wenton shook his head. *Dumb kids*, he thought.

Maggie suddenly froze and then crouched and placed a hand on the ground. "Everyone, stop moving for a moment." She cocked her head.

Wenton frowned. "What is it now?"

"*Shush*... I think..." She closed her eyes for a moment and then they flicked open. "I can feel something." Her eyes widened. "*Quake*."

From somewhere above them, a bread-loaf-sized rock crashed to the ground and exploded.

"Shit." Wenton turned one way then the other.

Behind them was the stone bridge, 20 feet wide and about two dozen thick. Ahead of them were several narrow passages. For a split second or two, he was torn between going back and going forward.

Their packs were over there, they needed them, so he decided. He pointed. "We go bac..."

More rocks rained down, and then in the next instant, a boulder the size of a Mack truck struck the bridge, dead center, and took the entire middle out of it. Wenton felt his heart jump in his chest so hard it actually hurt.

His options had been changed for him. "Into the cave!" he yelled and the group sprinted into the center crevice in the wall.

By now, the rocks shimmied and shook all around them. It was a caver's worst nightmare: being underground when the quiet earth "woke up."

Marcus took off down the throat of the middle cave. It was a crack in the wall, running up and out of sight, but with a good width of about three feet. The young man was like a jackrabbit and already 50 feet ahead of Bruno. Behind him was Maggie, then Harry, followed by Jamison.

Gravel and small rocks rained down on them, plinking on their helmets and bouncing from the shoulders of their toughened cave suits.

In seconds, the shimmy turned into a roar and the cave walls began to shudder.

Please open up, please open up, Harry prayed. He didn't like being in the "throat" when the ground was in flux. The earth seemed solid and immutable, but in fact during ground movement could be very malleable and even elastic—it bent, twisted, folded, and broke like glass when it wanted to.

A deep tremor also opened huge wounds, and then sewed them shut when it had a mind to. And that's exactly what began to happen—the walls started to close in.

"No-*ooo*!" Harry stopped dead, making Jamison crash into him from behind. "Maggie!" he yelled, and the woman stopped.

Faithful Bruno also slid to a stop, but Marcus was too far out in front to hear over the scream of the rock maelstrom.

The roar and grind was like a titan's millstone as the cave walls began to knit shut. There could have been a scream, but it was impossible to really tell with the cacophony of roaring stone. The group backed up, but in a few seconds the noise died, and the shaking stopped.

The group all stood breathing hard, not speaking, but waiting, ready to sprint one way or the other depending on what happened next.

"Is it over?" Maggie finally asked.

Wenton looked up and down the chasm. "I think so."

"Where is young man Marcus?" Bruno asked.

"He was ahead of us," Wenton said. "Come on, let's find him."

He moved quickly back down the narrow crack between the two cliff faces and the first thing he noticed was that it was a lot narrower than it had been before. And it began to get even more narrow.

After another few minutes, they were edging sideways, and Wenton was the first to drop his pack so he could slide through.

"*Marcus!*" Maggie yelled.

"Marcus, make a sound if you can hear us." Wenton held up a hand and the group quietened. After a moment, Wenton shook his head and pushed on.

Bruno, the stockiest, was left behind, and Wenton, Maggie, and Jamison slowly forced their way onward. Wenton was about to let Maggie slither past him to continue the search on her own, as it was getting too tight for him to move forward. Then his light revealed the final closure.

The wall had perfectly knitted together and all that was left was a line in the stone running from floor to ceiling to show where the narrow cave had once been.

"Oh God." That wasn't all that the line showed.

Maggie blew air through pressed lips and turned away, vomiting up some bile and water she had drunk a few minutes back.

Wenton grimaced, feeling like he had been gut-punched. He knew that what the Earth gave, it sometimes took back. And the cave they had chosen had now become just another rock face, making Marcus part of it.

But about two feet up from the ground, there were two fingers sticking from the crack. A line of blood ran down to the ground and the digits were swollen blue from blood pressure, and rod straight.

"Sorry, Jazz," Wenton whispered.

In a way, a small part of him was relieved that the young man wasn't missing, as they would have spent hours, days maybe, looking for him. At least now they had immediate closure.

Bad, sure, but it could have been worse, Wenton thought. *It could have been me.*

"We go back," Maggie said.

"How?" Jamison gave a mirthless laugh. "Our bridge has collapsed. And there's no ceiling to crawl across. Plus, we've lost most of our gear, supplies, and the only water we have is in our canteens we're carrying—a few days at best," he whined.

"Then we backtrack to the entrance and choose another. We have no choice but to press on." Wenton shared his most confident smile with them.

"Until when?" Maggie asked. "More of us get squashed. Or we run out of food, water, and batteries?"

"Krubera Cave has only one entrance to the surface, but it has hundreds of tributary caves leading to that. We'll find another path up, don't worry." He smiled. "Trust me. And if not, I volunteer to leap across that divide and rig a rope bridge, okay?"

"Yeah, right." She chuckled softly. "I'll hold you to that."

"We best press on," he said and went to turn away.

"Wait. That's it?" Jamison frowned. "Are we going to say any words over Marcus? He was our buddy, remember."

Wenton groaned inwardly, but then nodded. "Of course." He lowered his head and shut his eyes. "Farewell, Marcus, a good friend and a great professional. Thank you for your skill, courage, and friendship. We won't forget you."

Jamison nodded. "He died doing what he loved most."

Oh yeah, Wenton thought. Being crushed like a freaking grape in a press—what's not to love? He finally turned away. "Come on, everyone, let's do this, for Marcus."

They followed him out, no one speaking.

EPISODE 02

"What is darkness to you is light to me" — Jules Verne

CHAPTER 10

"This is it?" Andy looked up slowly. "This is what is supposed to lead to the center of the Earth?"

David exhaled. "I was expecting something better, or at least bigger."

The chamber they were in was around 80 feet wide and had multiple caves leading into it. The group stood around a hole 30 feet across and in its throat nothing but impenetrable darkness.

Ronnie looked around as he scratched and rolled his shoulders, and then peered back into the hole. "A void within a void," he said and grimaced. He continued to scratch his neck and under his arm.

"I think it's the gravity well." Michael continued to stare. "According to Katya's notes, yes, this is how they traveled to the center."

"I don't like it," David pronounced. "Doesn't make sense. The mantle is 6,000 miles thick. You want us to climb into a hole and keep descending until we drop down to a molten hell. Any wonder they said the woman was insane?"

"You see adversity, I see adventure." Michael smiled back at his friend. "You see an end of things, and I see the beginning."

"How did they do it?" Jane put her hands on her hips. "You know, a horrible thought just jumped into my head. What if Katya really was mad and she killed all her friends and simply left them down here? We have no way of knowing what she told you or wrote in her book was true."

"Some things can only be proven when we see them with our own eyes." Michael quickly looked around and spotted some loose stones. He picked up a few walnut-sized samples and returned to the hole.

He held one up. "Here's to science...being turned on its head." He tossed one of the stones into the center of the pit.

It floated.

"What...in the...hell?" Ronnie walked forward and held a hand out, waving it over the pit. "There's nothing there. No breeze, no anything."

"Not even gravity in there?" Angela picked up a stone and tossed it. Just like before, it hung in the air over the dark void.

"No, there's gravity, but it's in flux. I'm betting we can move with it and it can be traveled along." Michael smiled at the floating stones.

He grabbed up another stone and this time threw it downward. It traveled into the dark until it vanished. "I believe these are the Earth's arteries, and we can travel along them like a blood cell."

David shook his head. "We still don't have the time to float down 6,000 miles."

Michael removed Katya's book from his pocket and held it like an old-time preacher held the Bible. He opened it to find the page he was looking for. "We traveled along the gravity well downward and reached speeds of what Georgy estimated were 200 miles per hour. It took us two days, with one stop for resting."

Ronnie chuckled. "Come on, Michael—200 miles per hour? Even if it's true, you shoot along a narrow pipe for that long, sooner or later you hit a wall, and at that speed, you'd be obliterated." He scratched himself some more.

Michael shook his head. "They said the stream was strongest at the center but was like a cushion at the outer edges. If you got close to the wall, the gravity slowed and stopped you. You needed to be at the center to generate the vast speeds."

Michael studied the man for a moment, noticing he looked flushed and continued to worry his skin. "Ronnie, are you alright?"

Ronnie nodded. "Yeah, yeah, just itchy as all hell and got a damn rash. From not washing, I guess."

"Put some iodine on it and stop scratching it. You'll abrade your skin. You don't want to get an infection down here," David advised.

"Sure." Ronnie's jaw set.

"What now?" Angela asked.

Michael stared down into the impossible darkness. "Like I said, some things can only be proven when we see them with our own eyes." He lifted his head to smile at Jane.

"What are you going to do?" she asked.

"It can be done. It *has* been done." He took a deep breath as he kept his eyes on hers.

Michael's eyes seemed to blaze as he sucked in another huge breath.

"No." Jane lunged at him.

Michael stepped out over the dark hole.

And he floated.

Michael held his arms wide, threw his head back, and laughed.

"Holy shit." Andy clapped.

He swam to the other side and stepped down. He turned and held up a finger. "One more test."

He held his wrist light out before him, and this time he dove head-first into the pit. And vanished from sight.

Jane lunged forward to kneel on the edge and saw his tiny light grow faint and then disappear. "Now what?"

Ronnie leaned out. "Now what?"

"Now?" Jane folded her arms. "I guess we wait."

Sure enough, in five minutes, the dot of light appeared, and then Michael literally swam out of the pit and eased to one side to step down.

He rested his hands on his hips. "It can be done."

"What did you see?" David asked. "What was down there?"

"Nothing." Michel shrugged. "And I'm assuming there'll be nothing for hundreds or thousands of miles except for a featureless cave. But it proves that the gravity well can be traveled both ways without harm to us."

Jane exhaled. "I don't know."

Andy stepped out. "*Haha*, check this out." He held his arms out, hanging in the air over the hole. "Whoa...this is cool. Angela, try it."

Michael came and put his arm around Jane's shoulders. "This is it, Jane. This is where we make history."

She stared down into the hole. "And what if we travel down and find nothing but temperatures of three thousand degrees? We'll be incinerated before we can even turn around."

Michael smiled. "Katya and her team did it—we can too."

Jane's smile was lopsided. "No, Katya *said* she did it. We have no real proof other than her word."

"She said the gravity well existed. It does," Michael countered.

"I can't help feeling there's nothing but danger waiting for us." Jane grimaced up at him. "Sorry, I'm not usually the dark cloud on these things."

"I know. But it's time to let some light shine through those dark clouds." He squeezed her shoulders tighter. "We've come this far, and this step requires us to do nothing more than float."

David put his toes on the edge and then stepped out. He levitated. He held his hands out, fingers wiggling. "I can feel the force working on me. Interesting."

"I nearly fell asleep driving on the 65, between Montgomery and Hoover. Was lulled into a road trance. If I'm floating in this, I bet I'll do it again." Andy chuckled.

"*Hmm*, you bring up a good point." Michael nodded. "We should lash ourselves together to ensure no one gets too far ahead or behind. Katya never mentioned any side caves or branches in the tunnel, but we need to stay as a group."

Ronnie and Angela still hadn't stepped out to try it. Ronnie folded his arms, staring down into the darkness.

"Maybe a few of us should go first to reconnoiter."

"Sure." Michael rubbed his stubbled chin. "But I won't be traveling for 30 or so hours, to a potential world of wonders, and then coming back to get you." He shrugged. "But I'm okay with anyone wanting to wait here for us."

"I'm going." Andy swam out into the pit again.

"Yep," David said.

"Oh well, I guess someone has got to keep you out of trouble, you big kid." Jane's mouth was still quirked up in a smile.

Angela also agreed and gave the pit a quick test by floating across it.

"Good." Michael took off his pack. "I suggest a small meal, and then anyone who needs to take a piss do it now."

The group sat together and ate dried beef, some sultanas, and sipped water. A few pissed into their bottles and left them behind, and also spent a few minutes repacking their kits and securing anything on them that might be loose.

Jane went and looked down into the depths of the hole one last time. She knew that every time you entered a new cave, you stepped out into the unknown. But she felt this was on another level entirely.

An old quote seeped back into her mind: The cave you fear to enter holds the treasure you seek. *Who said that?* she wondered.

Michael stood beside her. "Penny for them."

"Just nervous." She turned and gave him a small smile.

"Your voice is the voice of reason in my head." He smiled, his teeth showing white in the darkness. "It's your counsel that stops me spinning off into space and doing the really dumb stuff."

She nodded toward the dark hole before them. "You mean like this?"

He chuckled. "Risk verse return. There will never be another opportunity like this in our lives, *ever*." He snorted softly. "I would die being consumed with curiosity if I didn't go. Or if I didn't and someone else did, then I would die with regret and envy."

She looked up at his handsome face. "Do you think Katya is happy she went?"

After a moment, he shook his head, and then turned away. "Let's line 'em up."

The group roped themselves together, about eight feet apart, with Michael out front, followed by Andy, Jane, Angela, David, and then Ronnie bringing up the rear.

Michael put his toes on the edge and stared down.

"Feet first or head first?" Andy asked.

"Head first," Michael said. "I found I could navigate with small movements of my arms. We'll be going at significant speed, so we should travel in a line like train carriages. But don't worry if you get close to the wall as it will only slow you down, not crash you." He smiled. "I think."

They lined up. "Just like we're getting ready to skydive." Andy's grin split his face. "I can't wait."

Michael took a deep breath. "*Go.*" He dove, and the team peeled off one after the other behind him.

CHAPTER 11

Harry Wenton squeezed through the cleft in the two jagged walls, feeling the dry stone chafe at his pack. The rift they followed was getting narrower, and though all cavers were exceptionally good at squeezing through the smallest of openings—with the maxim that, as long as your head and hips fit, you were through—he started to contemplate backtracking if it narrowed any more.

"Everyone okay back there?"

"All good," Maggie said from behind him.

"No problem," from Jamison.

There was a pause, and then, "Getting tight squeeze," from Bruno.

Wenton grinned. He expected that. Bruno was the only one with excess muscle, and though he was as strong as an ox, the ideal caving body was long of limb and good upper body strength, all on a stringy, muscled frame.

He'd give it another few hundred feet and if it didn't open out, they'd turn back.

Wenton had to start taking shallow breaths so his chest was less expanded, and for the first time, his helmet scraped. At the rear, he heard Bruno puffing and grunting as he literally muscled his way between the rift walls.

Then in the next few feet, his light didn't illuminate any more wall. And he popped free.

"Thank God." Wenton rolled his shoulders, shook out tight muscles, and walked a few paces forward as he sucked in deep breaths. Behind him, his team came out of the crack in the wall and he turned back. "Jamison, help Bruno out."

The young man went, stuck an arm in, and took hold of Bruno's hand. "Exhale on the count of 3, 2, 1, *now*." He dragged hard as the stocky man pushed forward, and then he was free. Bruno coughed and rubbed his chest.

"Don't know how you did it." Maggie chuckled. "That was getting tight for me, so it musta been hell for you guys."

"Think thin," Jamison said.

"What's that smell?" Wenton looked about.

After days of inhaling nothing but rock dust, ancient mold spores, and the various chemical compounds that are brewed deep beneath the earth, anything out of the ordinary was easily detectable.

"Sweet, sort of." Jamison sniffed deeply. He flicked on his wrist light and shone it around. A body scuttled out of his beam.

"*Shit*. What the hell was that?"

The thing had been about the size of a large dog and looked skinlessly translucent, but it moved too fast for them to follow.

Everyone's light now whipped around the dark cavern.

"Something's in here with us," Wenton said.

"Impossible," Maggie said. "The only things living down here at these depths are nematodes, and that's a big maybe."

"Little big for a nematode, wouldn't you say?" Wenton shone his light into an alcove. There was a lump there that had steam curling from an open-gut cavity.

"And what the hell is that?" Jamison's face contorted.

"Some sort of animal. Or was." Wenton crouched. "Hairless, and totally without eyes. A true cave species."

Maggie crouched beside him. She used her knife to prod at the creature. The thing was about two feet in length but had spindly legs that ended in sharp claws. The face had a long snout with a protuberant pink nose surrounded with bristles, and the open mouth displayed a row of flat, even teeth.

"No eyes, and not even any vestigial orbital sockets." Maggie pointed her knife. "Look at that long nose. It must have a great sense of smell."

"And I'd say how it found its food," Jamison added.

"What food?" Maggie asked. "And for that matter, what attacked it?"

"Something else. Something bigger." Wenton got to his feet. "This is a fresh kill." He looked at Jamison. "What did you see?"

"Like you said, something a lot bigger than this. Whatever it was, it beat it when I shone my light over here." He turned about. "That damn thing was in here with us."

"I don't like this." Bruno's deep voice had a brittle edge to it.

"Don't worry, we're a little big for anything to try and take down." Wenton also turned about in the pitch-black cavern while resting his hand on the butt of his gun. He started looking for tracks or a sign of where the thing had gone. There were multiple exits from the cavern they were in, some large, some just hubcap size.

"Yeah, but if the lights ever go out, I don't want to be down in these tunnels with something that big that is obviously a meat-eater. And can find you in the dark." Maggie grimaced. "Let's pack it in, Harry. We've come far enough. You've got your record."

Wenton nodded. "Okay, might be prudent at this time. Let's find a cave with an upward tilt." He turned back to the carcass. "Love to bring it with us. Even just the head."

"Please do not do that," Bruno advised. "The meat-eater will track us if you carry fresh kill with you."

Wenton looked at the man, knowing that was probably true and when they slept, they'd be vulnerable. "Don't worry, I get it. It stays."

"Let's…" he turned to the caves and walked toward them, examining each before making his mind up. "This one." He reached into his kit for some cave chalk and made a stroke on the rock. "Pathway one."

They headed in.

*****

Hanging above the group were three pale bodies that were hugely muscled and whose noses twitched at the strange smells. Though their distended eyes were totally white, they saw an image of the pack of new animals as thermal red-orange glows in a bipedal outline.

From the tall creature's exhalations, they could tell the new animals were carnivores, and potential rivals for meat. The pack saw them as one of two things: a threat or food.

After they had left, the creatures eased down to finish their meal. Then they would follow them.

CHAPTER 12

Jane couldn't suppress the smile as she flew. From time to time, she turned her head to see the rock wall flashing past faster than she could pick out details. The air inside the tunnel seemed to move with them, so there was no sensation of speed or any friction to singe or scrape at their skin. But she knew they were traveling at enormous speeds.

They'd been plummeting downward for hours. From time to time, a blue flash of light was glimpsed as they soared past, but as soon as she spotted it, it was already long gone. *Bioluminescence?* she wondered. Or maybe some sort of rare mineral that fluoresced.

Michael in front seemed indefatigable, and she wished she could see his face. She bet it was split by a wide smile as boyish enthusiasm overtook any fears he had.

After more hours, Jane began to find that the hardest aspect was staying awake, as the warmth from the environment and the cosseting they got from the almost sensation-free gravity well was like a soft cocoon.

It was after 18 hours that Michael out in front led them toward a huge shelf of stone to their left side. As he approached its edge, the air became thicker and they automatically slowed, and then slowed some more.

From behind, Jane saw he opened his arms and looked like he expected to land like some sort of mythical figure alighting softly on his feet. But even though they had slowed considerably, they still came in too fast.

Michael hit first, trying to run along the ledge, and fell, the others like train carriages all piling up behind him. Caving suits got ripped, elbows and knees skinned, and it was only due to their caving helmets that no one got a concussion or a skull fracture.

After they rolled for a few more seconds, Michael finally lay still, stayed down, and began to laugh. He turned to her. "What a freaking rush."

Jane sat up. "Is everyone okay?"

Angela groaned and hobbled to her feet. "Great landing. What happened to, *we'll slow as we close in on the sides*?"

"We did." Michael got to his feet. "But just by not as much as I expected." He stretched and rubbed one of his shoulders. "We'll get a few hours sleep here, take some food, and then start again."

They sat around in a group, a few talking, and all blindingly tired. David lifted bloodshot eyes.

"How far do you think we've come?"

Michael smiled. "Well, we've been at it for around 18 hours. And if we reached speeds of between 200 and 250 miles an hour, then I'd say we've come about 4,000 miles—over halfway."

"It seems impossible." David rubbed his face.

"It will continue to do so until we reach the end. And there we'll see what we see," Michael replied.

He turned to watch Ronnie for a few moments. He was the only one in constant motion. He continued to rub, scratch, and constantly worked on himself.

The poor guy, he thought. He could see that he was already coated in iodine, but whatever he was afflicted with was fighting back. He just hoped he improved.

After another few moments, they each stretched out on a flat surface, packs for pillows, and tried to make themselves comfortable. The air was warm, but not unpleasant, and slightly thick and humid. It smelled of ozone, but little else.

Jane went and lay by Michael. "Why aren't we dead? Forget about the heat—why isn't the pressure at these depths squeezing us down to something the size of a walnut?"

Michael waved his arm around. "These gravity wells." He turned. "I'm betting they're all over the globe and act like pressure valves, gently releasing the compressive forces." He smiled and shrugged. "It's my theory anyway."

"Best and only theory I've heard." She smiled in return. "This all makes me kind of nervous and excited. And I wonder what else Katya was telling the truth about?"

"The red sky, the ocean, and the strange animals?" He nodded. "I can't wait to find out." He stretched out and put an arm under his head. "Got to get some sleep…if we can."

Jane lay down as well. But images of a vast blood-red sea populated by huge beasts haunted her until sleep finally came and took her.

*****

Michael woke to muttering and curses. His eyes came fully open and he sat up. He suddenly remembered the strange spider-like things and kicked himself for not leaving someone on watch.

They had left a single lamp on, but he also flicked on his lights and looked one way then the other. But there were no intruders, human or otherwise. Just Ronnie facing away from the group, writhing and cursing as his hands moved over his body, hooked into claws as they raked his skin through his clothing.

"What's up?" Jane looked at him, hair mussed, and with one eye closed.

"Ronnie's having a nightmare, I think." He got to his feet and carefully picked his way through the group.

Jane rose and followed close on his heel, and only when she got closer did she use her wrist light.

First thing they saw was that his fingers had actually started to shred his clothing. Plus, the tips of his fingers as well by the look of the blood streaks.

"Ronnie," she said softly.

The man was still facing away from them and shuddering as though either laughing or crying. She placed a hand on his upper arm.

"Ron, *Ronnie...*" she grabbed his arm to shake him and felt his doughy flesh.

He rolled over.

"*Ack.*" Jane pulled her hands away from him.

"What the hell is wrong with him?" Michael stood over the man, his hands hovering but not touching him.

At his front, Ronnie's clothing had burst open in several places, showing large unnatural lumps of swollen red tissue, as if something was trying to break out of him.

"His...skin," Jane stammered.

What was worse was his face and hands were crowded with green knobby growths connected by ropey veins.

"*David, get over here!*" Michael yelled.

Ronnie groaned and opened his mouth, but it was impossible to see his throat or tongue as they were hidden behind swollen things, just guttural sounds emanating from within.

"Oh God." Angela was behind them now, with the others rousing with the commotion.

Angela gripped Michael's arm. "The water from the pool. It looks like the same stuff that was at its edges."

"That's impossible," David said.

Ronnie sat up, and his eyes were half-lidded and dull. He grabbed his torso and his mouth opened wider. His lips moved, but instead of words, a thick gush of greenish paste came forth and slapped greasily down on his stomach and groin. Oddly, instead of it splashing, it remained solid and stayed attached to the inside of his mouth.

Then to everyone's horror, the mass actually moved and clung onto him.

"*It's alive! It's alive!*" Jane backed away. "Something's living in him."

"Get back everyone." Michael threw his arms wide, keeping everyone behind him.

The thick pulpy matter oozed from his nose and ears now, and the man's arms dropped by his sides. His stomach gurgled and roiled and his entire frame swelled up, looking now as though there were small animals fighting inside it.

Ronnie fell back and his body shuddered, and then its outline became frayed before it simply lost its integrity. Ronnie…just…liquefied to become a huge, thick, green puddle with some tattered clothing at the center.

David's eyes were wide. "I've…I've never seen or heard of anything so aggressive."

Angela sobbed. "Ronnie, poor Ronnie. I told him not to drink the water."

"Could it be contagious?" Jane asked.

"I don't know, but I don't want to find out. Let's get out of here." Michael ushered them back to their small camp and hurriedly began to pack his kit.

Jane stared at the growing pulpy pool. "What about Ronnie? Should we bury him?"

"No, Ronnie is gone." Michael stood and lashed his kit tight on his body. "We shouldn't even take a chance of touching it. Or even going near it." He looked from the mass to Jane. "If it is a fungus, it might produce spores that could adhere to us. Or we inhale."

Jane placed a hand over her mouth and nodded.

"What even does that?" Angela pleaded.

"Nothing. Nothing we know of." Jane backed away.

"And what do you mean spores?" Angela's lips trembled.

Andy was all ready to go. "It means they could float off that crap and get in our noses, eyes, lungs. And infect us too."

Angela's mouth snapped shut and she looked like she held her breath. David, Jane, and Angela were ready at lightning speed. In moments more, they were all lashed together again. Michael moved to the edge of the stone shelf and took one last look at the solidifying mass that had been their friend.

"Goodbye, Ronnie."

He jumped, pulling the others with him.

CHAPTER 13

"Mr. Wenton."

Wenton stopped and turned. "What is it, Bruno?"

"I think we are being followed." The Russian ex-military man looked briefly over his shoulder and then back to the man.

"Who by?" Wenton frowned.

Bruno just stared.

Maggie frowned. "Are you sure? I didn't hear a thing."

Jamison looked back the way they'd come and crowded in a little closer to the group.

"Softly, like they're stalking us." Bruno squinted back into the darkness. "I think so."

Wenton walked past the group to stand by Bruno and stared back the way they had just traveled. "People?"

"Seriously? What sort of question is that?" Jamison demanded. "What makes you…?"

"*Shut it,*" Wenton bossed. He turned back to the Russian. "Well?"

"They are not people," Bruno replied emphatically.

"What?" Maggie asked softly.

The stocky man turned to her. "No, I don't think what is following us is a person. The footfalls are not…" he made a walking motion with his hands.

"Bipedal?" she asked.

"Yes, bipedal, two feet. I think comes on four."

"Oh shit, those things we saw in the cave. They're tracking us now." Jamison grimaced. "We need to get the hell out of here."

"And we will," Wenton replied. "Everyone, stay in tight. Bruno, cover our rear. Jamison, lead us out, but don't get too far in front. Everyone, stay sharp."

The gangly youth shot off into the darkness.

"Hey, not that fast." Wenton made a noise in his throat. "So much for staying in tight."

The group moved quicker than they should have in a cave that could have had drop-offs suddenly opening in front of them and falling away for hundreds of feet.

"Watch out." Jamison was waiting for them and threw his hands up to slow them.

"Damn it, this is exactly why we don't run in caves. Have you forgotten everything?" Wenton was about to give the kid another blast but noticed the piles of discarded clothing and kit. "Hey, what's all this?"

He walked toward the clothing and crouched, quickly sorting through the piles. He found some of the bags and equipment had labels.

"This belonged to Angela Andrews, one of Michael Monroe's group." He stood, holding the T-shirt, and then looked around the cave.

"Why'd they leave their spare gear?" Jamison toed one of the piles. "Did they need to lighten their loads?"

Maggie walked to the edge of the pit. "I'm betting so they could rappel down into there."

Wenton walked around the perimeter of the large hole in the cave floor. "I'm not so sure—there's no bolts sunk in anywhere and no footholds. I don't see any way to get down." He looked up at the cave ceiling for a moment, looking for spikes, expansion bolts, or even remnant carabiners. "Nothing."

Bruno was leaning into the cave mouth they had just exited from. "I think our other problem has not gone away."

"*Damnit,*" Wenton spat.

"What do we do, try one of the other entrances?" Maggie lifted her wrist light and pointed it, scanning more of the caves leading in to them.

"Hurry," Bruno pressed, and then worryingly, drew a long knife from a scabbard on his belt.

Wenton tried to think—the deep cave in the floor must be the answer, but he had no idea how it could be.

Bruno lifted his blade, held it before him, and stood across the cave mouth.

"Shit!" In frustration, Wenton balled-up Angela's T-shirt and threw it at the void, expecting it to flutter down into the darkness. Instead, it hung in the air.

They stared.

Jamison walked closer. "What's going on here?" He stretched a long arm out over the hole and waggled his fingers. "The air feels…strange." He leaned over, looking down. "There's no movement of air, and nothing that would cause...this."

"Well, something is causing it." Wenton stretched his own hand out and grabbed the T-shirt. He dragged it to his face and sniffed. There was no strange odor like some sort of fuel or gas infusion.

"Now I think we know where Monroe's team went and how they went," Maggie said. She put her hands on her hips and turned to them. "What do you think?"

Wenton turned about and saw that Bruno had squared up, shoulders hiked in front of the cave they had come from, and was staring intently into it, his long blade held out at chest level. The guy was ready to fight.

"What do I think? I think we first need to be as light as possible." Wenton pulled off his pack and began to discard anything he didn't think he'd need. He looked up. "Everyone, quick, lighten up—essentials only."

They snapped to it, and Jamison slowed when he came to the boom box.

"What about the dynamite?"

Wenton squinted for a moment, thinking. The box contained several quarter sticks of dynamite in short, red, paper-rolled tubes. These smaller-scale explosives were used to move tiny amounts of rubble out of the way. But in the box were also eight sticks of full-sized commercial dynamite. It was treated with respect, as it was shock-sensitive. Normally, you couldn't legally buy a stick of dynamite unless you had a demolitions expert license. But Wenton knew people. If he needed to open a cave or widen one, he needed the right tools.

"Leave it," he said. "Wait. Give me three sticks of the big stuff and a few quarters. You never know, right?"

Once done, they all looked to him, waiting.

"What now?" Maggie asked.

"We follow them."

"How?" Jamison frowned.

Wenton's heart hammered. *I'm insane*, he thought. He closed his eyes and stepped out.

"Holy shit, Harry," Jamison breathed out.

Wenton opened his eyes. He floated, suspended in the air over the dark pit. He swung his arms in a breaststroke and edged back to the side.

"That's how they did it. Somehow, gravity has been nullified or counteracted in the chute. They traveled, downward." He beamed.

"To where?" Maggie asked.

"Mr. Wenton? Our time is up." Bruno's face was pale in the light.

"To wherever that isn't here," Wenton said. "Maybe they were fleeing the same things we are. Or maybe this is where they wanted to come all along." He got to the edge. "I suggest we follow them. *Now*."

Jamison looked over his shoulder to Bruno. "Count me in." He moved closer and leaned on a large rocky outcrop.

Maggie and Bruno agreed, and Wenton moved to the edge, sucked in a lungful of air, and leaped.

******

The creatures burst into the cavern just as Jamison was the last to vanish into the dark hole. They immediately set on the clothing and packs, being intoxicated by the warm salty smells of the humans, and especially the bottles of urine.

One jumped to the rocks where Jamison had perched, then another, and a huge boulder that creaked under their weight became loose.

None of them would follow the bipeds into the hole as if they knew what was down there. As they skittered away into the depths of the cave, much of the group's belongings were scattered and the box of dynamite was kicked over the side where it began its long descent after the people.

In addition, the rock that Jamison had perched on and had probably stood in place as a silent sentinel for tens of thousands of years also toppled into the hole to follow the floating people.

The upper caves grew silent again, perhaps waiting for the warm and soft humans to return one day.

*****

Michael dreamed that he was Peter Pan soaring through the night air. His mother used to read him the story in bed when he was only six years old, and he hadn't thought about it since then.

He was leading Wendy and the Lost Boys to Neverland, a place beyond the horizon and bound only by one's imagination. But this time, Wendy had Jane's face, and the Lost Boys were Andy, David, and even Angela all shouting to him, waving small pointed swords and displaying immense bravado.

They were all being pursued by a flying pirate ship that before his eyes transformed into a giant amoebic green blob. The fungal blob screamed in Ronnie's voice.

Wendy shouted at him again, and he looked back dreamily to see her face contorted. He doffed his small green cap with a red feather in it and blew her a kiss, just before he crashed into solid rock.

Michael came instantly awake. He was lying at the foot of a huge stalagmite that reached a hundred feet into the air.

"*Ouch*." He rubbed his head and looked upward.

High above him hanging down to meet the stalagmites were equally large stalactites. Some had joined up and formed columns but most looked like colossal daggers.

Jane was immediately beside him. "We were yelling—you were asleep and wouldn't wake up." Jane gently wiped his forehead with a cloth. "You were smiling. Was it a nice dream?"

"Yes, Wendy." He winced and reached up to take the cloth from her. There was blood on it. He smiled at the concern on her face. "Don't worry about it. I'm okay."

"Don't feel too bad—we all probably nodded off. We've been floating for nearly 20 hours."

David, the only one with medical training, crouched beside him. "How do you feel?"

"Sore." Michael touched his forehead again.

"How many fingers?" David held up a hand, showing three fingers.

"Eleven." Michael pushed his hand away. "Three, I'm fine, I'm fine."

"Luckily, the gravity well ended and we were slowing down anyway. But even striking a stone column at little more than walking pace will give you a nasty headache." He waggled a finger at him. "Never sleep-fly, doctor's orders."

Michael laughed and carefully rose to his feet, hanging onto Jane's arm. "Where are we?"

Michael looked around, noticing he could see without the glow of the headlamps, and actually had to squint a little from the red light.

"We're here," Andy called from near another column. He turned to stare out again, his eyes wild and wide. *"We're at the center of the Earth."*

EPISODE 03

"What pen can describe this scene of marvelous horror; what pencil can portray it?" — Jules Verne

CHAPTER 14

Michael walked as fast as his stiff legs could manage to the columns of stone that formed colossal prison bars and jumped up to peer through.

His mouth dropped open. "Oh my God."

He blinked and tried to organize his senses. Imagine sweet music after years of silence. Imagine color after only ever seeing in black and white, or perhaps tasting fine food after living on gruel. After days and days in the pitiless darkness of the cave, and only seeing life within a halo of white light, this world tore at his mind.

"What do you see?" Angela called up to him.

"I dream with my eyes open," he whispered. It was one of his favorite quotes from Jules Verne, and it was never more appropriate than now.

Michael had read the works of Verne, studied Katya's notes drawn from her own experiences, and also as much of the legacy of the Russian alchemist who influenced the author, all with the intensity of a student cramming for a final exam. And after all that he had hoped, but still didn't fully believe, that what they wrote and talked about was real. And yet now, here it was.

"A world." He leaned forward. There was an endless pellucid sea, with small waves breaking softly on a coal-black sandy beach. Its water seemed a burnished red and his gaze was drawn upward.

He grinned open-mouthed and pointed. "Look." He turned briefly to Jane. "The sky."

There was a boiling red liquid furnace miles above them but still plainly visible. As he had suspected and as detailed in Katya's papers, it was the remains of the outer magma core swirling in its molten form.

He found it hard to get his head around that where he stood, he was upside down to the outer surface, and was staring upward at, and not down at, the core. Between that boiling magma and the atmosphere of this world was a layer of volcanic glass perhaps thousands of feet or even miles thick, providing heat and light insulation.

"I take it all back. Katya was right," Jane said at his side.

He shook his head. "I never really expected it to be real."

There was a splash from out in the ocean and their heads were dragged down. On the surface of the sea, huge ripples were moving away from something that had submerged just a hundred feet from the shoreline.

"Did something just fall in there?" Angela asked.

"No, see just a few hundred feet out to the left?" Andy pointed. "Those ripples moving along the water's surface are caused by a moving body in, or under, the water. There's something alive in there. And by the size of those motion waves, something pretty big."

Michael sighed. "Magnificent."

"What now?" Jane asked.

Michael turned to her. "I don't know. I never really expected to be here looking at this." He shrugged. "We explore, I guess."

David put his hand over his eyes and looked up, squinting. "For how long? By my estimation, we've been gone from the surface for around two full weeks. We have few supplies left, and I can smell brine, meaning that body of water is not drinkable."

Michael nodded. "I hear you. We'll spend a day or two resting, and then…" He leaned even further through a gap in the columns and looked to the side, "…I want to see what's along the beach. There's something down there." He pulled back in. "If it's seawater, with life, then I'm sure there'll be food if we forage."

"Just remember, we have no idea what's safe to eat or drink," Angela said. "Remember Ronnie."

"There's risk, and there's acceptable risk," Michael said. He straightened. "I'm going to take a quick look. Everyone else, wait right here."

Michael was first to climb between the colossal columns and leap down. His feet crunched on the black crystalline sand, and he walked a few paces toward the waterline.

The first thing he noticed was the amount of heat he felt on his face and neck. He felt giddily excited in his stomach.

The entire world was a giant cave of impossible proportions. And the humid sea glittered in a sparkling Titian under a red sky. It even had clouds suspended overhead. *It's so big, I bet it has its own weather*, he thought.

He inhaled the salty sea air, and then let it all out. "Hallo-*oooo*!" There was no echo, as it was too big.

He turned, his arms still spread, grinning. He saw his team still behind the massive columns that looked like colossal melted candles. The cave they were in wasn't easy to see, as it had mostly grown closed by the stone formations. Water ran down the sides of the columns and showed the layers of sparkling minerals were still being added to the stone growths. Eventually, the cave would be totally sealed over by nature.

Looking up, he saw that running on either side of him was a huge cliff face and its striations were all manner of layers that could have reached all the way back to the origins of the planet.

"Come on!" he yelled.

Before the words were even out of his mouth, Andy had leaped through to sprint down the sand.

When the group had all joined Michael, he laughed loud and held his arms wide. "I've dreamed of this." He turned. "Am I still dreaming now?"

"If you are, we are. I guess it's real, alright." Jane smiled broadly. "And I still don't believe it."

He pointed along the beach. In the sea-misted distance, Michael could just make out where the cliff faces ended and perhaps something started that might have been a forest of trees.

"Worth checking that out. If it's some sort of plant growth, then that might mean herbivores for us to catch for dinner."

"Herbivores also attract carnivores," Jane said and raised her eyebrows. "Just saying."

"Also fish or shellfish." Andy crouched and scooped up a handful of the sand. He held it out.

There were tiny shells in among the grains of dark sand. Some were the typical conical spirals, and others flat shells. But there were also purple, black, and dark-reddish spiked shells that looked more like tiny spiders.

"Notice the coloring," Jane said. "Putting on my biology hat, I'd say those colors are due to the red light influencing their design and also their camouflage palette."

"Are they the same as on the surface shorelines?" Michael asked.

Jane shrugged. "Some sure look like it. As you said, either some of the ocean poured in during a sort of great cataclysm in the long distant past, or there's been concurrent evolution."

Angela frowned. "Say what evolution?"

Jane got to her feet and dusted her hands off. "It's where similar species of plant or animal can evolve to look exactly the same as each other, even though they might have been separated by time, geography, or maybe even a common ancestor. The similar environments had simply created a creature to fill a niche that suited that environment."

"Sounds weird," Angela added.

The group walked along the shoreline, their feet scrunching on the sand and shells. Andy walked right down at the water line, his eyes fixed on the clear water.

"I can see fish, plenty of them, but they're only minnows."

"We could make a net out of our underwear, if need be," David said.

"David, I love you, but I'm not eating anything you catch in your underpants," Angela giggled.

David chuckled. "Come on, it gets a wash and we catch some dinner at the same time—everybody wins."

"*Whoa*, see that?" Andy pointed. "The fish all took off. They must have heard us talking about catching them." He walked a few paces closer to the water, his shoes actually at the lapping waterline.

Michael turned, half-distracted, and saw the v-shaped waves about a hundred feet from shore, heading arrow-like right toward the young caver. Alarm bells rang in his head.

"Andy, *get back*!"

"Wha...?" He turned, saw Michael's expression, and whipped his head back around.

In an explosion of water, a massive torpedo shape barreled up the shallows and came at him. Andy was fit and quick enough to react and he dove to the side as huge jaws snapped in the air where he had been standing.

"What the hell?" David's voice was high-pitched as they all stared at the monstrous thing that had beached itself.

The creature was heavily armor-plated and dappled with blue and gunmetal gray stripes. Large prominent eyes on stalks swiveled to watch Andy, as the huge jaws still worked, opening and closing as though its brain had forgotten to let the mouth know it had missed its opportunity.

It flipped, made a grunting noise, and flipped again, crushing the sand and shells beneath itself, before managing to turn its bulk back into the water. In another few seconds, a huge scythe-like tail thrashed, showering the shore in seawater before it headed back to the depths.

"What...the hell...was that?" Andy jumped to his feet. He pointed. "That thing tried to eat me."

"Did you see?" Jane said. "It knew it could get back to the water. It's used that ambush technique before."

Michael shook his head, but Jane put a hand over her eyes to stare out at the red ocean.

"That armor plating...I think it was a placoderm," Jane whispered, her eyes wide. "There was a time on Earth's distant past where the bony fish ruled. It was a long time ago during the late Devonian period, about 380 million years ago."

"*Dunkleosteus*," David said and raised his eyebrows.

Jane turned and nodded. "Well done, and yes, that's what I thought as well. But it looked different, bigger. They were huge, and got to be over 20 feet, but this thing looked twice that. And I can't be sure, but am I the only one who thought its eyes looked a little strange?"

"Yeah, I saw that. Not flat and glassy like a fish, but more like a lobster." Andy blew air between his lips. "Weird, and freaking scary."

"So, was it a dunkelosta thing?" Angela asked.

"Why not, or something like it? In this place, evolution could have stood still," Michael added. "The climate certainly wouldn't change from millennia to millennia, forcing adaptations."

"It came out of the water!" Andy yelled. "Right...out...of the...damn water to get me!"

"Killer whales do that," David said. "They beach themselves while trying to catch seals. It's a perfected attack strategy."

"Means they're watching from under the water," Angela said. "Did you see the size of those jaws? Andy would have been toast."

"Maybe I'm wrong, as I've only ever seen fossils, but Andy was right about the eyes—they definitely didn't have eyes on stalks." Jane continued to look back out at the water. "But one of the reasons those things developed such heavy armor was to protect against each other and bigger predators."

"Oh great! There could be something even bigger in there?" Andy threw his arms up and walked up the beach.

"We're not in Kansas anymore, Toto," Angela said softly.

"I suggest we stay close together, and also up from the water," Michael said.

"And there goes our fish dinner," David complained.

"Maybe not. That thing must have weighed several tons. If we find sand-banks or shallows, then it won't be able to get its bulk up on them." Jane turned. "But like Angela said, we need to pay attention, as this is not our world down here."

"So no wandering off," Michael said. "Even if you want to take a leak, you tell someone."

They headed down along the sand and Jane noticed in among the tiny shells were larger fragments. Some were half bivalve shells, and some looked like discarded crustacean shells, but they could have been the remains of bony placoderm armor.

"Make sure you leave some sort of markers so we can find our way back," Andy said.

"I've been thinking...it might not matter if we come back exactly here or not as there have to be other exits to the surface somewhere," Michael said.

"They could be hundreds of miles away." Angela frowned. "Our plan is to come back *right* here where we know we can return."

Michael walked backward for a moment. "Hundreds of miles on the surface. But we're walking upside down on the inside of a wheel. What is hundreds of miles up top might be only a few miles down here."

"Nope, we return here," Angela stated.

A line appeared between Jane's brows. "Yeah, come on, Michael, why swap an unknown for a known?"

"Okay, okay. All I'm saying is we'll probably have other opportunities to exit. And just imagine how cool it'd be if we entered via the Krubera and came out somewhere in, I don't know, Iceland maybe. The press would love it."

"*Ha.*" Andy scoffed. "Michael is already thinking ahead to his media appearances."

Jane put a hand over her eyes, and then pulled her collar up as she felt the tingle of something like sunburn. She held up her hand, palm down, and saw the red light beating down on her skin, and after a moment, it began to sting from a needling type of burn.

She wished she had a broad hat and sunglasses. But they weren't exactly things you needed when caving. She also wanted some binoculars to see what was ahead. Something else you never brought on a caving expedition.

They trekked along the sand unmolested for three-quarters of an hour, and Jane took a sip of her water. She didn't drink it all because there was little more than one sip left.

"I'm nearly out of water here." She jiggled her bottle.

Michael nodded. "I'm out already. I hope that the forest ahead will allow us to replenish our stores and our energy."

They were still at least a mile from what looked like a huge opening in the cliff wall that formed a valley, but now they could begin to see huge growing trunks and broad, green pads that could be palm leaves.

"I can see some sort of birds in there," David said. "See, flying over the treetops."

"They might not be birds at all," Jane said.

David turned, laughing softly. "As long as they've got meat on their bones, I don't care if they're as bony as that damn fish that tried to eat Andy."

As they approached the valley, they were nearing a small stream that cut the beach and ran from some cracks in the rock wall like a wellspring. By now, there was driftwood starting to be scattered on the sand.

David slowed a few dozen feet out and put his hand over his eyes. "There's a sandbank out there. This stream must sometimes run heavier to push out sand." He cautiously approached the stream; it was only about four feet across. He stared down into it.

"Shallow," he said.

Jane stood at his shoulder and saw the clear water was teeming with sprats. She walked along its bank and saw that it looked to be only a foot deep all along its lengths.

"Nothing too big is going to make its way in here."

"Those minnows are everywhere, and right about now, I'm prepared to eat them raw." David licked his lips.

"Well, you know the old saying about cooking a rabbit?" Angela grinned.

Michael answered. "Yeah, first, catch your rabbit."

"Step one; we need a dam," Jane said.

The group set about pushing sand across the stream to create a small blockage. The flow wasn't too great, but soon the end of the stream filled to create a pond, and the fish congregated in the deepening water.

Angela stood at the stream's beginning to keep watch, just in case anything weird showed up while Michael, Andy, and David formed a line to walk down the waterway herding the sprats toward Angela who had laid out one of her spare T-shirts that was a lightweight, synthetic mesh design.

Finger-length fish began to hop and jump as they crowded together. Angela held the makeshift net down.

"3, 2, 1… *now!*" She jerked her net up.

She hoisted it out of the water, netting about 50 of the small sprats. She closed the end in her fist, placing her other hand underneath the bag of live fish.

"Sushi is served." She grinned.

In a few minutes, the group sat with their backs to the cliff face, each with a handful of live fish, eating them like popcorn.

"Needs some soy and perhaps a little wasabi," Andy commented.

"Beggars can't be choosers," David replied. "Hey, we've been here little more than an hour and already we're eating the locals." He scoffed. "Look out, innocent new world, the top of the food chain has just arrived."

"You saw that thing that tried to eat *me*, right?" Andy chuckled, tossed the last fish into his mouth, chewed, swallowed, and then wiped his hands. "Hey, should we grab some more fish, you know, for after?"

Michael shook his head. "No, if we need to, we can come back, but I'm betting there's more game in the forest valley."

"We should release the dam, and at least try and leave everything as we found it," Jane said.

"Fine with me," Michael said.

Andy and Jane set to opening the dam and letting the water flow again. She noticed the fish swam hard to push against the increased flow and she guessed to stay in the safety of the tiny river and not be washed out into the ocean.

I'd be the same little fish, she thought. *Stay safe in here and avoid us big two-legged apes as well.*

"Hurry it up there," Michael said impatiently.

"Done." Jane slapped her hands together, wiping away excess sand.

They set off again, walking in a tight bunch. But as Michael and David led them out, Angela was tasked with keeping an eye on the ocean, and Jane on the huge cliff face to their left, while Andy's job was to make sure nothing crept up from behind them.

It took them another hour to cautiously close in on the huge valley-like tear in the cliff wall. Spilling out were monstrously huge plants, all the way down to the dark sand.

They kept close to the rock face and slowed as the sounds of life emanated all the way down the beach.

"Sounds like a jungle," David said.

"*Looks* like a jungle," Angela added.

"Everything is so big," Jane observed. "Remember the placoderm? It's like everything here is on a different scale."

Michael shielded his eyes and looked upward for a moment. "Maybe it's the perpetual light. There's no nighttime, so the plants continue to benefit from the light and heat. Maybe the animals are the same."

Something about that statement triggered a small feeling of unease within Jane and try as she might to understand why, her brain refused to provide any more answers. *It'll come to me later*, she thought.

"Should we go in?" Angela asked.

"Show of hands?" Michael grinned.

"Yep," Andy responded.

"Will it be safe?" Angela asked.

"Probably not," David replied.

"Still yes." Andy kept his hand up.

"Reminds me a little of Sumatra. I was there a few years ago doing some medical charity work. Very primitive." David's lips pressed flat for a moment. "There's tigers in Sumatra. Just a thought, but except for bolt guns, we're unarmed."

"It's not tigers I'm worried about," Jane said.

Angela frowned. "Then what?"

"She doesn't know—how could she?" Michael scowled. "Stop scaring everyone, Jane."

Jane scoffed. "No, you're right, I don't know. But Katya does. What did she have to say? Read her diary notes, Michael."

The sound was faint, but it traveled along the beach in a rolling wave.

"What was that? Was that a voice?" Angela said. "Where did it come

86

from?"

"Behind us," Andy said, squinting into the distance.

"Sounded like a yell, from a man." David looked up at the towering cliffs and then back along the beach. "Could there be people down here?"

"Interesting question," Michael said and turned to Jane.

"Maybe, but what would they be like?" Jane replied.

The group stared back along the beach for another few minutes but the sounds weren't repeated.

"Could have been a hundred things, or nothing. We don't know what the normal sounds of this place are yet," Michael said and turned away. "We're wasting time. We go into the jungle, find food and shelter, and when we're rested, I'll read the diary this evening." He chuckled. "Well, there's no evening, but I'll read it in a few hours' time. Deal?"

Jane took one last glance back down the beach but then nodded slowly. After all, she knew that if Michael wanted to, he could just make something up while pretending to read it. How would they know, as none of them read Russian? She looked at him for a moment. *Nah, he wouldn't do that*, she thought.

"Fine," she said.

"Good. Same formation as before, we stay low and quiet. David gets the honors to lead us in." Michael turned back. "Soft voices and careful steps. Let's do this."

He led them closer until they came to the opening in the cliff wall. The group stopped, crouched behind an outcrop of broken rock, and just stared.

"Wow," Michael whispered, his eyes glassy.

Jane also felt a swell of excitement in her chest as she stared. The crack in the cliff wall was only a half-mile or so wide, but deeper inside, the valley opened out, and the jungle continued on for as far as the eye could see.

Jane leaned forward on the stone and placed a hand at her brow. She saw there was a low mist clinging to the tops of the towering trees and also curling in among the lower boughs. Near ground level were huge palm fronds, some as large as sedans, and they all combined with the boiling ceiling to give a reddish-tinged twilight onto the forest floor.

"I don't even know what those are," Jane breathed out.

Tall plants rose on straight trunks, looking like stalks of asparagus with spiked heads and rising a hundred feet in the air. There were also primitive-looking trees with spreading limbs like monstrous banyans and were a hundred feet around at the trunk. Things like orange bead curtains were strung across some of the lower branches that could have been fruits or seeds.

Jane lifted her gaze. Above her, in their massive canopies, things rustled leaves or flitted from branch to branch, some on wings and some leaping madly about.

"Holy shit, it's all massive. Like a giant's kingdom," Andy said.

"Yes, it is." Michael smiled and nodded. "And it's all ours."

"Ours?" David grinned.

"Yeah, why not? Under UN conventions, nations can claim everything within 12 miles of their coastline as territorial waters. But none of them can with this place as it's 6,000 miles from anywhere. It's here for the taking."

David laughed. "Looks like someone has given this some thought."

Michael shrugged. "Like I said, why not?" He put his finger to his lips. "Quiet now. Let's push in a little way and just watch for a while."

They crept in and immediately were assailed with the smells as the humid air was an intoxicating bouquet of fragrances of plant resins, hidden blooms, and rich soil that were filled with rotting plant material, and something else that smelled of sweet almonds that was just out of sight.

The air was also crowded with the thrum of insects and though things leaped among the branches overhead, there was no bird song. However, there were rattles, clicks, and squeaks hidden within the thick foliage.

They found a tumble of boulders with vines hanging in a fringe over its front, and Michael pulled them back, staring inside for a moment before waving the group in.

They huddled there, peering out and watching the strange new world with a mixture of awe and excitement. Jane looked at their faces and remembered David's comment about them being top of the food chain; in reality, they were little more than a tiny band of hairless primates, a long way from home.

CHAPTER 15

Harry Wenton was first to land and rolled for a while before coming up on his hands and knees. He was disorientated, giddy, and also in disbelief of what they had achieved.

The rest of his group crashed down around him; Maggie first, then Jamison, and finally Bruno, the heaviest, coming in on his belly, striking hard and bouncing twice. He grunted each time in pain.

Haven't you ever heard of tuck and roll? Wenton thought and got slowly to his feet. He turned. "Hey, there's light."

Maggie groaned and rose behind him, and Jamison still sat rubbing his face. They had been traveling non-stop for over 30 hours, and frankly, they were flying blind. It was a leap of faith, as he had no way of knowing where they would end up.

For all he knew, they were drifting straight to some lower chamber in the bowels of the Earth or perhaps even the Earth's molten core itself. He snorted; at least it would have been a quick death.

Smaller rocks and other debris followed them, with some crashing into the wall, and either floating or dropping to the ground. *Someone must have dislodged it when they departed*, he thought and cast a glance at Bruno's large boots.

He approached the columns barring the end of the cave and climbed up on one's base to hang from its side and stare out.

"Holy shit. That bastard Monroe must have known about this all along. No wonder he was so secretive." He clapped his hands once and began to laugh. "It's a whole new goddamn world out there." Without waiting, he climbed through and jogged a few paces down along the black sand.

"There are tracks." He followed them for a while.

"Why is everything red?" Maggie called from the cave.

Wenton placed a hand over his eyes to shield them and looked up. "It's

89

some sort of fusion light up there—yes, red, and damned hot."

Maggie climbed out to join him. She walked open-mouthed down the dark sand. "It's an ocean. At the center of the Earth." She turned about. "Am I still lying in some cave, unconscious?"

"Then I am too." Wenton smiled.

"It's enormous. It's not just a cave—it's a world." She reached down to grab a handful of sand, seeming to only want to hold it to prove it had physical substance and was real. She squeezed it, eliciting a squeak of dry sand crystals.

"Then we're all in the same dream." Jamison put his hands on his hips and gazed out at the red-tinged water. "You know, many people actually thought this might be real. And we've just proved it is."

"But we're not the first." Wenton pointed at the tracks leading along the sand. "Monroe and his team went that way, and I don't think they're too far ahead."

"So they got here first," Maggie noted. "There go your naming rights."

Wenton shrugged and his mouth momentarily turned down. "We arrived around the same time. I'm sure when we meet them, it'll be agreed it is a joint discovery. After all, Michael Monroe is a reasonable man. As am I." He grinned as he arched an eyebrow. "Well, truth be known, he's far more reasonable than I am anyway."

Wenton then clapped his hands. "Let's double time. I want to catch up with the old boy. First, let's check to make sure we haven't left anything behind." He turned and marched back up the sand, stopping at the stalagmite barrier.

He peered in and then frowned.

Jamison looked from Wenton's face to the interior of the cave they'd just arrived in. "What is it?"

Wenton pointed into the air about halfway up near the cave wall. "He-eeey, is that…?"

Hovering near the rock face was the boom box.

"Must have fallen in." Jamison snorted. "Guess it wanted to come with us. Good, might come in handy."

Out of the darkness, the huge rock came soaring toward the rock wall. In a split second, Wenton knew exactly what was about to happen.

Bruno was still gathering himself in the cave, and Wenton screamed at the man.

"Get out, get out!"

The Russian simply got to his feet and sprinted for the opening. The rest scrambled as the rock smashed into the cliff face, sandwiching the boom box between it and the stone. The dynamite did exactly what dynamite was supposed to do—it blew up…all of it.

CHAPTER 16

A light rain had begun to fall, and Jane held out a hand to catch some of the drops. After a moment, she let it trickle into her mouth—it was clean and tasteless.

"Big enough to have its own weather, but is it big enough to have its own separate continents, islands, and tides?" she asked.

A deep boom rolled across the landscape, and the group spun in its direction. No one talked for a moment as they stood listening.

"Speaking of weather, was that thunder?" Andy asked.

"Could have been. But we don't know enough about this place to know what's normal and what's not yet," David said.

Michael looked back the way they'd just come. "Thunder, rock slide, animal noise…" After a moment, he shrugged and turned away, "…who knows?"

They continued to push through the dense foliage until Jane threw her arms out.

"*Shush*." Jane put a finger to her lips, and then she used it to point to a place between two palm fronds a hundred feet out to their left.

As they watched, an animal that looked a little like a stocky, three-foot-long armadillo pushed through the foliage to stop and burrow a little into the soft earth and leaf detritus.

It continued on and began to move parallel to them. "Are you seeing what I'm seeing?" Jane whispered.

Michael spoke over his shoulder. "If you mean all those extra legs, then yeah. Is it an armadillo or not?"

"Doubtful," she said. "I'm thinking now it's more like some sort of big millipede."

"A freaking insect?" Andy's mouth dropped open. "But it looks like an animal, and it's enormous."

Angela wrinkled her nose. "Gross."

As it neared them, they could see the pointed ends of the legs like spikes. What they thought originally was armadillo plating, based on hardened keratin, was actually sheets of something like overlapping shell. The underlying brown armor shone with iridescent highlights and made for excellent camouflage in among the dead wood and foliage.

"Do you think we can eat it?" David asked.

"Sure you can." Jane grinned. "But I think I'll wait and see if there is something a little more palatable." She bobbed her head. "You know, this is a totally new species. Maybe we should examine it to at least document what we're seeing down here."

"It's the first land creature we've seen, but I'm betting there'll be a lot more. Let's not waste time on this big guy," Michael said. He looked around. "And after that fish attack on Andy, I'd like us to have some weapons. We should at least make some spears."

The thing ambled a little closer, now being only a few dozen feet from them.

"Looks like a big mouse in a shell. Kinda cute." Angela grinned.

"I say we capture it. We may not get an opportunity to catch something so easily." David kept his eyes on the thing.

"Still thinking of your stomach, *huh*?" Andy grinned.

"Jane, want me to grab it for you?" David whispered.

"Not with your bare hands...and not netting it with your underwear either." She laughed softly. "What else have you got?"

David took off his pack. "I've got a spare T-shirt to wrap it in." He drew forth the shirt. "Michael, okay?"

Michael sighed. "Okay, fine. Andy, go with him."

David held the T-shirt in front of himself and he and Andy crept out from underneath the foliage. Around them, the jungle had gone quiet, and Jane frowned, looking about.

"I think the jungle knows we're here," Michael whispered.

Jane looked around slowly. "I don't know if it's us." She shook her head. "Something's wrong."

Andy and David continued to inch forward and were now only about eight feet from the snuffling creature.

Jane's mouth dropped open but no words would come. All she could do was point as the foliage close to the men moved—a creature, green, and standing about eight feet tall, lunged forward, impaling the millipede-mouse thing with two long, spiked arms.

The smaller creature squealed and thrashed as dark blood welled up. Even now revealed, the predator's camouflage was so good its shape was still hard to fully discern. But of what they could see, it was an upright-standing thing on four large legs at the rear and two held out in front.

The head swiveled to the two men, and both Andy and David froze. For one second, Jane thought it might have been contemplating discarding the bug for one of the humans, but perhaps it was also just as surprised by the strange new creatures as they were of it.

It turned back to the thrashing millipede and lifted it to its mouth. Long jaws opened and glass-clear, backward-curving teeth were revealed. It crunched down on the smaller creature's head, instantly shutting off its squeals.

It stopped its meal to take one last look at David and Andy and then vanished into the foliage.

The pair of men scurried back to the group, and when he arrived, Andy bent over, hands on knees and gulping air.

"I think I'm going to be sick," he said.

"That *thing* was there the whole time, watching. And we didn't even see it," Angela said softly and then whipped her head one way and then the other. "Are there any more?"

The others quickly looked about.

"It was so well-camouflaged, it was nearly invisible," Jane said. "I've never seen anything do that—even chameleons."

"Like you said, plant-eaters attract meat-eaters. We just saw one," Michael said. "Astounding."

"We need to go back, get the hell out of here," David said. "That monster was easily big enough to have killed one of us."

"Not yet. This is amazing, stupendous. Don't you see? They'll be talking about what we learn here for generations to come." Michael crouched down, resting his elbows on his knees. "But I definitely think we do need those spears for protection."

Everyone just stared. Michael pressed his hands together. "Humor me, just another hour or two."

Angela pushed her hair back. "Jesus, Michael."

He looked around and then motioned with his head. "That looks like an animal trail we can follow—make it easier for us to travel."

"Not a chance," Jane scoffed. "That big thing was staked out near a trail. That's what predators do. It knew that the small animals would come along it, and all it had to do was wait. If we're going to continue on, and only just a *little* more..." her eyes bored into him, "...then we grab some spears, right here and now. And stay off trails."

"Okay, okay." He smiled, and then mouthed, *thank you*, at Jane.

The group moved in under one of the banyan trees. Above them, the foliage had come alive again, obviously now that the threat of death had moved on. They each found or cut a six-foot spear for themselves, most not so straight, but at least they put a good point on their ends.

Michael hefted his spear. "Are we ready?"

Andy was looking up into the higher branches where things raced back and forth. "So, not birds after all."

They followed his gaze and saw that the bird things were the size of eagles, but their wings were stiff and membranous. Also, many were congregating around a structure that looked like a 10-foot papery ovoid, with a hole in the bottom. They landed on it, clung, and then walked in the jerky movement of wasps to disappear up inside it.

"Chicken's off the menu," David said.

"They're like big paper wasps," Angela said. "How could this be? How did these things get so big? I mean, they're all freaking bugs, right?"

"So far." Jane shook her head. "In fact, no. Remember those sprats we ate? They were real fish." She looked up. "It just seems that the arthropods might be the dominant species here."

"How could that happen?" David asked. "I know from our primordial past that insects grew big, but they never got this big."

"I have a theory," Jane said. "Two, actually." She half-smiled. "Theory one, look at your faces."

Everyone turned to each other and then back to her.

"That's not sunburn on your cheeks, but it *is* a type of burn. UV solar radiation burns our skin, but we have melanin cells evolved to try and cope with that. There's no sun down here, but a lot of other types of radiation. The big one is the primordial heat left over from the formation of the Earth and also the heat from the decay of deep radioactive elements." She looked at Michael. "Remember Katya's cancers? I think I now know how she got them."

"What? We could get cancer down here?" Angela's eyes were wide. "We need to get under cover like right now."

"So you're saying that the constant heightened radiation has maybe mutated the creatures?" David added. "Some mutations are beneficial, but with radiation, most are destructive."

"What's your other theory?" Michael asked.

"Well, this is a long shot. But around 400 million years ago when amphibians first came out of the water, they were in a race. The arthropods were also evolving to colonize the land. At that time, the amphibians only won because they were quicker at developing efficient lungs, and also creating egg cases that didn't need to be laid in water. But it was close."

She tilted her head. "The result was, the amphibians grew big, fast, and pushed the arthropods back to the water for a few more million years. Bearing in mind, the sea scorpions were nearly 10 feet long by then. The amphibians won, and eventually became us."

"You think down here maybe the amphibians didn't win, but the arthropods did? So this could be Earth's plan-B?" Andy asked.

"It's a theory," Jane replied.

"It's fascinating, is what it is," Michael said. "Do you see how important this is? It's like we've just dropped onto an alien planet. We are true explorers."

"True explorers?" Jane gritted her teeth for a moment. "Remind me again, how many of Katya's team survived?"

"We'll learn from their mistakes." Michael held up a hand flat. "Promise."

"What now?" David asked.

"We head in." Michael quickly looked to Jane. "Like you said, just a little further. At a minimum, we need to look for supplies before we head back up. Remember, it'll take us a long time to ascend to the surface. We can't do that on empty stomachs and little water."

"He's right. Full ascending in those caves, we'll burn up too much energy. And there aren't enough fish in that stream to feed all four of us for two weeks," David accepted.

"So, you're okay with bugs then?" Andy raised his eyebrows.

"Only if we can find one that tastes like chicken," David responded.

Michael chose a place to enter the jungle and the group followed him in. The group moved slowly, with Michael constantly holding up a hand for them to freeze, only to wave them on again an instant later. From time to time, he would reach out to touch a fern frond or tree trunk, as if testing its texture.

To Jane, the plants looked the same as surface species but different. As soon as she thought she recognized something, it would then reveal as having some leaf design, fruit, or shape that changed her mind.

She couldn't decide if they were primitive versions of things that now existed on the surface, or something else entirely. But the one thing that set most of the plants apart was their size—everything was damn huge.

Jane inhaled the tang of some sort of citric resin, and slowed to examine something like a long, emerald-green worm bunched up on a slender branch.

As she watched, eye buds pricked up like on a snail, and it regarded her for a moment before the thing retracted in on itself, bunching up even more, and then springing to launch itself from the branch it was on to dart 10 feet across the path to land on another branch, where it immediately slithered higher into the canopy.

"Spring worm," she named it, softly.

After an hour, they had only moved through a few hundred yards, and already they were covered in scratches, welts, and burns from acidic sap.

"This is impossible," Angela said.

"Yeah, this is costing us a lot of energy," David said. "I'm exhausted already."

"Michael, we need to rethink this," Jane called softly.

"Keep going. I see something up ahead," Michael replied without turning.

"Something good, I hope," Andy said under his breath.

In another 10 minutes of squeezing, scratching, and muscling through the dense foliage, Michael pushed through a curtain of hanging vines at the edge of a small clearing.

"Thought so." He grinned.

The group followed but flattened along the line of jungle and didn't step out into the open. However, just a few dozen feet ahead was a river—shallow but meandering slowly through the jungle on its way to what might be the interior.

Lace-winged creatures the size of robins bobbed and darted over the top of the red-hued water, the fusion light from above shimmering on their diaphanous wings, as the river babbled and jumped over small round stones at its edges.

Michael turned and held an arm out. "You wanted a highway into the jungle, you've got one."

Angela shook her head. "No way. We've seen what lives in the water."

"Looks pretty shallow, I think." Andy craned forward. "Too shallow for anything of size to live in."

Angela squinted at the river and brooded, not conceding just yet. Andy looked up along the waterway until it vanished between some trees.

"Why is it traveling away from the ocean?" David asked.

Michael shrugged. "Maybe the land is below sea level further in. Or maybe there's another body of water in there."

"Makes sense. So, how do we travel?" David asked, and then his brows shot up. "Please don't say swim or wade."

"Nope," Michael replied. "I've been seeing a lot of these weird trees about. They feel like cork." He walked toward a towering trunk that just had a few fronds right at its tip. He took out his knife and slid it down along its length, cutting off a foot-long piece of the bark.

"It seems dry, like rolled paper." He squeezed the material for a moment and then handed it to Andy. The young caver bent it and rubbed a thumb against it.

"It's so light, almost like cork." He looked up. "You mean we make a raft?"

"Yep." Michael grinned. "We travel Robinson Crusoe style."

Jane took the shard from Andy and flexed it in her hands. She nodded. "Might work. And we already have rope to lash them together."

"That's the spirit." Michael clapped his hands once. He turned back to the jungle. "I think we'll only need about four of the big ones. It cuts easy, and once we lash them together, they'll have more strength and should hold all of us."

Michael turned to Jane. "That sound okay?"

"Just remember, we only give it another few more hours before we turn back." She looked up. "Wish there was nightfall. But as there isn't and we'll be more exposed, I suggest we make some sort of hats to keep the sunli… I mean, the *core*-light… off us."

"Just one thing—the raft building time doesn't count," Michael chuckled. "Okay, we better get to it." Michael glanced back at the thick foliage. "David, Angela, and I will cut down these tree trunks. Andy and Jane find something that'll act like a canopy and also as a light shade." He went to turn away but paused. "And one more thing—everyone, keep your eyes open."

They set to it, and in a few hours had cut through the soft pulpy wood of the trees and cut them to length. Cross-stays were added from the off cuts, and all were lashed together with the climbing ropes.

Andy and Jane had used more of the stiff branches to create a framework for some huge fronds to go over. And quicker than any of them expected, they had a 20-foot raft that seemed strong, light, and they hoped, buoyant.

Andy held up a hand. "I dub thee, the SS *Verne*."

"And long may she sail." David saluted. "Or at least float," he added with a grin.

Michael wiped a forearm across his wet brow and then stood with his hands on his hips. "Well, looks functional. Let's see if it does what it's supposed to."

"Wait, can we take a rest break for a while?" Angela pleaded.

"Why?" Andy asked. "Soon we'll be traveling languidly down a river on a raft, spearing fish, and drinking cool drafts of clear river water. We'll get plenty of rest, as we can't do anything else but sit or lay down."

She smiled. "Well, that doesn't sound too bad."

"We'll be using our spears to push ourselves along, but we can do that in shifts. Let's get the raft in the water." Michael crouched and grabbed one end.

Together, they dragged the raft to the small river and succeeded in pushing it onto the water. Michael held on, and to his delight, it sat high and buoyant on the surface.

"Jump on, one at a time."

They carefully clambered aboard, with Michael last. The raft bobbed and shook until they each found a place that balanced the load, and then it settled perfectly on the water.

"Ready?" Michael used his spear to push off from the bank. "Heave ho."

Michael and David took to each side and pushed again. They used their spears to pole slowly down the river and after a while, they just let the gentle current draw them along with only a shove now and then to keep the raft in the middle of the shallow stream.

The canopy that Andy and Jane had constructed to fit on the raft was only high enough to crouch or lay under and they took turns getting some rest. Jane had also fashioned some broad-brimmed headwear from stiff fronds to keep the sun off their faces and necks.

The hours rolled by and they caught sight of numerous denizens of the hidden world coming down to drink. If the group stayed low and silent, the creatures didn't seem to be bothered by them, or tried bothering them back. Perhaps their scent was so alien the beasts didn't recognize them as being food or a threat.

It was David who spotted the first fish darting across the river bottom, and together they lifted their spears and waited. Luckily for them, the fish seemed to like trying to shelter beneath the raft, and Andy stabbed down hard and hauled a three-foot specimen onto the raft top.

"Looks like even more normal creatures have evolved down here," David said. "I didn't really relish the idea of dining on giant bugs...*yet*."

They quickly pulled the skin from the fish, cut it into strips, and wolfed it down.

"Delicious," Jane announced.

After a while, the fish was gone save for the head, backbone, and tail.

"Do you want to use it as bait?" Andy asked.

Michael looked at it for a while and then shook his head. "Nah, in the heat, fish goes rank really quick. I don't want anything smelling like carrion close to us. Best dump it over the side."

"You got it." Andy slid the fish carcass over the raft edge, where it spiraled down the few feet to the bottom in a cloud of blood.

Jane turned to watch it as the raft sailed on and she saw that a few smaller fish came to investigate the body before something large swooshed across and took it whole.

"*Whoa*." She sat back.

"What is it?" Michael turned.

"Something just ate the fish body. *All of it*," she replied.

Michael looked over the water. "Oh well, as long as it sticks to eating fish and not bothering us, I say we ignore it."

They drifted on, and Jane found it disconcerting that the light and the shadows never moved. There was no sunup, no sundown, or the cool blessing of twilight. Just an eternal light, like a lamp left on in a room night and day.

"Check that out." David pointed to the shoreline.

There was a patch of the jungle that had been pressed flat. It was about 50 feet wide, and they could see that it led from the depths of the jungle all the way to the water's edge.

"Something came down to drink. Something freaking big." David turned to Michael.

"Blue whale. Big," Andy added.

Angela exhaled. "You know, in this place, I think we're the bugs."

"I'd like to see it...from a distance," Andy chuckled. "*Plenty* of distance."

"Me too," said Michael. He turned. "Should we?"

Jane scowled, and he shook his head.

"Just kidding." He winked at Andy and mouthed, *No, I'm not.*

"I saw that," Jane shot back.

The group continued to meander down the river and marveled at a large, open field of strange purple grasses that were being mown down by a herd of animals the size of hippos but had lustrous, hard bodies, and six stump-like legs. Their mouths lowered and jaws opened, but inside there were no teeth, instead having something like a shredder that sawed at the grass, and then small feeder arms at its edges grabbed the tufts and pulled the food inside.

In the longer grasses at the edge, they spotted two lethal-looking creatures that watched with a predator's intensity. They had long, muscular legs, two out back and two out front, and their bodies were coiled and ready. Multiple front-facing eyes crowded wolf-like faces as they watched the herd, with special attention being given to one of the smaller creatures that was wandering just a few extra paces from the main group.

"It's like watching a nature documentary about Africa," Angela said.

"What did you call it, Jane? Concurr...?" Andy asked.

"Concurrent evolution," Jane replied, keeping her eyes on the scene. "It seems nature likes a certain model and repeats it with whatever raw materials it can find."

"New Zealand," David said softly and turned. "It was only inhabited about 1,200 years ago by the Maoris. When they arrived, they found all the biological niches filled by birds—the huge grass-eaters, the carnivores, giant raptors—eagles—big enough to carry off a full-grown man."

"And so we think down here it's the insects?" Andy asked.

"We haven't seen everything yet." Michael turned. "Making a call on

99

that now would be like venturing to the Amazon and making a judgment call based on traveling up the first river—we'd think the land was filled with snakes, alligators, and rainbow-colored parrots."

"You mean it isn't?" Angela asked.

Michael laughed. "No. This is far stranger, but you must admit, it's pretty cool."

They glided onward, and the river broadened. In the thick foliage on either side of them, the branches were alive with movement, but rarely was anything seen. From time to time, a huge tree limb would bend down toward them as if something of considerable weight moved to the thinner end to get a better look at them.

Andy and David had their spears cocked and Michael had his bolt gun in his hand, but nothing ever emerged. Or perhaps the camouflage was so good, they just couldn't see it.

A half hour later, Andy had speared another fish, this one flatter and broader, and they set about pulling the skin from it and slicing it up again. The meat was a little muddy-tasting on this species but still nourishing and it revitalized them considerably.

This fish being bigger meant it bled out all over the raft.

Michael scowled. "Andy, will you wash that blood off the raft? We look like a floating abattoir."

David helped Andy splash water on the raft's logs, but it soaked into the cracks of the cork-like wood and became a never-ending job while Andy still held the dripping carcass.

"Andy, get rid of it. Toss the damn body overboard," David said and looked over the side. With the widening of the river, the depths began to increase. "Crap, I can't see the bottom anymore," he whispered.

Andy also looked over. "*Shit.*" He pulled back, dropping the fish to the deck and falling onto his ass. "Something big under the raft."

David immediately yanked his hand back just as they felt like they hit a submerged rock and the raft lifted a few inches.

They froze, just drifting, but a little lower in the water.

"Did we just hit something?" Angela whispered.

"Or something hit us," Jane finished.

"Ah, guys." Michael was standing, legs spread, while trying to use his spear as a paddle. "I think... I think we should try and get a little closer to the bank."

David got to the other side and began to try and paddle as well. "We've stopped moving."

Andy was still sitting down when right beside him a foot-long dark spike punched up through the raft. From its center, a long tendril emerged to lash about.

100

"*Shit.*" He scrambled backward, and Jane and Angela backed up to the raft's edges.

"What is that?" Jane held her knife out at the thing.

The spike withdrew for a second or two only to punch up through the raft in another area. The tendril lashed out again, flicking and writhing over the raft where the fish carcass had been lying.

"The blood... It's after the fish blood," Jane stammered.

Andy swept his spear across the dark spike, but the thing seemed harder than iron and didn't break. In a flash, the spike was drawn down again.

"The blood, it's coming after it," Michael said softly. He held his spear up. "Can anyone see it?"

From the left side of the raft, a claw emerged to grip the wood, pressing down and sinking in.

"Yeah, I think I do." Andy lifted his spear.

The same came from the other side.

"Just how big is this thing?" Andy backed up.

"Bigger than our raft," David said.

"It's hanging onto us," Michael said. He lifted his spear and smashed it down with all his strength on one of the claws. It released, and the raft jerked and jumped for a second, but then the claws simply reattached in another area—one, two, four, six.

Michael looked over the side and could make out a huge outline, longer than the raft, broad and flat-looking, like a stingray. It was clinging to them upside down.

Jane was up on her knees. "Must be some sort of water beetle. They're carnivorous," Jane said. "Get the fish over the side. That's probably all it wants."

Michael raised his spear high, and then jammed it down into where he thought the thing's head might be. The spear struck something solid, and he held on tight. But the creature jerked backward, taking the spear, and Michael with it.

He flew about 10 feet from the raft into the clear water, and as soon as he hit, he opened his eyes and looked back to see the enormous dark shadow under the raft. He came to the surface spluttering—he would never want to fall into a river in the Amazon, but the thought of falling in a river here chilled him right to the bone.

He was frozen in indecision. *Carnivorous*, Jane had said. He saw her expression was one of terror as her eyes were as round as saucers and her mouth worked as she yelled something.

He didn't know whether to swim back to the raft or not as that meant getting closer to where the creature was hanging on.

"The fish! Throw the fish," he finally heard Jane demanding.

Andy picked it up and threw it 20 feet out and away from Michael. It slapped onto the water's surface and slowly began to sink.

Their raft was immediately released as the beetle went after the fish body.

Michael thrashed to the raft and came up over the side like an eel to lie on his back, gasping. He turned over and vomited, undoubtedly from fear.

"You're okay now. Breathe easy," Jane said, cradling his shoulders.

He coughed, spat out some bile, and pointed. "Everyone, let's get to shallow water, quick."

Michael's spear was floating on the surface and Andy reached out to grab it. He handed it back to Michael who used it to lift himself to his feet. He felt his legs were still like jelly, but he helped to paddle as best he could with the narrow spear-oar.

It took them another 10 minutes to approach the bank and see the bottom again. They paused a dozen feet out, and Michael sunk his spear in, anchoring them for a moment. He sat down hard.

"What now? Do we take to the land or continue and hug the riverbank?" David asked.

Michael turned back to the river. It stayed wide for another half-mile before it disappeared around a bend. It made sense that the deeper and bigger the river got then it would support bigger predators.

He slowly looked along the waterway. It seemed nothing but a placid river with a gentle flow, but he knew below the surface there were dangers now. And at this point, none of them could even imagine what those dangers might be.

Michael looked over the side into the clear water. He'd always thought of spiders and insects as alien-like creatures, and the idea that they were huge scared the shit out of him. But he'd never admit that to Jane.

He turned back to the jungle. Thick vines criss-crossed everything, broad palms like massive hanging tongues dripped water, exotic flowers hung like bells the size of garden pails, and there were tree trunks, some as large around as an office block that created a giant's garden.

He exhaled softly, still feeling the nerves at play in his stomach. The jungle was as dark and impenetrable-looking as ever. But just in the distance, there was a hill that lifted above the treetops and didn't seem as heavily forested.

Michael wiped his eyes and squinted. "Hey, call me crazy, but what does it look like on that hill in the distance?"

The group all stood, some on their toes. "Wish we had binoculars," Angela stated. "But it looks like huts or some sort of village."

"You're kidding. There are people here?" Andy said. "Thank God."

Jane raised her eyebrows. "You think they'll be people?"

"What?" Andy's forehead creased.

"For all we know, it's the lost members of Katya's caving team," David said as he turned to Michael. "She never actually said that they *all* died, did she?"

"Yeah, she did. They're all dead. Except for maybe her sister, who she said she lost in the caves." Michael smiled flatly back at the doctor. "Maybe this is something new. Maybe they're not people, but they at least might be intelligent life. It'll be a true meeting of species." He turned back to the hill. "I wonder what they'll be like."

"It only looks like it's about a mile or so. We need to leave the water anyway, and maybe they know a shortcut back," David said. "In my opinion, I think it's worth leaving the river."

"I agree. Anyone opposed?" Michael waited a few seconds, and when there weren't any dissenters, he nodded once. "Gather everything up. We'll head up the valley and approach from the right side of their village." He adjusted the brim of the makeshift hat Jane had made as he gazed up at the small structures. There was no movement at all, and it was hard to judge the size of the structures, but he didn't think they were very big.

Michael felt a shiver of excitement run through him. The thought of an intelligent non-human species down here was akin to finding life on Mars. It had to be worth the risk, even if it was just to catch a glimpse of them.

They filled their water bottles, placed the packs on their backs or over their shoulders, and finally hefted their spears. Before they set off, they dragged their raft up and out of the water onto the bank.

Andy grinned. "We're probably going to seem like gods to them."

"Yeah, sure, and I'm betting they'll probably make you their king, right?" Angela said and shot him a short, barking laugh.

"Keep it down," Michael urged.

They headed into the dense foliage, and immediately were relieved to be out of the oppressive heat of the blood-red sky. Just as before, they avoided game trails, and once again, it made the traveling arduous and slow.

It was about 20 minutes in that Andy spotted the tree. He stopped underneath the small, fleshy plant and stared up at one of the swollen-looking purple fruits.

"Looks like some sort of melon."

The fruit was pear-shaped but larger and the most magnificent royal purple any of them had ever seen. The tree was absolutely covered in them.

In the upper branches, there was something like a three-foot-long caterpillar that was happily munching away on a fruit and ignoring the spectators below.

"Obviously not poisonous," Andy said.

"To them," Jane replied.

Andy got on his toes, reached up, and took hold of the fruit. "It's soft." He twisted and tugged.

It popped free and fell into his hand. He brought it close to his face to smell then rubbed it vigorously against his shirt and smelled again. He smiled widely as he held it out. "Smells like a strawberry."

Jane smelled and thought it was a bit more tart than that, but close enough to some sort of berry smell anyway.

"Should I?" he asked, grinning.

"I wouldn't," Michael said.

Andy looked at it for another second and then took out his knife, slicing into it. The flesh of the fruit was a deep-red wine color and dotted with small black seeds. He sniffed again at the open fruit and used the blade to pick out some of the seeds.

He shrugged and used the knife as a spoon to scoop out some of the flesh and put it on his tongue. He chewed and rolled it around his mouth for a second or two.

He looked about to say something when his eyes went wide and he spat the mouthful out. With it came a gobbet of blood.

"Jesus Christ, it burns." He threw the fruit hard to the ground and spat, each time more blood coming out.

"Wash it out, wash it out." Jane pointed to his canteen.

Andy got the message. Moaning and with fumbling hands, he unscrewed the small flask and tipped it up, filling his mouth and spitting out the red fluid. This time, several of his molars came free.

He sunk down, whining with his tongue out. It was red, covered in white blisters, and streaked with mucousy blood.

"Easy, easy." David crouched beside him and had him open his mouth so he could look inside. "Okay, yep, I'd say we just found the world's hottest chili." He looked into the young man's eyes. "Just be thankful you didn't swallow any, or you'd have a constricted throat and could be choking to death right now."

"*Ih, uking, urts,*" Andy croaked.

"I'll bet it does," David replied. "But lucky for you, injuries in the mouth heal quickly."

Andy groaned and Michael pointed up in the tree to the large caterpillar. "That thing up there probably has mouth parts like steel sheers. Plus a gut to match. We all better keep that in mind before we start chowing down on anything new."

"Or drink. Remember poor Ronnie," Angela said.

Michael nodded, and then looked down at Andy. "Can you walk?"

"Ess." Andy winced.

"Then up you get, and let's get on our way."

It took them another hour to reach a point where they had climbed the steep hill from the right side which lifted them almost equal to the small group of huts or domes set on open ground.

"Is it really a village?" David asked.

"They look like igloos except made from some sort of fibrous material." Angela peered from behind a tree trunk. "I can see they have something in pens, maybe livestock." She turned. "So they're intelligent."

"Farmers? Is that what they are?" Jane asked.

"Maybe we should walk in and introduce ourselves," Michael said.

"Yeah, right," Andy mumbled through swollen lips. "Where are the doors?"

They all looked back at the domes and noticed Andy had a good point; there didn't seem to be any doors or windows on the rounded structures.

It was hard to exactly judge size from this distance, but Michael guessed that most of the structures must have been 30 feet around and about 10 high. At the top was an opening, a bit like in some Native American tents where they let smoke out and only kept the heat in.

In the center of the group of huts was a larger construction, like the others but twice the size.

"So what now?" David asked.

"I want to meet them." Michael hiked his shoulders. "Plus, they may have food, and answers." He turned away.

"Answers to what?" Jane asked.

He turned back. "To how this place came to be. How *they* came to be. For all we know, we're looking at the most intelligent species down here." Michael straightened. "And don't forget, they may know a quick way home."

"We're just going to walk across the face of the hill, out in the open, and say hello?" Andy shook his head. "And you all think I was crazy for taking a bite of that damn fruit."

Michael grinned back. "No, I go in first." He then felt a shock run right through his body as he stared at a point just behind Andy's left shoulder. "Hold that thought. I think I'm going to be able to say hello right here, right now."

Andy spun around, followed by the others. Standing not a dozen paces behind them was a creature about three feet tall. It had six limbs, but the back two operated together to allow it to stand upright.

It stared back at them with a cluster of dark and shiny button-like eyes crowding a face covered in bristling insectoid hairs and plastic-looking gargoyle features.

Michael lifted his hand, slowly. "Hello." He then placed the hand on his chest. "I am Michael, and we come in peace." He lifted the hand again in what he hoped was a universal sign of friendship.

The thing had a tube-like mouth that opened at the tip emitting a chittering-clicking noise that made Michael think that learning each other's language would be damn impossible. In response, other creatures appeared from the jungle.

They moved fast and the one that had appeared first scuttled forward, keeping its eyes on Michael as it rushed up to grip his hand and run one of its own hands up his arm, squeezing and pinching at what must have seemed strange skin to it.

It raked its claws down, scratching his arm but not breaking the flesh.

"Ouch." Michael gently pulled his arm back.

They clicked and twittered and even more appeared from the jungle. Some took the hands of the humans, and others pulled the spears, the packs, and other equipment from their hands.

"It's okay, I guess." And Michael let his hand fall. "A sign of good faith, and to show we come in peace. We'll get our gear later."

The creatures then began leading them out from the trees.

"Guess we've been welcomed already," he said.

"These guys are very cool." Andy grinned down at them. "Hi, I'm Andy."

The hard-shelled face stared up at him for a second. It was impossible to read any expression in the oil-dark cluster of eyes and Andy went to touch its arm, but it emitted a louder squeak and recoiled.

"It's okay, it's okay." He looked up. "I think they're a little scared of us."

"You would be too if you came home to find a group of massive bipeds watching your village." David looked down at the waist-high things holding his hands. "But if this is this world's top sentient beings, then you're right, we must seem like gods to them."

"Well, we arrived from their Heaven," Angela added.

"Or their Hell." Jane tried to tug her hand out, but the thing just chittered louder and gripped her tighter.

In a strange procession, the people were escorted toward the domed huts by a phalanx of the small, dark insectoid people. They constantly looked up, with their blank twisted faces, and as they approached, the group saw more of the things erupt from the top of the domes.

"That's what they are—they're like hives," Jane said. "We should have guessed."

One of them tried to remove Andy's knife. "Sorry, buddy, I need that." Andy pushed the hand away. It tried again, and Andy was a little more forceful, giving the little being a push. "*No.*"

The creature hissed and it spat something at him that landed on his pants.

"Oh nice. Is that a way to welcome your new king?" He grinned over his shoulder at Angela.

"Hey, your pants." Angela pointed. "Look."

Where the thing had spat at him, smoke curled from a darkening patch.

"Don't touch it, Andy. I think it's acid. Must be some sort of defense mechanism," Jane said.

As they entered the village, the whole tribe was out in the open and the twittering grew in volume almost like cheering.

Michael could now see that the fenced-in area was more like a cage with a roof over it. Inside, the corralled animals were the size of dogs and scuttled away on multiple legs, trying to press themselves as far back from the creatures as they could get. Also, there were several different species of beetleoids in there, some jet black, some mottled, and a few striped like tiger cubs, except with antenna and folded wings.

They were led toward the fence, and Michael suddenly got a sinking feeling in his stomach. "Oh shit, no."

Other creatures opened a gate, and one by one the people were pushed in and then the gate closed.

"Not exactly what I was expecting." Andy scoffed and turned to grip the bars. "I'm thinking something got lost in translation."

"What just happened?" Angela folded her arms.

"I have a horrible feeling…" Michael sighed, "… that might have been a hunting party."

"A hunting party? What does that mean?" David asked as he tried to keep away from the other creatures in the enclosure.

"It means we just got hunted," Jane finished.

"So we've just been taken prisoner." Andy snorted. "That first contact thing didn't go to plan, did it?"

"What do they want from us?" Angela watched them through the wooden bars.

Michael looked at Jane who shook her head. He turned away.

"I don't know yet, Angela. Let's just work on a plan for getting out," Jane said.

"We're bigger and smarter than those little fellas. We should just break out," Andy said. "We have all the advantages."

"Do we?" Jane sighed. "If they're based on insect morphology, which they certainly look it, then they have superior vision and can see in spectrums we can't. They have armor plating, are faster, and by the way, they'll probably be stronger than we are—did you know the average ant can lift 50 times its own body weight? The strongest human can only just lift its *own* weight."

"But we have the brains, and therefore the ultimate advantage," David added. "But only if we use them."

There was commotion among the huts, as the group who brought them in all congregated outside the large central hive.

Then from the hole in the top, a group of the things emerged dragging something. Something big. It was obscenely bloated and they pushed and pulled the long grub-like thing free.

Once exposed, the beings rushed to lift and comfort it and its true form was revealed.

"All hail the queen," David said softly.

The huge creature was about 15 feet long and though the front third of its body was the same multi-limbed gargoyle as the creatures that captured them, its back end was a huge, distended sack that pulsed with an unnatural life.

"Put on your best smiles, people. We're about to be introduced to royalty," Michael said.

The swarm spent a few moments handing the queen some of the items they had taken from the people, and in turn, she spent a few moments examining each. Her long, fingered claws took many minutes turning them over and feeling their surface, hardness, and composition, and holding them up in front of her multiple eyes.

Finally, the massive thing looked up, and whether a signal was given or not, it was carried closer to the cage.

The group pulled back a little from the front of their prison, as the inscrutable button-like eyes stared in at them. The grotesque head turned, slowly examining each of them—the two smaller women, the skinny and tall Andy, the muscular Michael, and the shorter and stouter David.

After another moment, there was a chattering call from the queen and the swarm surged forward. The door was pulled open and the horde came surging in like a wave of hard skeletal bodies.

The smaller creatures in the pens with them went crazy and screamed in terror as they tried to get behind the people.

"*Piss off.*" Andy threw one off, and Michael rushed to try and put himself in front of the women, but all of them were quickly overwhelmed, and with so many bodies in the pens, they quickly lost sight of each other.

Even though the creatures were half their size, as Jane had suggested, they were extraordinarily strong and the humans were quickly subdued or held down flat. Michael now noticed the smell was revolting, and he detected something like formic acid and an odor of stale almonds.

The group yelled and struggled, but in another few seconds, the horde started to withdraw. When the cage cleared, they noticed they were one down.

"Shit, they took David." Michael rushed to the cage door as it was pulled closed.

The doctor struggled and thrashed, being held by a dozen of the small beings as he was pulled up the hill toward the queen. When he was before the grotesque thing, its lumpy body bent so it could bring its upper segments closer, it reached out to feel his body, pressing, prodding, and then it brought its face even closer as it was obviously smelling him.

David was held flat on the ground with many of the things holding each of his arms and legs and body. He stopped struggling and stared back into the inquisitive queen's face.

"We mean you no harm," he said with a shuddering voice.

The queen recoiled for a moment, but then sensing no danger, her horrifying face inched closer to David once again. She examined David's hair, face, shoulders, and then limbs.

She looked about to pull away, but instead shuddered for a moment before vomiting onto one of his arms.

David turned away and grimaced. *"Blech."*

He turned back to look. But then his face contorted and he howled in agony. Smoke rose from the mucous-covered arm, and immediately the flesh reddened, softened, and began to liquefy.

The queen was eased forward by her dozens of attendants and the tube-like mouth elongated and fixed on the liquefying flesh of David's arm. She began to suck it up.

Angela shrieked in horror, and then turned away to throw up.

"Oh God, no." Jane grimaced.

As if a signal was given, the other creatures began to eject the acidic bile onto David's other limbs, and the man was literally melting and being consumed alive as a feast.

Michael backed up, going to barge into the gate, but Jane grabbed him and held on. She shook her head. He looked down and saw that her face was wet with tears.

"Please no, we're not ready yet."

Michael bared his teeth in anguish and tried to shut out his friend's pitiful sobs as the creatures worked their way up his limbs toward his torso.

The queen moved grub-like toward his face and stared down with her emotionless insect eyes. As she hovered over David's pitiful, tear-streaked face, her mouthparts bloomed open once again.

"Noooo." Michael felt his sanity slipping, not just at the thought of what was to come, but that this would be their fate as well.

David howled non-stop in insane agony and his eyes swiveled in his head. The queen was inches from him with her mouth fully open, just as a shot rang out. A small red hole appeared in David's forehead and he fell back, silent.

The creatures froze, and Michael and the group swung to the sound. Standing just a few dozen feet away were Harry Wenton and a small group of people.

Wenton fired again, and this time the bullet smashed into the bag-like body of the queen, and with a screeching and flailing of chitinous limbs, she was dragged back to the large domed hive, and then just as quickly pulled up its side and into the hole in its top.

In a few seconds, the field was clear, as the horde had vanished either into the huts or into the jungle.

Wenton and his team ran forward and opened the cage. "So sorry about your friend. Wish we had gotten here sooner."

"You shot him?" Angela glared.

"And thank God he did." Andy fell through the gate and ran to David.

They hugged Harry and introduced themselves to the new group. Wenton turned back to the domed hives.

"What the hell were those things?"

Jane also turned. "Maybe in our world they're ticks, or fleas, or who knows what. Down here, they're hunters, monsters."

"And we were all on the menu," Michael said.

Wenton saw that Angela still glared at him. "I'm sorry to shoot your friend, but..."

"It's okay, you did the right thing," Michael said.

"Thank you." Wenton exhaled and holstered his gun. "We better move. One gun against dozens of those monstrosities is not going to scare them off for long."

"You're right," Michael said and called Andy back in. "We need to grab our stuff."

"Then we head back." Jane turned to Michael. "We are not prepared for this, any of this. We go back now."

Michael nodded. "Agreed."

"Yeah, about that." Wenton grimaced. "The cave we came in on, and the one I assume you did too... It's sort of blocked, now."

"That sound we heard...that was an explosion and not thunder. That was you?" Angela's scowl deepened.

Wenton nodded. "An accident, I assure you."

"You damn idiot," Angela wailed. "Now we're really screwed."

"Hey, back off." Maggie jabbed a finger into Angela's face. "He said it was an accident, because it was." She then pointed at David's remains. "And just so we're all on the same page, if it wasn't for Harry, that'd be you next."

"I think that's enough." Wenton's eyes bored into Angela for a moment. "No use expending energy on something that's already history." He sighed and then looked about. "So, you seem to know this place, Monroe—what's our next steps?"

Michael sucked in a breath. "Katya and her team also thought there might be more exits via other gravity wells."

"Is that what they were? Gravity wells? Cool." Jamison grinned.

"Who's Katya?" Wenton asked.

"Doesn't matter now. Our problem is we need to find one of those exits and ride it all the way to the surface," Michael replied.

"Just how big is this place?" Maggie asked.

"We think it's an entire world," Jane said.

"And in this *entire world*, we don't know where those wells are. Well, that doesn't sound like a needle in a haystack at all." Wenton rolled his eyes.

"Really, Harry?" Jane scoffed. "We wouldn't need to search for that needle if you assholes hadn't blown up our existing route home."

Wenton grinned. "No need to be rude, Jane. We're all in this together now."

"Okay, first thing we need to do is get as far away from here as we can," Michael said.

"What about David?" Angela asked in a small voice.

Michael shook his head. "Unfortunately, we don't have the time or can risk trying to bury him, or even take his remains with us. He stays here."

Angela's mouth turned down. "Michael."

He turned.

"I think you brought us to Hell." Angela walked away.

Michael watched her go and Jane reached out to grab his arm. "She's just upset."

"I know." He sighed. "But she's right."

CHAPTER 17

"*Lemuriya*." Michael smiled. "That's what Katya called this place. It was a mythical lost continent."

"Seems apt," Wenton agreed.

Michael had the notebook open at a page that held a map. "The interior." He looked up. "That's where Katya and her team ventured to—they were following the path of Saknussov. She eventually came back from there with her sister...*just* her sister."

"Saknussov?" Wenton chuckled. "Really? That old Russian fable was a real person?"

"Look around, Harry." Jane waved an arm at the towering jungle banyans. "I think the time for skepticism is long over."

"Yes, true, but I thought he was an invention of that French author." Wenton raised an eyebrow.

"He was real, alright. In the late 1400s, Arkady Saknussov had been telling anyone who would listen that he believed there was a world within a world, and he could find his way down here. True to his word, he set out with a team of explorers to prove his theory." Michael drew in a deep breath. "Katya and her team got access to his notes, and later followed his path. I'm sure they thought it was all just a legend as well when they began."

"And we followed Katya, and here we are," Jane added.

"And that French author, Jules Verne, was also a believer," Jamison said.

Michael nodded. "Yes, he must have obtained some of Saknussov's notes, or perhaps had been intrigued by the legends he'd heard."

"Well, whichever, you've got to admit his story was amazingly prescient." Wenton turned to the walls of jungle. "A few have come, and even fewer have returned."

The group sheltered beneath one of the huge trees whose limbs spread so wide they touched the ground, creating a green cave beneath. Each of them had recovered their spears; Maggie and Jamison had done the same, with Bruno carrying a stout club.

Their clothing was soiled, torn, and Andy's was acid burned in places. Jane noticed their expressions were haunted and fatigued.

She looked up at Michael. "The *interior*…is that where she lost the rest of her team?"

He slowly lifted his eyes from the notebook. "Mostly."

She pulled in one of her cheeks. "I'm guessing she didn't exactly say how or what the risk was?"

"No, other than writing that it was a land of giants." He half-smiled. "And there were caves in the column mountain."

"Another way out?" Angela almost pleaded.

"I think so." Michael didn't meet her eyes.

Wenton lifted a finger. "Question."

"Go." Michael waited.

"If we do manage to get our expedition out of here, I know some very good publicists. We can all be famous—something to look forward to." Wenton's eyes gleamed.

"Our expedition?" Michael snorted. "You came second and then joined us."

Wenton looked pained. "And you'd be dinner by now if not for us, dear boy."

"Bullshit." Michael's jaw clenched. "And by the way, we could be halfway home by now if you hadn't closed our front door."

"Don't make this ugly." Wenton squared his shoulders.

Bruno came and stood at Wenton's shoulder. Andy did the same behind Michael.

"Seriously? You're going to do this now?" Jane cursed under her breath. "Everyone, take a step back and shut the hell up so we can work *together* on getting out of here. You guys save the pissing contests for later."

Michael grunted and sat down; Andy did too.

Wenton waved Bruno down. "Helpful is my middle name." Wenton smirked. "But I want to see that notebook."

Michael tossed it to him and with a grim smile watched as Wenton opened the book and after a moment, his brows came together.

"Yeah, that's right." Michael's grin widened. "How's your Russian?"

"I get by." Wenton continued to flip pages.

"*Ty vsegda byl durakom*," Michael said in Russian and waited.

Bruno chuckled. Wenton glared at him and then snapped the book shut and tossed it back. "I'm a little out of practice."

"Yeah, sure you are." Michael opened the book to the map again. "We head inland, skirt around some sort of large body of water, and then find the column mountain." He handed the book to Bruno.

The stout Russian took it and looked through it. After a moment, he nodded. "This is what it says."

"While we're stuck here, we work together." Michael took the book back. "For now, let's all just pray there's another gravity well waiting for us."

CHAPTER 18

The clearing wasn't big, maybe 10 feet by 10 feet. The group was walking in single file, some in the footsteps of the person in front, and some meandering a little now that they had more space.

Jane saw Angela veer a few feet to the left and cross a patch of something that looked like white threads spread over the earth.

As soon as the young woman did, the worm came out of the ground so quickly it had Angela by the leg before anyone could even react.

The thing was like a jack in the box, in that it had a trapdoor set in the center of the silk mesh and from within it the muscular creature sprang forward, obviously after it felt the vibrations from her footfalls.

The worm, about 18 inches around, extended six feet to grab her with two wicked-looking red pincers each as long as a man's finger and curving back toward its feeler-ringed mouth. The rest of the worm was still anchored in the silk-lined tube it came out of.

Michael was first to ram his spear into it, followed by Maggie doing the same. But it was leather-tough and strong, and seemed to be made of solid muscle, and already it was pulling back and taking the screaming woman with it.

"Don't let it get me in there! Don't let it!" Angela screamed.

Michael clenched his jaws, pulled his spear, and rammed again. As far as he was concerned, there was no way he was going to lose another team member, especially not by getting pulled into a hole and probably devoured alive below the earth.

Bruno slammed his club down on its head, but it didn't look like it even felt it. Jane held Angela as the rest of the group joined in the attack and while they yelled, stabbed, and bashed at it, the worm pulled another few feet back into its hole.

"Shoot it! Shoot it!" Michael yelled.

Wenton ignored him and continued to jab his spear at the worm. Jane then let go of Angela, rushed around behind the creature, and pulled out her bolt gun. With expert hands, she loaded a pin and held it down on the back of the thing's neck, where she could just make out a thin line of grey running just under the skin like in a shrimp. And fired.

In an instant, the worm simply stopped moving as if frozen. The pincers slowly opened and Angela fell free, crawling away and holding a bleeding leg.

Jane pushed the bolt gun back into her pouch on her hip. "Invertebrates don't have a brain as we know it, but more a thickened brain stem as a chord. The bolt severed it."

The thing flopped to the side.

"But I think it's still alive," she said.

Andy and Maggie tended to Angela who continued to shake from fear on the ground and Wenton approached the thing, one hand on his revolver.

"You could have shot it, you know," Jane said.

He nodded. "I could have, but you had it under control." He turned to her. "Just remember, once the bullets run out, then all the gun is, is a piece of steel. And your boyfriend just finished telling us that the interior is where the real danger lies, yes?"

Jane's lips pressed into a line, and Wenton placed a boot on the thing's head.

"Any ideas what it is?" He cocked his head.

Jane looked back down at the monster. "There's something called a bristle worm that's carnivorous and uses ambush to catch its prey. But they live in the ocean and only get to a few inches long."

"The land of giants," Andy whispered.

Wenton grunted. "Well, there is one upside to this little mishap."

"Really? What the hell could that be?" Jane's brows knitted.

Wenton smiled. "We now have fresh meat."

*****

"Has anyone ever eaten alligator?" Andy said between mouthfuls. "Tastes a bit like this."

"I have," Maggie replied. "But this is a hellova lot tougher." She spat out a chunk she had been working in her mouth for a few minutes and it bounced away into the foliage like a rubber ball.

They had made a small fire and cut slabs from the neck of the massive worm. Michael had expected it to be sort of mushy inside, like the small ones in your garden. But this sucker was a column of solid muscle. With effort, he swallowed the last piece he had. He knew he needed the calories.

"You know, maybe there's better cuts on the thing, and we just ate the wrong bit." He tucked another morsel into the corner of his mouth and chewed it like a wad of tobacco.

"I'm sure it would have said the same thing about Angela," Andy guffawed.

Angela gave him the finger, and then looked back at the huge pipe of meat hanging out of its hole. "There's probably another 1,000 pounds of meat in there. What a waste."

"How's the leg?" Jane asked.

Angela reached forward to squeeze the bandages that were only slightly discolored. "Damn sore, but luckily it didn't lacerate me too badly."

"For now, we'll keep the iodine up and change the bandages daily until it stops weeping," Jane announced.

They broke camp and once again headed toward the interior. For a while, the trees started to open up, and the ground became marshy. There were low ferns and also huge living poles, a hundred feet tall and covered in bark that was like fur and with just a few stalks of green on their very tips. They soon became the dominant plant.

"The going is a little easier, but I don't like there being so little cover for us from these damned plants," Wenton grumbled.

"Not plants, I think. More like a type of primitive fungus," Jane observed. She pulled the frond she had on her head down a little more. "And I would suggest you guys get some more sunshades out of anything you can find. That's radiation you can feel on your skin, and not solar radiation."

"Oh freaking great," Maggie scoffed. "You sure know how to show a freckled girl a good time, Harry."

Wenton grinned. "I do my best."

Michel held up his hand and the group paused. He slowly tilted his head for a moment.

"What is it?" Andy whispered.

Michael continued to concentrate. He could feel it right up his legs—a shaking, not like an earth tremor, but slow and rhythmic. He began to hear it then; a thunderous sound that shook the earth and made the puddles at his feet shimmer with impact ripples.

He turned. "Take cover."

The group scrambled to find some sort of shelter or concealment. They hunkered down, waiting.

Michael placed a hand against the nub of a rock sticking up from the marshy landscape. As he crouched there, he saw what looked like tadpoles flicking about in the small pools.

Good to see a few more of you made it, he thought. It comforted him seeing something else recognizable so far from home.

Jane came and joined him under the fronds of a low palm and the pair then lay belly down in the muddy water.

They all heard it then: the thunder-like pounding, followed by the splintering of wood and then from their east, trees started to fall and thump to the ground.

From out of the jungle, came a mountainous creature.

"Oh my dear God," Jane whispered.

The thing was easily 100 feet tall, and twice that in length. The neck was long and covered in over-locking plates that also ran down over its shoulders and flanks. The nubs of false wings were tightly folded on its back, and its six legs were each as thick around as redwood trees.

The colossal creature paused to lower its head, and the group could see compound eyes that were an iridescent green and the size of wagon wheels. There were tiny feeder arms on each side of its mouth, and they plucked at a tree and sucked in every bit of green into mouthparts that worked like machines, churning, cutting, and grinding up the tough fronds.

The neck lifted again, and the plates made a sliding scraping sound over each other.

"Herbivore, thank God," Jane said softly.

The creature lifted its head high and then made a deep trumpeting sound. Perhaps it was the all-clear as from behind it more titanic beasts pushed out of the jungle.

"Just like the massive sauropod dinosaurs," she said. "In fact, these are probably their arthropod equivalents."

The herd beasts, once fully revealed, showed huge blotches of muddy brown and some of the darkest purple. On the end of their feet instead of the stump-like feet of elephantine columns, they had claws that looked capable of grasping things if need be.

On their backs, tiny flying creatures landed and they squabbled over some sort of vermin they caught there. The massive insectoids probably never even noticed the flying creatures were there. Or perhaps they did and approved of them ridding their bodies of annoying parasites they could never hope to reach.

"*Thunder lizards*, they used to call the most massive dinosaurs," Michael said as the ground shook as the massive creatures began to pass by them.

"Thunder bugs?" Jane replied.

Michael went to stand to get a better look, but Jane grabbed his arm. "Stay down. They've got young, and sometimes carnivores follow big herds—like lions follow elephants."

Sure enough, once the first creature had begun to enter into the far tree line, from behind them came the first of the predators.

They looked tiny compared to the huge beasts, but they were easily 20 feet tall and up on their back four legs. These things were striped like tigers, and Michael remembered Jane talking about concurrent evolution, and it was obvious these hunters were built for speed and for jungle camouflage.

They had long faces, snouts that were filled with teeth of a bony material and not embedded in jaws, but rather set into their external exoskeleton like cutting shears. Michael had no doubt they could cut through the toughest of arthropod armor plating, so humans would be like soft candy to them.

He held his breath as the pack came out of the tree line and a few stopped to lift their heads and test the air. Eyes on long tendrils moved independently, and he bet their vision might have extended to infrared and thermal. He just hoped the ambient warmth was enough to mask the human's body heat profiles in their concealment.

There came the deep trumpeting of the herd leader of the titans that was answered by the softer sounds of the smaller creatures, the young probably, and the predators took that as a cue, put their heads down, and ran, blindingly fast into the jungle in pursuit.

"Like Angela said, we're the bugs here," Jane whispered.

Michael blew air between his lips. They stayed hunkered down for another 10 minutes, but nothing else came out of the jungle. Michael waved his arm in the air, and they crouch-ran to the forest line, quickly vanishing into the humid shade of the massive pad-like fronds.

Michael felt a sinking feeling in his stomach when he noticed Angela had begun to limp. Plus, her wound was leaking—not blood, but something repellently yellow.

Infection, his mind lamented. And he knew they didn't have the medicine to treat it.

To her credit, Angela marched on, and it was still another hot and exhausting hour before they finally broke free of the jungle. Before them lay two very different paths forward—one a huge expanse of water and the other, closer, a plane, devoid of life and strangely shimmering in the red heat. And beyond that, rising like a geological colossus, was their goal.

"The column mountain. Just like you promised," Wenton said. "So that's what your Russian friend meant."

Just visible, rising up in the far distance, was a huge geological formation that literally touched the boiling red sky. It was many miles around at its base and the cone-shaped mega-mountain kept steepening until it formed a huge column of rock that touched the ceiling.

"Somewhere around that, on that, or *in* that thing, might be the pathway we seek, and perhaps our best hope for getting home," Michael said. "All we need to do is get to it."

"Easy choice. The shortest path is across that plane. It only looks to be a little over a mile, and then just a few more miles of jungle beyond that." Wenton turned his head slowly as he studied the open space. "Looks the least dangerous, and we can cross that open area at a jog in a few hours, even with our injuries." He glanced briefly at Angela.

"No, it's not as straightforward as it seems. There was something Katya mentioned about that plane." Michael quickly retrieved Katya's notebook and flipped through pages.

He stopped and ran a finger down the scribbled notes for a few moments before looking up. "*Razdavit' zemlyu*—crush land." He lifted his chin higher, squinting up at the red ceiling miles above them. "And that might be it. Look."

Overhead was a black dot on the red ceiling. It looked to be only the size of a pea, but Michael was sure that up close it'd be hundreds of feet across, and it was hanging directly over the empty, lifeless plane.

He read some more. "Katya said the plane can be crossed, but only once a month it is safe. At all other times, it is deadly."

"I have no idea what that even begins to mean," Jamison said.

"Neither do I, but I can hazard a guess," Jane said and placed a hand over her eyes to look up at the speck on the red ceiling. "The Earth's pressure here, everywhere, should be deadly. But it's somehow mitigated by the gravity wells, and also I think by the volcanic glass shield overhead. That dot we see might be an area where there is a solid ball of matter, probably a super-dense iron-based composition that is allowing the gravity to be focused, like a lens, in the places directly underneath it."

The group looked back out over the plane; the air shimmered and seemed heavy.

She waved an arm out over the flattened geography. "Notice the way there is nothing above ground level—no tree, rock, or even blade of grass? Everything there is super compressed and pounded down. I assume if you tried to cross it, you'd end up the same."

"But Katya said it can be crossed, but only once a month it becomes safe," Andy replied. "How? When?"

"What's the one thing that happens once a month that affects our gravity and even pulls hard enough to affect our oceans?" Michael asked.

"The moon," Maggie answered.

Michael nodded. "My money is on the gravitational pull of the moon, somehow dragging those iron-based focal points back just enough to reduce the gravity concentration."

"By how much?" Jamison asked.

"Does it matter?" Jane shrugged. "If it's ten-times normal gravity, or a thousand times? Look at the plane—everything out there is pounded to nothingness."

Andy bent to pick up a fist-sized rock, cocked his arm, and threw it with all his might. The rock sailed toward the plane, and when it arrived at the edge, it simply vanished.

"Where'd it go?" he asked. "Did anyone see it?"

"Atomised," Jane said. "Pounded down so hard and fast, it was crushed to dust."

"Ouch," Andy acknowledged.

"So, when is the next full moon?" Wenton asked.

"By my calculations, there's no full moon due for weeks. We can't risk it." Michael turned away. "So, what else have we got?"

"Then we have two options." Wenton held up two fingers and curled one of them. "Option one, we go around the outside of the lake and spend maybe a week doing it. Plus expend a lot of energy unnecessarily." He curled his other finger. "Option two, we sail across in a direct line, as the crow flies. Save ourselves days."

Andy laughed but with little humor. "Listen, buddy. I was nearly made fish food by some armor-plated monster from the deep that looked like a bear trap with fins. And that was when I was still on the shore. I can't imagine what's lurking out in the center of some giant lake in this hellhole."

"But that was the ocean, right?" Wenton raised an eyebrow.

"Yes, it was, but he's right, Harry," Michael replied. "And for that matter, we got attacked just recently when we were on a raft by something that punctured the wood. Something pretty big. And that body of water wasn't very large." He pointed. "Look at the size of this so-called lake. I can't even see the other side. It's more an inland sea." He dropped his arm. "Big lakes, mean big lake occupants."

"Risk verse return," Wenton replied. "Look at us. We're dressed in rags now. Angela there has a festering wound on her leg that no one wants to talk about."

"I'm fine," she protested.

"Of course you are." Wenton half-bowed. "I'll pretend not to see you hobbling along as well. And when your leg starts to smell and attracts the carnivores, I'll simply look the other way."

"You're a real asshole, Wenton," Andy spat.

"Perhaps, but an asshole who tells the truth." Wenton folded his arms. "Will you at least hear me out?"

"Piss off." Andy jabbed a finger toward Harry Wenton's face.

Michael grabbed Andy's arm and pulled him back a step. "All plans and suggestions are listened to. Go ahead."

"Thank you." He briefly smirked at Andy. "Let's examine your previous effort." He held up his first finger. "Your raft was vulnerable because it was small. So, we make a bigger, sturdier raft. You were vulnerable because you were slow, so we make something faster. And finally, you were vulnerable because you didn't have proper weapons. We now have a gun."

"We have a handgun that looks like it's probably a 9mm. It'll be a pea-shooter against a real monster. You did see that thing that made the ground shake a while back, didn't you?" Andy shook his head. "Suicide."

Wenton reached into his pack and pulled out the sticks of dynamite. "Oh yes, I forgot, we also have a few things that'll blow the head off even one of those big bastards." He briefly glanced down at Angela's leg. "Every day, every hour counts now."

Michael looked at Jane. She looked back at him and gave an almost imperceptible lift of an eyebrow.

"One condition." Michael held out his hand. "I take the dynamite."

"One other condition." Wenton smiled. "Joint expedition naming."

Michael began to laugh. "You never give up, do you?"

"No, and I never will." He held up the dynamite—there were two sticks of dynamite plus several quarter sticks. "And we share them equally. Do we have a deal?"

"Deal." Michael took half the dynamite and stuck it in his pack.

"Ah, shit," Andy cursed and stomped away.

"Andy." Michael followed him, and when he got close, the young caver spun back.

"I don't trust that asshole."

"Neither do I," Michael said. "But you know as well as I do that Angela's leg is infected. We spend another week pushing through a humid jungle, and she'll have gangrene. It'll stink, and then..."

Andy put a hand over his face, but Michael could see his mouth was turned down. After another moment, he nodded.

"Good man. We'll get through this. All of us." Michael grabbed his shoulder. "Now come on, we need strong backs as we've got a boat to build."

CHAPTER 19

Bruno was a master. Turned out the Russian ex-soldier came from a boat-building family, and he had the group all squatting in a circle as he drew in the sand and explained what he wanted to create, and who would be doing what tasks.

Michael was impressed, and the Russian was delighted to have another Russian speaker in the group. He could explain the intricacies of the build and also tell his jokes that were only funny in Russian and never translated well into English. Michael noticed Wenton wasn't too impressed by the budding relationship.

Michael thought the work would take an entire day. But that concept made little sense in a world that didn't have nights or days. But after 10 hours, the group had a rough outline of a boat with narrowing bow and stern, and a flat bottom.

It reminded Michael a little of a Viking ship in design, and there were even seats. Bruno also emulated Viking craftsmanship by drilling holes in the beams and using wooden pegs and plant resin to lock it all together. Plus, the upside of having port and starboard side gunwales was it simply felt a lot safer than a flat raft.

In addition, following him telling Bruno about the thing that punctured their boat, the Russian reinforced the bottom with an extra layer of wood.

With the boat nearly finished, they took a break, to stretch backs, bathe blistered hands, and also splash water onto their faces. Michael, Jane, and Harry Wenton stood on the shoreline and looked out over the vast expanse of water.

"Maybe this world is another planet's hell," Wenton said softly as the pair turned to him. He smiled. "An author by the name of Aldous Huxley said that nearly a hundred years ago. Maybe he was onto something."

"Well, there definitely is an underworld. And right now, we're in it," Jane replied.

"Populated by monsters and devils, no less." Wenton continued to watch them. "Dante with Virgil's help ascended from Hell. They climbed all the way up from the center of the Earth."

"After passing through the nine levels of Hell." Jane snorted and turned back to the lake. "How many levels have we been through already?"

"I think we have a few more challenges just yet," Wenton said.

"What's that?" Michael put a hand over his eyes. "On the horizon?"

"I don't know. It's dark, touches the sky…could it be another land mass?" Jane asked.

"Could it finally be some sort of nightfall approaching?" Wenton turned. "It's coming fast, whatever it is."

Bruno joined them, with the others now standing just behind to watch the approaching wall of purple and grey. He made a guttural noise in his throat.

"Is storm. Big one. Might be waves with it."

"Holy crap. I knew this place was big enough to have its own weather systems." Andy folded his arms and watched.

"Lucky we haven't launched the boat yet," Angela observed.

Wenton rubbed his chin. "If it's a cyclone, we have no choice but to wait it out." He turned to look into the distance at the column mountain. "But if it's just a storm, even if it's a bad one, we should take advantage of it."

"What do you mean?" Andy frowned. "Wait, I hope you're not thinking about…"

"Yes, we launch," Wenton said matter-of-factly. He glanced back at the approaching wall of boiling cloud momentarily. "What's our biggest threat crossing the lake?"

"Being attacked," Jane replied.

"Exactly. Being attacked from something below the water. That could see us on the surface, while we can't see it." He pointed at the approaching storm front. "But what if the surface is obscured, by rain, and waves, and foam?"

"They can't attack what they can't see." Michael half-smiled. "Crazy logic…that might just work."

"Michael, seriously? You want to put it out into that storm? I mean, the objective of building the boat was to keep us out of the water, right?" Andy glowered at Wenton.

"That's right. We have a sail and paddles. We'll keep the sail furled until we see just what the wind speed is like. As long as there's no breaking surf, we can do it." Michael looked around. "We should push out and get out a little from the shoreline before the storm hits. Be hard to do in the face of a gale."

Andy pushed long hair back from his forehead. "This is madness."

"No, this is Sparta." Michael grinned back at him.

The young caver laughed. "Okay, very funny."

Michael slapped his arm. "Help get Angela into the boat."

The first zephyr of wind began to move past them. Michael sniffed. There was little new odor, but the air was cooler, laden with moisture. And he knew there'd be rain coming as well.

He turned to the jungle and saw the last of the flying creatures that he couldn't really call birds take to the treetops. He hoped below the surface of the water, the denizens of this mighty lake would either do the same by retreating to deeper water, or at least the storm would render their boat invisible on the surface.

"Is everyone ready?" Michael asked.

"No." Andy smiled flatly.

Michael had to raise his voice over the wind. "Andy, get Angela onboard and then you take starboard rear oar. Jamison, port-side oar. Harry and I will take forward oars, and Bruno to steer."

Angela was carefully placed inside the boat. He sniffed and smelled an earthiness carried on the breeze...maybe ozone.

Time was against them. The wind began to whip at them and the rags of their clothing flapped madly. The group was all around the boat that had considerable weight on land.

Wenton, at the front half, turned. "On the count of 3, 2, 1, *hea-aaaave*."

The boat slid forward on the sand and then stopped a few feet from the water.

"Once again, and *hea-aaave*," he yelled over the breeze.

Small waves had begun to break on the shore, and above them, the blood-red sky suddenly went dark. This time, the sliding boat went into the water, and Michael was delighted to see it was rock steady and extremely buoyant.

They pushed it a little further out, and then one last push set it in motion as everyone clambered over the side to drop into their positions.

"And we're away," Michael yelled as they grabbed their oars and started to pull out from the shore.

As they stroked away from the shoreline, they saw that the depths increased dramatically. The water here was fresh, so it proved that all those trillions of gallons of liquid that geologists had said were locked up in the Earth's crust and mantle had found a home.

Around them, the first drops of rain began to fall—big drops and warm as blood. Then the wind increased and in just a few moments more, it began to come down in driving sheets that made talk impossible.

Jane lit one of their lamps and laid it in the bottom of the boat as finally the blood-red heat and glare from the boiling fusion overhead was shut out completely, leaving them in near darkness.

In moments, the little lamp was underwater, and luckily they'd done a little forward planning and had at-the-ready giant empty seedpod-like gourds to use to bail the excess water out.

Bruno stood at the rear, holding the long steering oar. His eyes were closed to near slits from the pelting rain, and Michael wondered whether he could actually see where they were going. They had to cross the lake at an angle and cut out a huge swathe of the jungle.

They expected it to take them a day to cross, and as yet, he wasn't sure if the storm would help or hinder them.

The wind and rain blasted them so hard it stung their exposed skin, and their boat rose up the peaks of waves, and then slammed back down into the troughs, almost throwing the occupants of the boat to the floor. Michael had no idea whether anyone got seasick among the group, but right about now, as long as no one went overboard, he didn't care how sick they felt.

Bruno yelled his orders in Russian, his urgency meaning his brain probably didn't have the time to translate. Michael did the job, yelling himself, ordering one side of the boat or one specific oar-person to pull harder or stop rowing for a few seconds.

Several times, waves crashed over the side, pouring thousands of gallons of water into the boat, and everyone had duel jobs of keeping the boat stable, while also getting the water out—the lower they sat, the more waves came in.

The sky above boiled an angry purple shot through with veins of red, and the rain, though painful, was warm and slick. There was no sign of it abating, and for the first time, Michael started to have doubts about the wisdom of them setting out. At least nothing below had bothered them, so at least it was doing its job of masking their passage.

He hoped that when the rain and blasting wind left them, they'd be close to their destination. But in reality, he had no idea which way they were actually heading. The wind was their master now, and it might be luck that dictated where they ended up.

The boat lifted again on the crest of a huge wave, and they seemed to be suspended in the air for ages. Michael held his breath, clamped his teeth, and sure enough, the impact from striking the wave's trough was loud, hard, and jarring. But the worst noise of all was the sound of splintering wood. Somewhere, their boat was losing the battle of durability verse gale force.

The wind was a living thing, pushing, pulling, and battering at them. Michael knew now it had to be forcing them further than they were rowing.

Everywhere around them were darkness, foam, and machine-gun rain, and good as Bruno was, he knew that the man's focus was keeping their nose into the wind, more so than their direction.

"We need to get to shore," Michael yelled. He switched and yelled the same again in Russian, and Bruno looked to him briefly, but then shook his head. He flicked water from his eyes, took one hand off the steering oar, and pointed.

"*Konets shtorma.*"

Michael followed where he indicated and saw that there was a line of red on the horizon—as Bruno had said: *end of storm.*

Michael nodded. "Pull, pull," he yelled, and they all set to dragging on their oars to keep them moving forward into the teeth of the maelstrom, but toward the red line marking its end.

And then as quickly as it started, it ended. The rains eased and then stopped. Then like a giant's purple blanket being pulled back, the clouds continued to rush onward, now moving away over the interior world's horizon.

In another few moments, light began to move over the lake, as if there was a sped-up transition between night and day. The darkness of the storm vanished and once again they were under brilliant, and hot, red light.

They stopped bailing and the group looked around. About 500 yards from them was an island that seemed no more than a few hundred feet around. Trees were at its center and golden sand ringed it, making it look like a child's birthday cake. But that was all.

Michael rose up in his seat. "Where's the shore?"

"Oh no," Angela said.

Bruno looked about. "I think we get turned about, maybe."

"No maybe." Wenton stood. "I'd say definitely."

Michael saw that the cloud was vanishing toward the horizon. "The storm came at us from what I think was probably the northeast and has headed southwest. Therefore, we originally wanted to head parallel to the storm. I think we need to be going that way." He pointed. "I think."

The group turned to where Michael indicated. There was nothing that way or in any other direction, save the small island behind them.

"How far?" Andy said.

"I don't know." Michael sat down.

They continued to row slowly toward the small island. Michael looked around, trying to get his bearings. Any sign of land on any horizon would have helped. The wind now had dropped away to dead stillness and with it the lake became a sheet of red glass as it reflected the blood sky.

"And if we're wrong? Instead of heading toward land, we're heading further out into the center of this inland sea," Andy asked. "We're a long way out already. Maybe already too far to get back." He shook his head. "And now very visible to what's underneath us."

"Andy, just being negative isn't going to help. We all agreed to this plan," Jane said.

"No, I didn…" he stopped talking, sighed, and sat down heavily. "What the hell anyway. We're literally all in the same boat now, right?"

The boat rocked a little and Michael turned to Bruno who had his head turned to look over the side. The Russian continued to stare, and Michael didn't like the look on his face.

"Bruno?"

The Russian still didn't turn. "Something."

Michael slowly stood and saw that a few hundred yards out, the millpond-like lake surface now had ripples emanating from the spot Bruno was watching.

"What was it?" Michael asked.

Bruno shrugged. "Something came up, but when I looked it was already going back down. Very big."

From the other side of the boat, there was the tinkle of falling water, and once again when they whipped their heads around, there were just the signs of something having been there and now gone.

"It's playing with us," Wenton said just above a whisper.

"And I don't know whether that makes it better or worse," Michael replied. "Listen, guys, why don't we pull a little harder toward the island? I suddenly like the idea of having ground under my feet for a while."

They began to row, deep strokes and hard, but all trying not to create too much of a disturbance on the water.

Bruno did his bit, using the oar as a sweep to get a few extra ounces of speed from their boat.

Michael and the other rowers were faced toward the rear, with the rest fronting forward. He half-turned. "Someone count off the feet to the island."

"300," Jane immediately responded.

Michael leaned into it and pulled back, grabbing the oar cup full of water and pushing it back as the boat moved forward. Their small craft was sturdy and built for stability, and safety, but definitely not for speed. Every inch of progress was hard-fought and done with muscle, not design.

"Any sign, Bruno?" Michael called, looking up at the Russian.

With legs planted wide, he slowly turned, but shook his head. "All is calm now."

They pulled hard, and Michael felt his hands becoming sore and rubbing. He shifted his grip to ease the pain and friction, but knew the blisters would form, then they would burst, and then he'd be rubbing against raw skin.

"200," Jane yelled.

200 was nothing, Michael thought. *A few more strokes, and we'll hit the sand.*

Michael turned to look up at Bruno just as the man's eyes went wide and he sat down in the boat for a moment.

"What is it?" Michael quickly asked.

"In water. Thing underneath boat. Big eye. Look up at me."

"Ah, shit," Michael said between his teeth. "Come on, everyone. Last few strokes, pull hard now."

Bruno got warily to his feet but stayed in more of a crouch as he took the sweep oar again. He carefully looked over the side and then down. He shook his head.

The rowers pulled hard, but the boat slowed and then stopped. And no matter how hard they dragged on the oars, it remained stationary.

"Have we run aground?" Jamison asked.

Bruno looked over the port side and then the starboard. He shook his head. "No, still deep water."

Michael turned to look over his shoulder. The small island was so close he felt he could get out and almost run to it. The upside was that he felt if need be, they could swim it.

"Might be a reef outcrop." Andy leaned over the side. He turned back. "Hold on to me, will you?"

Jamison grabbed the back of his pants, and Andy leaned out even more, his face now just inches from the water.

He squinted down into it and lifted a hand to hold over his head to try and shield himself from the red glare from the sky.

"Can't see anything." He turned back while still hanging over the side, his ear nearly touching the water. "We might be in a patch of weed. Someone might need to go over and free us."

"No, come back in," Michael said.

As if in response, the boat suddenly pulled forward, almost throwing Andy over the side. He sat down hard and turned with a grin.

"See, like I said, musta just been weed or something."

In another few minutes, the boat scrunched in on the sand and Michael and Wenton were first out to grab the gunwales and hold the boat steady. After each leaped out, they all pulled the boat in a few extra feet to ground it.

Wenton pointed to tide marks on the sand. "Seems we have an ebb and flow of tides. We'll need to watch the boat."

They gathered in their group. Angela hung onto Andy and kept one leg up off the ground. Michael walked into their center.

"I'm not going to kid anyone that without sun or stars we have no real navigation guides. We have no working GPS anymore, or even a toy compass. Without doubt, the storm blew us off course, so we'd be guessing on a direction to take."

"Suddenly, coming by water isn't looking like such a game-changer after all," Maggie sighed.

"For now, we rest up. Fatigue is doing nothing for our decision-making abilities or our normally good humors." He half-smiled. "First up, we need to do a scout of the island to make sure we haven't just blundered into anyone or anything's backyard."

Jamison scoffed. "Too bad if we did. We can't exactly start up the outboard motor and zoom away."

Michael ignored him. "Keep a lookout for anything to eat. Then we can make some sort of shelter, and take turns grabbing some shuteye. Choose a partner and do a quick scout. It's not a big piece of land so meet back here in 15 minutes. And shout out if you see anything…concerning."

He turned and noticed Bruno by himself near the shoreline, and he went to stand by the stocky Russian.

"What is it?"

The Russian turned. "I think it was that thing that stopped us just off the shore. But then let us go." He turned. "Because maybe it wants us here."

"That's not a comforting thought," Michael said. "Why?"

Bruno shrugged. "That is good question." He looked quickly along the shoreline, and then waded into the water a few feet to grab at something. He lifted it out and walked quickly back up the beach.

He held it out to Michael. It looked like a piece of shell or exoskeleton, and on its side was a perfectly round hole the size of his fist. He put his fingers through it.

"Maybe is tooth mark."

Michael groaned. "Maybe. Let's keep it to ourselves for now. But we stay alert."

"*Da*, always." The Russian tossed the fragment back out into the water. "*Michael.*"

"Yo." The call came from Andy, and he turned and jogged up the beach and headed into the thicket of trees at the center of the island.

Andy and Angela were standing by a pile of earth as the others joined them. The mound was about seven feet long and three feet wide, and at one end a caving pick used as a marker.

"A grave," Andy said.

"Whose?" Wenton asked.

Michael crouched and started to clear away some of the sandy soil. He came across a canteen, Swiss army knife, and fragments of material.

130

He shook the canteen and something rattled inside it. He tossed it to Jane. "Check this out."

He rubbed a thumb on the knife case and read the name. He scoffed softly. "Georgy." He looked up. "Katya's team leader." He then opened the Army knife, folding out a few rusted implements, but also a tiny compass. He tapped it, seeing the small needle wobble to life.

"*Yes*, we now have a compass."

Jane had opened the canteen, stuck a finger inside, and drew out a tiny roll of paper.

She shook her head and held it out to Michael. "It's in Russian."

Wenton grabbed it and handed it to Bruno. "What does it say?"

Bruno read the note. "*Here lie, great friend and leader, Georgy Azarov. We press on: northwest.*" He turned it over and frowned. "Can't read, some faded. But this bit strange: *beware the water*."

"Beware the water?" Jamison said. "That's not very helpful."

Bruno turned back. "I think they mean, beware *what's* in water."

Maggie seethed. "Oh for Chrissake. I mean, we're on a freaking island—there's water all around us."

"Yeah, we've got no choice *but* to go back out on the water," Jamison sighed. "We can't exactly stay on Gilligan's Island."

Michael held up the Army knife. "They went back out. And now we know which way they went—north—and also more importantly, which way north is." He stood, dusting off the sand. "Let's finish our scout for food and anything else that might be useful. We'll make a quick shelter from the heat with the palm fronds, catch a few hours' sleep, and then be a bit better equipped and ready to head back out."

"What about…?" Jane started but Michael raised a hand to stop her.

"Rest first. Problem-solving is easier when we all have clear and refreshed minds."

They erected a small structure that had a roof of fern fronds held up by sticks, and only about three feet off the ground. It would serve as a shade from the red heat constantly beating down from above.

When foraging, Maggie found a fleshy plant like a cactus that when broken open or cut, leaked water—it tasted a little bitter but was nourishing. Later, Jamison located some eggs, and the group sat around looking at the gold ball-sized leathery things. They came from the local flying creatures that looked like a cross between a seagull and a dragonfly that had stiff, feather-like fronds for getting airborne, six legs, and multifaceted, compound eyes that glinted like stained glass in the red light.

Bruno lifted one of the eggs and squeezed it for a moment before biting into it. Silvery viscous liquid spilled out into his fingers. His nose wrinkled a little, and he bobbed his head.

"Taste like almond and…" He pondered for a moment and then just shrugged, sucking the rest of the yolk out.

"Insect eggs for breakfast, lunch, or whatever time of day it is. This place is just heaven…*not*." Andy tried one and grimaced. "*Yech*."

Jane and Maggie both held one, and Jane looked at hers between finger and thumb. "I'm only eating this because I need the energy." She bit it and sucked it down, her nose wrinkling. They all did the same.

After another few minutes, they allocated the job of designated lookouts, and the rest crawled under the shade of their structure. Bruno would take first watch, Michael next, and then Wenton.

Michael closed his eyes and tried to shut out all the discomfort he felt and concerns he had. He needed rest more than any other time in his life. They depended on him. He had brought them here, and then it had turned out far more dangerous than he could ever have imagined. He owed it to them to get them all home.

When sleep finally took him, it was crowded with images of burning skies, monstrous many-armed creatures, and a bottomless sea with things looking up at them with a hundred eyes.

Bruno woke him after two hours and Michael still felt exhausted. Bruno lay down and was out cold almost immediately so Michael got comfortable for his time on watch. He saw that a few of the group slept soundly, but Angela and Andy tossed, murmured, and spoke in their sleep.

He smiled down at Jane, watching her for a while. The strain had painted lines around her eyes, but she was still carrying the innocence of a child in the curve of her lips.

I've got to get them home, he thought. *If it's the last thing I do.*

He cursed Katya and her notes for being so vague. She had come here and not mentioned many of the dangers. It was like her brain had refused to store some images, perhaps because they were too onerous or psychologically debilitating and she found she could only make the smallest of mentions of the horrors assailing them.

But she had tried to warn them; even threatening to go to the police rather than let them come. Michael exhaled. He couldn't blame her for leaving blanks. Some things were just too painful to remember.

She had told him that Georgy was her lover, so it was here she had lost him and said her final goodbye. Maybe her mind was simply protecting her.

When his shift was over, he roused Wenton, who grumbled and then wandered off a ways to empty his bladder. When he returned, he sat down on the sand and waved Michael off.

Michael almost immediately fell back into his disturbed sleep once again.

*****

Angela giggled in her sleep. "Andy, stop it. Your hands are cold."

She dreamed she was floating, gently hovering above everyone else. She knew they were all tired so she was careful not to wake them. Andy held her like a baby, and his arms were so strong.

Something moist went over her mouth. His lips? She kissed them back.

*****

"Angela?"

"*Huh...?*" Michael woke to the sound of Andy's voice. "*What is it?*" He sat up immediately as the others were also roused.

The young caver was on his feet, looking about.

"Where's Angela?"

"She was right next to you." Jane sprang to her feet.

"Is she taking a leak somewhere?" Jamison asked.

"I checked and she's *nowhere*," Andy wailed.

Michael spun. "Harry, you were on watch, where'd she go?"

The man hiked his shoulders. "She must have slipped past me when..."

"Oh for God's sake. When you nodded off, right?" Michael bared his teeth in frustration.

Wenton just looked sheepish but didn't apologize. Michael looked up and down the beach. There were no new tracks. "Come on, it's not a big island, so let's spread out and find her." Andy went to run ahead. "Hey, work in pairs."

Wenton went with Maggie along the north coastline. Jamison and Andy went into the interior, and Michael and Jane went south. Bruno stayed with the boat.

In only a few minutes, the beach searchers joined up, and then headed to the interior. And then it took them only minutes more before they met at Georgy's grave.

Andy looked stricken with worry. "What happened? Where is she?"

"She can't have just vanished," Maggie said. "Is there anywhere else on the island she could be?"

"No, this whole island is no larger than a few football fields. There are no caves, and nowhere to hide," Michael said.

"Maybe not." Wenton tapped his chin. He looked up slowly. "Remember Captain Lawrence Oates of the Tera Nova expedition to the Antarctic?"

Michael frowned as he tried to recollect the name...and then he did. "Oh, bullshit."

"Who's that? What's bullshit?" Andy asked.

Wenton turned. "We must face the possibility that she 'walked off into the snow,' as Captain Oates did in 1920. He was dying, knew it, and didn't want to slow down his friends anymore. He was suffering from frostbite and knew he couldn't go on, so…"

"Piss off." Andy threw his hands in the air and walked away.

Michael looked down at the ground and tried to think it through. Angela was exactly the sort to self-sacrifice. But she was hardly at the end of her tether—he'd spoken to her, and she was like all of them, dragged down by fatigue but certainly not despondent.

"I don't buy it," he said. "She didn't leave a message, didn't even give away a hint she was feeling that way." He shook his head. "It doesn't seem right."

"She could have just hidden it well." Maggie hiked her shoulders. "I don't think we're going to find her again."

Michael looked up. "We're not leaving here until we at least find her body then. Like I said, I don't buy it."

"Come on, Monroe. We're dying here, and every extra hour we stay, we get closer to someone else walking off into the snow." Wenton pointed a finger at Michael's chest. "This is my expedition too, you know."

Michael folded his arms. "And?"

"I say we take a vote." Wenton straightened and lifted an arm. "All those in favor of departing for the mainland right now, please raise their hand. All those in favor of staying, do nothing."

Maggie raised her hand along with Wenton. Jamison also raised his but didn't meet anyone's eyes.

Michael kept his arms folded, and so did Jane. Andy had returned and just glared.

"Three apiece," Michael said.

They all turned to Bruno, and after a moment, he still hadn't moved.

"Bruno?" Wenton frowned. "Are you with us?"

"Yes, sir." He kept his hands by his sides. "But I think we should find out what happened to girl first."

"*Damnit*," Wenton spat.

"There you go again, Harry, overestimating your popularity again." Andy gave him the finger.

Wenton looked to take a step toward him but Michael stepped in front of the man. "Save your strength for rowing."

Wenton shook his head, muttering, and walked off a few paces to stare out at the endless red water.

Jane came and tugged at Michael's elbow. "I just had a terrible thought."

"What is it?" he asked.

134

"Remember that worm that grabbed Angela? It came out of the ground, and if we weren't there, it would have dragged her down, closed its trapdoor, and not left a trace. We might not have ever found her." She blanched. "Do you think…?"

"Damn." He rubbed a hand up through his unkempt hair, snagging his fingers in the knots. "Yeah, yeah, that's possible." He sighed and then turned. "Listen up, people. We're going to do another sweep of the island. But this time, we're looking for another of those trapdoor holes, like the one the worm came out of. She might be, *ah*, underground."

"*What*? You think another one got her?" Andy looked skyward and crushed his eyes shut.

"We form a skirmish line and look for a hole, a crack or crevice, or anything that might indicate an entrance, or something large enough to take her down."

Bruno pointed at the boat. "You want me to come or mind after this again?"

Michael looked at the calm water and clear sky and shook his head. "No, come with us, we can use your eyes. This won't take long."

Bruno saluted and joined them. The group spread out in a line about 10 feet apart and began a slow walk into the thatch of trees in the center of the island.

They came across a few more clutches of eggs, and another long creature like a snake but it had multiple eyes, and bands of plates instead of scales. They walked slowly, using their spears to prod bushes, rocks, and anything else that might have concealed a trapdoor. But in around 15 minutes, they exited the other side of the thicket and then onto the opposite shoreline.

"Nothing," Andy said. He rubbed his face. "We do it again, on the way back. Take a step to the left so we cover new ground."

"Okay." Michael knew it was probably hopeless, but a small hope was better than no hope at all. "Let's start again."

They re-entered, and this time went even slower, but still finished in around 15 minutes and were back where they started.

"Hey, is tide come in?" Bruno pointed.

Their boat was about 50 feet from shore, just hanging in the water as if anchored.

"Ah shit, how did that happen? Was there a wave or something?" Michael looked about and saw no evidence of a tidal surge, as the sand was dry to a waterline that was exactly where they left it.

Bruno didn't hesitate but walked straight into the water. Michael didn't like it, but one way or the other they needed that boat.

Bruno swam in an over-arm motion to the craft, and when he was about six feet from it, he vanished.

"Hey." Michael frowned and craned forward. "What's he doing?"

"Did he just dive under?" Jane asked.

"Maybe he got a cramp." Andy began to jog down the shore to the water.

"*Stop!*" Michael yelled.

At the water's edge, Andy turned but pointed. "He'll drown."

"The boat. Look at the boat," Michael said. "Even with all the splashing that Bruno was doing, look."

They turned. The boat stayed motionless as if it had run aground on a bank.

"It's not moving. At all. Just like when we came in," Maggie observed. "It's caught on something."

"Or something is holding it in place," Jane said softly.

Andy began to back away from the water, and as soon as he did, a tendril shot forward from the sea and wound around his legs. Then another came after him. Michael charged and used his spear to jam it into one of them, but they were like leather.

Jamison joined him and together they hacked and stabbed until the thing let go. Michael and Jamison dragged Andy back up the beach.

"*Look!*" Maggie pointed out at the water.

Just a dozen feet from the boat, a lump started to rise. It lifted more, displaying an insectoid face crowded with large dark eyes, with a pair of powerful-looking pincers on each side of its mouth. Surrounding the lump were long, muscular, and flexible legs like tentacles. One of them was coiled around the lifeless body of Bruno that hung limp in its grip.

"Oh my God. It was trying to trap us, lure us into the water after the boat." Jane backed up.

"It must have got Angela when we slept," Michael said.

"Oh no, my poor Angela," Andy wailed.

"It's just like an octopus, or this place's equivalent of one." Jane watched the thing as it watched them back. "Or a spider."

"A sea spider," Michael replied. "Another example of your concurrent evolution."

"It's smart," Jamison said. "I think it was toying with us, enjoying a little game before dinner."

"Poor bastard," Wenton said of Bruno. "Without the boat, we're not getting off the island. And with that thing out there, even if we had the boat, we're still not getting off the island." He kept his eyes on the creature as it slowly sank below the surface.

"We're not safe here. It can get us on land—it's already proved that," Jane said and hugged herself. "For the first time, I'm glad there's no night period. I'd hate to think of that thing sliding up out of the water and taking us in the dark."

"Seems we need that thing dead as much as we need the boat. Right now, maybe more." Wenton folded his arms.

"We need a plan," Michael said.

"Plans are what I do best." Wenton smiled.

"You have one?" Maggie asked.

Wenton flicked an eyebrow up. "Of course. And I only need one thing to make it happen—dear old Georgy."

*****

Jane held her breath as they uncovered the nearly 50-year-old corpse. But she didn't need to; the dry sand had desiccated it down to bone, sinew, and a skull with mouth gaped wide in the perpetual scream of the dead.

"Doesn't smell too bad," Jamison said.

"That's because he's like a big piece of jerky by now," Andy replied and scraped more sand off the body.

"Try and keep him intact, please. It's important." Wenton supervised from the edge of the grave.

Luckily, Georgy wasn't sunk deep, and after another 15 minutes, they had the skeleton free.

"He's missing a foot," Jane observed. "And by the look of the splintered bone, I'd say it was torn off."

Maggie fumed. "Our many-legged friend in the water, maybe?"

Jane crouched. "The bone shows no evidence of healing, so I'd say that's what killed him." Her forehead creased. "There's nothing else on this island that'd tear a limb off, so yeah, probably."

Michael walked through the trees to stare out at the boat still stuck fast, probably held in place by one of the creature's limbs. And sure enough, there was the lump of the head, just at the surface, watching them. *Perhaps with amusement, hunger, or was it making plans of its own?* he wondered.

Michael thought about the thing's intelligence and predatorial abilities. It had taken Angela, selected her, from among them without waking any of them. Then it tricked Bruno into coming into the water where it was waiting for him. What would it try next, and who did it have its eyes on?

He was still furious with Katya. She and the remains of her team had left them a cryptic warning about the beast, and Georgy's missing leg told him they obviously encountered it.

They had escaped the island but failed to mention what they did to achieve it. If he ever made it back to the surface one day, he'd be sure to ask her how.

Michael walked back to rejoin the group. "It's still there, watching."

"Good," Wenton said as he stopped Andy from climbing out of the grave. "Please bring dear Georgy out of his grave. And be gentle with him."

Jamison and Andy carefully lifted the ancient body up. It was like wood and seemed to weigh next to nothing. The pair held him up and Wenton walked a little closer.

"Dear Georgy, we are in need of your help, my friend." He turned and grinned at the group, but then faced Andy. "Andy, please loan Mr. Georgy your clothing."

"What?" Andy scowled.

"Just the shirt," Michael said.

Andy grumbled as he shed the remnants of the shirt he wore and handed it over. Wenton then carefully pulled it over Georgy's skeletal frame.

As he did, Michael tried to imagine the tall, handsome man that Katya had described to them. But in the skeletal remains, he could see nothing but death. The old woman he had met in the hospital had buried her long-lost lover down here nearly half a century ago. And now they were going to desecrate her work.

"Sorry, Katya," he muttered. *But your silence left us no choice.*

The next task Wenton had them perform was to create a stand out of a flat piece of bark and a straight stick. They used some of their remaining rope to lash Georgy to it, so he stood upright, with the new shirt adding to the lifelike ruse.

"Ready for action." Wenton smiled. "And now to add something to give our many-armed friend a little indigestion."

The man set about tying his full stick of dynamite to Georgy's back. He finished by pushing a detonator pin in but held off setting the timer.

"All set." He rubbed his hands together and then turned. "Mr. Monroe, the floor is yours."

"Why Michael?" Jane's mouth dropped open. "Harry, it's your idea, you do it."

Wenton shook his head as he continued to adjust the clothing on the corpse. "I supply the brains, my dear. Plus the dynamite. Michael supplies the brawn." He stood back. "Now, do we want to get off this island or not?"

Michael shrugged. "I'll do it."

"Good man." Wenton smirked. "Take Mr. Georgy down the beach away from our boat. Wouldn't want to damage our ride now, would we? Oh, and good luck."

*****

Jane watched as Michael lifted the stiff corpse and walked it a few hundred feet down the beach and away from where the boat was stuck.

138

Immediately, from out near the craft, the lump submerged, and she knew it was following Michael and the corpse from under the water, because the boat drifted along beside him.

At the water's edge, she saw Michael reach behind Georgy and set the timer. Then they waded into the water, and Michael began to yell and thrash. He backed up, and from a distance, it looked to her like it was two people standing on the shoreline. And she hoped it looked that way to the creature as well.

Michael began to back up, leaving the rigid corpse propped on its stand on the shoreline. From the water, a long tentacle shot out and took hold of the corpse. Another thick tendril lifted from the water and went after Michael.

The creature lifted higher in the water to get a better look at the fleeing man, and now with more revealed, the size of the thing made the breath catch in Jane's throat.

It was a spider, as big as a house, but the legs weren't stiff like a normal arachnid but more rubbery like tentacles. The eyes were crowded forward at the front and were all hubcap-sized as they fixed on the fleeing man.

Jane was amazed at the speed of the thing. Michael was 20 feet from the water now, and the tentacle still pursued him. And in a couple of seconds, it had him.

Jane screamed and went to run from the trees, but Wenton grabbed her. "Wait."

Michael turned and pulled his knife to stab down on the long, rubbery limb. He didn't have a hope of cutting the thing, but he undoubtedly hoped to irritate it enough to make it let go.

The limb unfurled maybe to get a better grip elsewhere, but Michael immediately rolled over and turned to sprint in a zigzag up the beach. The creature watched him go for a second or two and must have decided it could catch him again later.

It sunk below the surface of the water, taking its prize, Georgy, with it. "Get down," Michael yelled.

The explosion blew water in a giant spout into the air, and they felt the shock wave from the beach to where they sheltered behind the trees. After another moment, Michael jumped to his feet and ran back to the waterline, searching for any evidence of a kill.

"Did we get it?" Jane yelled.

The water was still all froth and chop in the area, but there was nothing else—no chunks of flesh, and with the water already blood red, it was impossible to tell if there was anything of the monster in there among it.

"I don't know." Michael walked along the shore, hand shielding his eyes.

"Do you think it found out that the thing it grabbed wasn't alive and tossed it?" Andy had joined them.

"Let's hope not. We haven't got any more corpses, so we've just played all our cards." Maggie pushed greasy hair back off her face.

"I'm sure we got it. The plan worked." Wenton half-smiled.

"What makes you say that?" Andy cocked an eyebrow.

"The boat, of course. Look," he said confidently.

They turned—their boat was now drifting parallel to the shore.

"There's nothing holding onto it. I think our beast is now safely in Davey Jones' locker." He turned. "Jamison, be a good chap and retrieve our boat."

"*Say what?*" The young man's brows shot up so high they threatened to escape into his hairline. "There's no way I'm swimming out there."

"Yeah, Mr. All-talk. Why don't *you* swim out there and get it?" Andy glared.

Wenton continued to smile. "You want *me* to swim out to the only boat we all have? The one with the last of our supplies, the last sticks of dynamite, and the only means of escape we, *you*, have?"

"Let me guess, and in a moment of madness, you decide you want to go home...by yourself," Michael chuckled. "We draw straws, and quick. Before our boat is further away from the shore and in even deeper water."

"Good call," Wenton replied. "After all, we don't know if our explosion will attract even more ferocious denizens of the deep."

Jane found a reed of even thickness that she broke into six pieces. She held them in her fist, and then held them out.

"Who's first?"

Michael took one—it was a long stick.

Andy, then Jamison, also drew long sticks.

Maggie closed her eyes and took another, drawing a long stick. She exhaled with relief.

There were now two sticks left.

"That leaves just you and me, Harry," Jane said.

Wenton drew a stick—the last long one. He smiled at her with mock sadness.

"Ah shit." She held up her short stick.

From behind the group came the splash of water, and Jane spun.

Michael was already in the water and swimming out to the boat.

"*Hey,*" she called. "Don't you damn be a hero, you big, dumb..." She jogged down to the waterline, "...magnificent man," she finished softly.

*****

Michael breaststroked out to the boat. He'd lost two friends because he dragged everyone down here on his personal quest to find out if an ancient legend was true. So he'd be dammed if he let anyone else die doing something he could do himself.

Especially not Jane, he thought.

The water was warm, but he felt himself shriveling regardless. The island must have been some sort of volcanic peak, because just a dozen feet from shore, the clear, but red-tinged water fell away to an unimaginable blackness. It meant he couldn't see down, and frankly, he didn't want to.

Every stroke he took seemed to bring the boat no closer, and he had a terrible thought that the many-armed spider-thing might still be beneath the boat, but instead of holding it in place, it was this time gently taking it away, inch by inch, to lure him ever further from safety.

He finally closed in on the boat. Now six feet, now five feet—his heart was galloping in his chest—four feet, three feet—if the thing was underneath the boat, it would take him now.

Then he reached up to grab the gunwale, and with almost superhuman strength brought on by absolute fear, he leaped up and into the boat and lay there, eyes closed for several moments, letting the heat from above warm his fear-chilled body as he shivered.

Michael finally opened his eyes, blew a breath out hard, and sat up. He waved to the group on the shore. They all waved back except for Jane who looked like she was shaking a fist at him.

Michael grinned and then picked up two of the oars and began to row back to the beach. In a few minutes, he felt the bow being grabbed and slid forward.

"You dumb bastard," Jane said, leaning on the rail. "I coulda done that myself. I'm no damsel in distress, you know."

He nodded. "I know you would have and could have done it. That's why I wouldn't let you." He gave her a crooked smile. "I'm not ready to lose you."

"Hey!" Andy mock scowled.

Michael chuckled. "Okay, not you either."

"Well done, Monroe." Wenton slapped his shoulder. He turned to Jane. "Don't be too hard on him. After all, this mad world needs more volunteers like this guy." He snorted.

"Well, am I the only one that wants to get off this island?" Andy asked.

"Yeah, let's move out. We now have a compass, a direction, and no reason to hang around for another minute," Michael replied.

It took them a little longer as Jane suggested they gather more of the eggs and also some of the fleshy plants that stored water—after all, they had no idea how long they'd be onboard this time.

Still, within half an hour, they were all back onboard. Michael had unfurled the sail. Even though the breeze was near non-existent, he decided that for now the splash of oars should be kept to a minimum.

Michael tightened the sail made of rags, the remains of tattered sleeping mats, woven through with tough reeds. He checked the small compass one last time and then pointed.

"North, and to home."

EPISODE 04

"There are no impossible obstacles; there are just stronger and weaker wills." **Jules Verne**

CHAPTER 20

Days.

Many days.

And they were hot and listless days.

No one spoke now, and the food had run out even though they had rationed the last of the glutinous eggs. The broad and fleshy leaves of the water-bearing plants were as dry now as the tongues in their mouths, and their lips felt like flaking paper.

There was not a breath of wind so they'd turned the sail into a canopy that shielded them from the fierce heat of the red ceiling, as Jane was insistent they not receive further radiation burns. But even under the canopy, the heat still found them.

The boat seemed far more spacious now that they were down two friends. Michael missed Angela, and oddly, also the big taciturn Russian. He'd take the more crowded boat any day if it meant he could have them back.

Some splashing out on the surface made Michael lift the brim of his sagging reed hat an inch and open one eye to squint out in its direction.

Silver torpedoes broke the surface, dove, and then surged back again. He smiled; they looked exactly like dolphins, but he knew that more than likely they were some form of arthropod that had evolved to keep pace with the fastest creatures in the inland sea.

Concurrent evolution, he remembered. He reached into his pocket and pulled out the small knife with compass—*northward*. He liked to think they were still headed in that direction, but without wind, they just floated, a hostage to whatever currents were working in the seeming endless body of water.

He heard a scrape from behind and he turned, ever mindful of some weird denizen of the deep coming up to investigate them.

144

Everyone was lying down or hunched over, sleeping. It was for the best, because activity burned calories and water. Best to hibernate until something broke. And hopefully, it wouldn't be their spirits.

He turned back and once again his eyes grew heavy, and he let his forehead rest on his arms as he had leaned forward on his knees. In another few seconds, he drifted off to join his friends.

Scra-*aaaape*.

Michael's head jerked up.

"What was that?" Andy muttered drowsily from behind him.

Michael turned about but saw nothing but a haze on the horizon. Then he looked over the side, and in the crystal-clear water saw they were traveling over some sort of chasm, and at the top of the valley peaks on each side, some of the rocks and corals were only a few feet below the surface.

"Some sort of outcrop or reef, I think." He continued to stare down into the depths. "We better get on the oars again as it really shallows out in a few areas."

There were some groans, but Wenton, Andy, and Maggie joined Michael rowing. Jane kept watch over the side.

They gently rowed across the glass-still surface, the sounds of the water dripping from their oars the only sound.

"Getting shallower. Stop rowing," Michael said. He quickly grabbed up his spear and used it to hold onto the rocks just below the surface and anchor the boat. He held it in place for a moment as he stared over the side.

"Let's get out. The reef here is only inches below the water, and there's bound to be some sort of shellfish or sea life we can scavenge."

They carefully climbed over the side, unwinding limbs that had been folded for days. Together, they hoisted the boat up onto the rocky platform and they picked their way forward using their bags or shirts to scavenge anything that looked edible.

Jane came to the edge of the reef and crouched to gaze into the deeper water of the chasm. She placed a hand over her eyes to cut down the glare. "There's something down there."

"Something edible?" Andy asked.

"Yes, there is, but that's not it," she replied, squinting into the depths. "Water is so clear I can't tell if it's 20 or 120 feet deep. But other than schools of fish things, I think, there might be a pathway—cobblestones."

"No way," Maggie said.

The group came and joined her, lining up on the edge of the reef that was like a valley wall.

"Are you sure?" Wenton asked. "After all, there are many natural geological formations that resemble interlocking stones. In fact, on the coast of…"

Jane rolled her eyes. "Yes, Harry, I know all about quartz bricks, shale tiles, and rhomboids, but this isn't what I'm seeing. It actually looks like paving stones, and with something along their sides that could be a wall. Or once was a wall."

"Are you saying there's a civilization down there?" Maggie's brows knitted.

"No… I don't think anymore," Jane replied. "Maybe it once was, but it looks like it sunk long ago. Maybe tens or hundreds of thousands of years."

"Maybe more," Michael said. "This is fresh water, so it's far less corrosive."

"So, no fish people then." Andy half-smiled.

Michael also cupped his eyes to see better into the deeper water. "Nice try, but I doubt it's Atlantis, Andy." He turned. "That's under the snow and ice of the Antarctic. Haven't you ever read the leaked report on the dark web from that Harvard linguistics professor? Matt Kearns I think his name was. He said he traveled there as part of a secret military mission."

"Yeah, he sounds sane. But I'll look it up when I get back." Andy also turned to stare down into the depths.

"Oh my God—they're columns, and some ruins." Jane pointed. "There really was a civilization here once."

Michael looked around. "Maybe this was another island once that eventually sunk. Or the lake level rose." He stood and walked along the valley peak to stare down into the deeper crystal-clear water.

"I wonder what they were like?" Maggie said.

"Like bugs, I presume," Wenton said. "Now that would be something to see—intelligent bugs."

"If they were on an island, and they were smart enough to build these structures, then I'm betting they were smart enough to leave when the water rose, or their land fell." Jane shielded her eyes and looked into the distance. "Yeah, I'd like to know what they were like as well."

"Hold that thought." Michael got to his feet and quickly rummaged in his decrepit pack.

"Yes, and still intact." He pulled free a small set of swim goggles he had packed on a whim. He held them to his face and leaned over, placing his face in the water.

He sat back.

"What is it?" Maggie asked.

He grinned, not believing what he just saw. "Might be something interesting; just give me a minute." Michael pulled the goggles over his head.

"What? Are you freaking nuts?" Andy's eyes widened. "Did you not see that thing that attacked us on the island?"

"I give up." Jane sat back, her lips pressed into a line. "Suicidal."

"I'll be quick. This is important and may answer one of the great questions of our time," he said.

"How quickly can a man get himself killed?" Wenton smiled.

Michael laughed, his lips pressed out from the goggles digging in under his nose. "No—are we alone?"

Michael took one last look below the surface and then slipped over the edge and into the sunken reef valley.

*****

Jane sprung forward to lean over and watch Michael descend. His tattered clothing fluttered in streamers from his arms and legs as he stroked toward the bottom. He paused for a moment to pinch his nose and she guessed he was equalizing the pressure. It was obviously deeper than he thought and the clear water was as deceptive as she expected.

He stroked on again, his body becoming smaller and less distinct. Fish came to check him out and what seemed like minnows from the surface, when next to Michael, were half as long as his body. For a fast moment, she wished he'd reach out and grab one and bring it back for them.

He reached the bottom, close to one of the weed-covered columns, and tugged at something at its base. In another second, he was propelling himself back to the surface.

The long silver fish things followed him and she wondered whether they could be like piranha and were thinking of taking a few chunks from the soft-bodied creature as it tried to escape from their domain.

In another moment, they helped Michael back over the reef edge and he dragged off his mask, still gasping for breath.

"Got it." He grinned.

He sat up and pushed hair off his face. Then he reached inside his shirt and produced what he'd found. Everyone craned forward to see.

"Well, well, Michael, I think that answers your question," Wenton said almost reverently.

Jane stared at the object. It was a small broken statue, of a person, or at least the top two-thirds from the knees up—two arms, half legs, a head, but with the features worn away and pitted, and grown over with algae and weed.

"No multiple legs, no arthropod plates, not even eyes on stalks." Michael looked up at her. "Could it be? Could concurrent evolution produce another version of, *us*, down here?"

Jane hiked her shoulders. "With enough time, anything and everything is possible."

"The structures could be early Roman or perhaps even Greek. They're not, of course, but the architecture has a similar design." Wenton continued looking over the side. "While our ancestral roots went on to found even bigger and better civilizations, this race seems to have vanished."

Maggie looked up at him. "If you fell from the sky and landed in the center of the Amazon jungle, the desert, or even Antarctica, you might walk for days or weeks without seeing another human being. There still could be thriving civilizations down here." She looked back at the figurine. "We just don't know where to look."

"But human or proto-human? That is the question, isn't it?" Wenton said as he slowly straightened. "I assume your Russian girlfriend made no mention of this either?"

Michael shook his head as he wrapped the artifact in a rag and placed it in the remains of his kit bag. "No, so maybe that means on her path home they never came across any evidence of people, human or otherwise."

"Should we," Wenton raised his eyebrows, "look for them?"

"No, our sole objective is to find a way home," Jane said forcefully. "If someone wants to come back and mount a bigger, and better-prepared expedition, then feel free."

Wenton held up his hands. "Just checking." He turned away to look out toward the horizon. "I just wonder what they'd be like. What they would say to us if we ever met. We'd both have compelling questions, I should think." He turned back. "Maybe I will come back one day. I'll meet them, and I think they'll like me."

"Yeah, sure they will, Harry. And by the way, you can only come back if you get home first. Let's make that priority number one, two, and three," Maggie said.

The group climbed back into the boat and shared the results of their foraging. There were shells, creatures like soft-bodied crabs, and starfish. They only ended up with a few mouthfuls each, but it was better than nothing.

They set off, rowed for another half hour until spent, and then finally a breeze gently lifted. They gratefully unfurled the sail once again and scudded forward. In the distance were some type of flying creatures in the air, and Andy pointed.

"Birds, or whatever they are. But it means there'll be land close by."

"Unless they're like the albatross," Jane replied. "They can fly entirely around the world without landing."

"You should do motivational speeches." Wenton saluted her with a finger.

She chuckled. "You're right, Andy. More than likely, it'll mean there's land close by."

In another few hours, the horizon showed a line of a dark rising up that had to be land.

"Did Katya say where they landed?" Jane asked.

"Yes, yes, she did, if I remember correctly." Michael quickly reached for the notebook and began flipping pages until he came to the place he wanted. "The field of flowers."

"That sounds nice. At last, something that doesn't bite, sting, or peck. I approve." Maggie held up a thumb.

"But she also says, 'hold your breath,'" Michael added.

"What does that mean?" Maggie frowned.

Michael shrugged. "That's all she wrote—'hold your breath.' Maybe she didn't like the smell."

"Are you sure you're translating that correctly? Let Bruno…" Maggie sighed and turned away. "Doesn't matter."

They continued on for another hour until the landscape dominated the skyline. It was a familiar jungle they recognized; however, here there was a riot of color and the tall trees gave way to more grassland dotted with the flowering shrubs in all the colors of the rainbow. Interestingly, the birds skimmed the treetops, but there didn't seem to be any over the clearing and the flowering shrubs.

"Should we avoid it?" Jane asked.

"There's thick jungle everywhere else. Katya's notes weren't exactly a warning. Not sure if she meant hold your breath because it stinks, or hold your breath because they were nervous." He clicked his tongue in his cheek. "Damn, wish I could ask her."

Wenton sat upright. "It seems the safest landing spot for miles. How about this: a few of us can go ashore first and scout. Everywhere else looks to be a near-impenetrable tangle anyway." He turned. "Besides, your friend made it okay, so why shouldn't we?"

Michael decided. "I agree—we land. Andy and I will…"

"No, I'm the biologist. No disrespect, but you guys have no idea what to even look out for. I'll go in first," Jane stated.

"I'll go with you," Andy added. "Jamison?"

"Yeah, okay." Jamison turned to check with Wenton who gave a small nod.

"Take your spears," Michael said.

She smiled. "Of course. I'm hunting wild flowers."

"Humor me," Michael added.

The boat nudged in at the muddy shoreline and Jane and Andy stepped out. Their feet squelched into the glutinous muck and Jane inhaled deeply and then shrugged.

"I'm not smelling anything significant." She looked along the flowering bushes and shrubs. The field of flowers extended several hundred feet before it entered a forest. She exhaled slowly through her nose. *But hold your breath*, Katya had written. Something in here had made the Russian woman apprehensive.

There was only one way to find out what it was. She turned to wave Andy and Jamison on.

She led the young men into the start of the blooming masses. She tried to watch for anything crouching in among the blooms or camouflaged but couldn't help but be distracted by the plants.

They were of myriad colors and shades, and they were like nothing she had ever seen on the surface. Some had broad leaves of brilliant vermillion, with yellow throats, some like trumpets of soft blue, and tightly rolled rosettes of a red so dark it was like clotted blood. The ground also had a thick carpet of green that was dotted with small purple bells.

On the tips of some of the branches, it looked like tiny seedpods with wing-nut leaves and blood-red centers.

"I'm not seeing or smelling anything," Andy said. "But my parents would kill for a few of these in their garden."

She grinned, and then couldn't help laughing at the thought. She half-turned. "No samples."

She heard Michael yelling at them and she turned to give him the *it's all good so far* sign. She'd give it another few dozen feet and then call the group in; as far as she could see, there were no signs of any threats.

The further the trio pressed inland, the more she felt better about her predicament. This place wasn't so bad. And in fact, wasn't a threat at all. She turned and looked back at the blood-red ocean, with the fields of flowers now between her and the boat.

She wondered what it would be like having a small house here. Coming home to find Michael sitting on the porch, two cold beers, and him with his shirt off. She felt herself blush.

Where did that come from? she wondered.

She laughed softly again, and only stopped when from behind she heard a soft scrunching sound. She turned to see that Jamison had sat down. Andy was doing the same.

"Hey, you guys. What're you doing?" She crossed to them.

The pair sat cross-legged and sipped their water. Andy raised his canteen. "Damndest thing—I wished this tasted like wine. Then I took a sip, and guess what? It does. How cool is that?"

A small voice told her that was ridiculous and she knew they didn't have time for this, but she couldn't resist sitting down with them. She unscrewed her canteen.

She closed her eyes. "Champagne." She then sipped. Her mouth dropped in an open smile. "Oh my God, you're right. It does taste like champagne."

She toasted them and sipped again. She looked up at the sky and saw the sun—it shouldn't have been there, but it was. Rainbow-colored birds flittered from bush to bush, and she sighed and lay back.

The birds came to land close by and sang the most beautiful song to her. She smiled down at them as they hopped onto her and began to gently caress her skin.

"I love it here. I really do," she said dreamily.

*****

"What the hell are they doing?" Michael stood up.

"Did they just fall down?" Maggie also stood.

"No, I think they all just, *sat down*, like they were about to have a damn picnic," Michael replied.

Wenton squinted and walked to the front of the boat. He perched on the forward gunwale and craned his neck for more height. "I don't believe they're sitting anymore. I think now they're lying down."

"That's it. I'm going in." Michael leaped over the side.

"Wait. We'll all come," Wenton said. "Let's get everything together."

"No time, we go now." Michael frowned.

"We're not coming back. Your friend got through this, so will we. And one more thing, I have a hunch—wear a mask. Soak a rag and tie it over your nose and mouth." Wenton began tossing everything they needed out of the boat and onto the sand.

Michael quickly loaded his pack, took out a tattered rag that once was a shirt, wet it, and wrapped it around his lower face. "Ready?"

Wenton and Maggie nodded. Michael began to jog in to where they had seen Jane and the men's last position.

In a few minutes, they came across the prone bodies.

"What the hell?" Maggie's eyes widened.

The two bodies were covered in red flowers the size of silver dollars. Michael went to his knees and started to rip them free. Every time he did, he left a small smear of blood where the rooting tendrils had pierced the skin.

"Bloodsuckers. Where's Jamison?" Wenton said as he ripped and scraped the things from Andy.

"*Jamison!*" Maggie yelled. "Ouch." She slapped at her neck and looked at her hand. One of the floating plants had tried to alight on her.

"We need to find him, fast." She began to circle the group, trying to locate her friend.

"Let's at least get these two the hell out of here," Michael said.

"Not without Jamison," Wenton said.

"We'll come back for him. Maggie will find him." They grabbed the slumbering bodies of Jane and Andy and dragged them through the clumps of flowers. In a few minutes, they were at the edge of the jungle and in the shade, and once out of the red light, many of the blooms started to drop off.

Michael turned back. "Harry, stay here with them. I'll be back." He sprinted back to where Maggie was searching.

In a few more minutes, the pair finally found him. He had crawled a hundred feet through the flowers and was curled up beneath a bush. Jamison was hard to see at first, as he was totally covered over by the parasitic blooms.

Michael hauled him out and together they ripped and wiped him as free of the blooms as they could manage.

"Let's go." They pulled him to where Wenton waited with the others.

Jane and Andy were groaning as they began to come round. But Jamison looked pale and a little shrunken.

"I think he's lost a lot of blood," Maggie said.

Michael pointed. "Maggie, see if you can rouse Jane. We need her expertise here. She's the biologist."

Michael looked back down at the young man. His mouth was open, and even though they had removed the visible blooms, he saw that where a lot of them had alighted, they had managed to embed their tendrils into the skin. And some had broken off.

As he watched, his eyes widened. "Oh shit." He saw them spreading below the skin surface like tiny worms, elongating and thickening.

"Oh God, what…just…happened?" Jane sat up and put a hand to her head.

"A little help here." Michael was trying to pull some of the tendril threads from Jamison's skin, but his fingers were becoming slippery from the blood and the fine hair-like threads broke off and then snapped back below the skin surface. "Damnit."

Wenton joined him and took out his knife. He looked up at Michael who nodded. "Go for it."

The man started to cut into the skin, tracing the larger tendrils that seemed to be forming veins. They'd spread, formed a little nodule below the skin, and then branched out from that nodule in different directions, to then make more nodules.

"Oh no, oh no, oh no." Maggie put a hand over her mouth.

Jamison's mouth dropped open, and from deep inside his throat, a tendril lifted free, broadened, and then a small bloom opened on its end.

Michael froze, staring at it as if in a trance. Even though his logical mind was revolted and in a state of panic, a small voice in his head was urging him to lean closer and inhale the flower's fragrance.

He began to lean in toward the young man's face.

"*Get. Away. From him.*" Jane groggily dragged at Michael's arm. "*They must. Be giving off. Some sort. Of gas.*"

Michael fell back and shook himself while Maggie and Wenton continued to pick at the young man, scrape at the blooming flowers, and cut into his flesh.

But Jamison began to swell; his stomach, his thighs, and even his throat.

"He's dead, get back," Michael said.

"He's not," Maggie wailed.

As if in response, Jamison let out a long and low moan. He seemed to take an enormous, deep breath as his chest swelled.

"He's not dead, goddamnit." Maggie ripped his shirt open to get at his chest, but the body was just a network of spidery veins and lumps that pushed up through the skin now to open as new blooms.

"Don't breathe it in." Andy got to his knees, his swollen eyes blinking as if sensitive from the light.

In another second, Jamison's body split open like a melon and spilled a bloody tangled mesh of roots, flowers, and questing tendrils.

Wenton and Maggie fell back, and Andy and Michael grabbed at the pair to pull them backward. As they watched, the body of Jamison threw out roots that dug into soil. Branches lifted from him to quest out from under the tree canopy toward the sky and further blooms opened on their ends.

The group pulled back into the darker jungle and stopped to stare. The young man was no more and the only sign was a vaguely human-shaped root ball at the base of yet another flowering shrub.

"*Hold your breath*, Katya told us." Jane wiped her eyes. "I wonder whether one of her team members is out there in among that field of flowers."

"They drugged us," Andy said. "They put some sort of gas in the air and made us fall asleep so those, *things*, could land on us and try and take root."

"To feed on us," Jane said. "We have carnivorous plants that use scent to attract their prey. But these things take it to another level. They use it to take down large animals, and then just…consume and use them."

"That's how they spread as well." Michael looked up briefly at the tree canopy overhead. "But seems they don't like shade."

Andy grimaced and scratched at his stomach. He suddenly stopped. "Shit." He ripped open his ragged shirt and pulled down his pants until he was just standing in very sweat-stained underwear.

"*Check my back, check my back.*" He pointed over his shoulder.

"Stay still," Michael said and spoke over his shoulder to Jane. "You're next."

Michael found one spot of the tendrils on Andy's neck and scraped them off with his blade. Luckily, they hadn't penetrated below the epidermal layer of his skin. And more good news was Jane was spore free.

Michael turned back. "Remind me in my notes to say something a little less cryptic than: *hold your damn breath*."

"Amen to that," said Andy as he pulled his tattered clothing back on.

Michael turned back to the forest. There were tall trees like redwoods and carpets of fallen leaves. In between the mighty boughs, fern fronds the size of small cars hung heavy with dripping moisture, and the further in he looked, the darker it got.

Andy finished pulling his rags back on. "I feel we're back where we started."

"Yeah." Jane leaned up against a tree trunk for a moment. She looked at Michael and gave him a watery smile.

"I don't know how much more I've got in me."

He nodded. "I understand. But we'll see the surface again. Just remember, every step we take is a step closer to home now."

"You promise?" she asked.

"I guarantee it." He smiled confidently and then hugged her to him and kept the smile on his face.

But behind the façade, he couldn't help feeling a sinking ache of doubt deep in his chest.

CHAPTER 21

After a little over a mile, the land began to slope downward and the huge trees began to thin as smaller species took over. Beneath their feet, the jungle floor squelched and became slippery, and even the feeder roots began to lift from the waterlogged soil.

They could smell it before they saw it: the stench of rottenness as the thick air filled with the odor of fetid gases, fungus, and death. And just as Michael hoped it would begin to dry, they passed through a stand of broken rock and there before them was the bog. And it seemed endless.

"Oh God no." Maggie leaned forward to place hands on her knees and Michael also slumped against a rock.

"How long did you say this Russian woman was missing down here?" Wenton asked.

"A year." Michael turned. "But I don't think she went this way."

"What? Have we lost her trail?" Andy asked.

Michael shrugged. "She can't have come this way because she said they followed a river. She didn't say which way it was."

"Maybe she did," Jane said. "Maybe 50 years ago this was the river. But now the land is saturated and spoiled."

"You might be right." Michael held out the compass. "North is right through the center of this damn swamp."

They turned back to stare at the belching morass. There were thick, green pools of algae, some the size of bathtubs, and some hundreds of feet across. Bubbles of methane popped and let loose eggy-smelling vapors.

"Wait here." Michael walked a few paces ahead of the group and turned slowly. The gigantic tree branches cut out most of the light, and the murky water plus too many shadows made for a deadly mix.

He stood with his hands on his hips for a few moments and could feel eyes on him. He walked back slowly to the group. "I can't see any sort of path."

"We'll never make it," Maggie said. "How far is it—a few hours, a day, a week?" She shook her head and slid slowly down to sit. "Someone just shoot me now."

"Alligators," Jane said.

"*What*? Where?" Michael craned forward.

"Or something like it." She rubbed her face and then looked up at him. "Remember what I told you about nature hating a vacuum? And also if it found something that worked, it recreated it from any raw material it could find?" She raised her eyebrows.

"Yeah, I do," Michael said, already guessing where she was going.

"Alligators and crocodiles are some of the most successful creatures on the planet. I mean, the surface of the planet. Their form is largely unchanged since the first crocodilians of some 250 million years ago." Jane turned to look back out over the dismal swamp. "I'd bet my last dollar that there is some sort of insectoid equivalent of an alligator in there."

"Oh Jesus. I *do not* want to meet that," Andy said softly. "Everything in this goddamn place is huge and wants to eat us."

"Don't know if anyone else noticed, but it seems that soft-bodied creatures are very popular down here." Wenton half-smiled. "But levity aside, going in the right direction is one thing. But it's not very advantageous if that means going the hard path. We need to get our bearings." He looked up, and up.

Michael followed his gaze, and then nodded. "Yeah, I get it. Someone needs to climb to the top of one of these trees and let us know what…" he turned to Andy "…he sees."

"Oh yeah, make the young, dumb but handsome guy do it." Andy grinned. "*Nah*, I would have volunteered anyway." He looked up into the high canopy. "Might even be a cool breeze and fresh air up there."

Andy searched around until he found a fallen stump leaning up against a huge tree. He lightly walked up it, hands out, until he got to the bottom branches.

The branch was enormous and he stood with hands on hips as he looked along its length.

"We could camp up here. Out of the swamp and up from danger." He stared upward again. "Okay, this is gonna take me a while." He began to climb.

*****

The trunk and limbs of the tree were so huge Andy used more of his rock-climbing expertise than his tree-climbing skills.

He leaped and levered himself ever upward, and after 20 minutes was already 150 feet above the ground. He looked down and saw that the team had done what he suggested and moved to one of the broad, lower limbs for rest and security.

He craned upward again. He still had at least 200 feet to go. He knew redwoods could get up to 370 feet, but they were tall and straight, and this guy he climbed was around that height easily, but broad like some sort of massive banyan or ficus fig tree.

He went to reach out for another branch and something hissed at him, and he pulled his hand back. On the branch were crash helmet-sized beetles with glossy black bodies and red stripes. They were mostly round with smaller heads, and they reminded him of overgrown ladybeetles.

"You know, where I came from, you guys are small, friendly, and everyone loves you."

The beetle closest to him hissed again and this time reared up, exposing wickedly sharp nippers.

"Oh, piss off." Andy batted it away, and it fell backward off the branch and plummeted for a few dozen feet before taking flight and zooming away into the tree canopy.

He continued on, stopping several more times to ease his muscle strain and sip from his now brackish, warm canteen water. He started again and finally made it near to the top.

Andy then edged out along one of the branches as far as it would allow his weight to travel. He moved sideways, a foot at a time and held onto an overhead branch. He only stopped when the limb was creaking and bending downward.

He reached forward to open the branches and gaze out at their hidden world at the center of the Earth.

"Wow," he whispered.

The red world stretched on until it vanished in the distance. Huge treetops with the dots of flying creatures moving in and out of the impenetrable foliage made it impossible to even see the ground in some areas.

There were pools of open water, gleaming like some sort of molten-red metal under the brilliant and bloody-colored sky. In the distance were the cones of smoking volcanoes, and also the massive column mountain that rose up above all others. It narrowed but instead of forming a cone, it continued on up and into the red ceiling.

"Bingo," he said.

Andy tried to edge out a few more feet and dragged the branch in front of him aside a little more. He saw that the miasmic swamp they had entered ran for several miles, and there was no sign of the river that Katya and her team had taken. He wondered whether it had dried up, or as Jane suggested, over the half-century since the Russian woman had been here it had stagnated and become the swamp.

Thankfully, the densest parts of the jungle swamp didn't seem all that big and running through them he could make out large areas where the smaller trees and grasses had been stamped down, like massive animal tracks.

He exhaled. "Not easy." There didn't seem any other way of crossing it other than trekking right through the heart of the miasma. It would be dangerous, energy-sapping, and inevitable if they were to get to the column mountain.

Leaves rained down on his head and he hunkered down, momentarily expecting attack. He looked up.

The tree shook and more leaves rained down on him and all around him.

"What the hell?"

Andy gripped the branch and was about to clamber back toward the central trunk, when the trees in the distance shook. Then the next one shook, and he began to get an idea of what was happening.

He waited a few more moments and then he saw it—the huge backs of a couple of the titanic insect-like sauropods moving through the jungle forest. He stared down on the things as they went to pass by within only a few hundred feet of him.

Once again on their backs were the bird-like arthropods hitching a ride—all up high and out of trouble from the swamp below.

"So you big guys are the ones making those giant animal tracks, *huh*?"

He watched for a few more moments as an idea began to form.

"Maybe, just maybe."

He carefully weaved his way back to the trunk to begin the long climb down.

*****

"It can be done," Andy announced.

"Ride on the back of the equivalent of a sauropod insect?" Wenton snorted. "Yes, sounds perfectly sane to me."

"Go on," Michael said.

"I noticed on their backs that the flying insects just sat there and weren't disturbed by the giant creatures. It might not even know they're there. Or even care." He shrugged. "If they can do it, why can't we?"

"Because they can fly there, and if the crap hits the fan, then they just fly away," Maggie said. "That thing is a moving mountain." She folded her arms. "How do we climb them, and while they're moving? I'm not saying it's a bad idea, but those things are enormous. We'd get crushed just trying to get close to them."

"I've thought of that…we don't climb them, we drop down on them from above. Just like the flyers." Andy smiled. "We wait in the trees and when they go past, we drop down and join the parade."

Michael stared out at the swampy jungle and rubbed his chin for a moment before turning back.

"Was there any sign of the river that Katya mentioned?"

"I saw there was water that might have been a river, but it was miles to the northwest. I don't think it was the same one," Andy replied.

Michael nodded. "So we can either slog through the swamp, or we can try and catch a ride on one of the behemoths that's going our way."

"Which is the greater risk?" Maggie asked.

"Both carry different risks. But the biggest separator is that if we trek through the bog, it'll take us days. And we have no idea what's living in those fetid pools," Michael replied.

"Or what diseases are brewing in there," Jane added. "I vote we ride."

Michael turned to Wenton. "Harry, what are your thoughts?"

Wenton inhaled deeply and then let it out slowly. "If we trek through the swamp, we could die a slow and miserable death from corruption and disease, or maybe even be eaten alive. Or we ride a monster and could die from falling off the back of a beast from the Earth's core." He smiled. "But at least that'd be damn exciting. So, I say we ride."

Andy rubbed his hands together. "We ride."

Maggie tilted her head. "How do we know which tree they'll pass underneath?"

"I saw there were huge paths cut through the forest. I think these things have been moving back and forth for years, centuries maybe. We just need to scale a tree over the trail and wait. Use the ropes to rappel down," Andy explained.

Michael nodded. "It'll be nice for someone or something else to do the walking for a while. Andy, find us the best tree, and then I guess we just wait."

The group scaled to a position mid-canopy and waited for six long hours. The branches were so wide they were able to sit or lay down. Many times, they watched below as herds of creatures passed beneath them.

"My kingdom for a camera," Jane said as she rested her chin on her hands and looked down toward the ground.

Creatures moved along the trail that defied logic, or maybe only so because they were so alien to anything they knew on the surface—long-necked things like giraffes with six legs and diamond-shaped heads. Once, a snake-like creature slithered below, black bands along all 50 feet of its length, and its large armor plates sliding smoothly over each other to make it near soundless. A small herd of spiked balls marched so tightly together at first they thought the things might be a single creature, until they broke apart to swarm around the stalk of a large palm frond.

Death was ever-present as well. A barrel-shaped creature wandered along the path, and then paused, looked like it sniffed the ground for a moment, and then backed itself into the thick foliage.

Jane could just make out its head in among the ferns and mosses as it waited. In a few more minutes, another creature sauntered along, this almost as large as the first, longer and with a whip-like tail with a wicked dagger point on the end.

When it got close to the hiding barrel-on-legs, the hiding creature shot out something like a mesh that covered the scorpion thing completely. It screamed, hissed, and struggled frantically in its confines.

In the next few seconds, Jane heard the first crackle of shell, and as the net was pulled tighter, the captured creature screamed as more of its carapace crumpled.

Inexorably, the web structure was hauled back in toward the ambush hunter, and as the net got tighter and smaller, the captured animal was crushed down to a long pipe of meat and shell fragments.

It was then fed into the maw and bite-by-bite was completely ingested. Jane shuddered, not able to stop her memory taking her back to David's fate. She turned away.

More time passed, and it was when they began to move into their seventh hour that they first felt the tree begin to shudder.

"Heads up," Andy said. "I think our ride is on its way."

They moved along the branch over the trail and tied their ropes in a release knot on the limb. If everything went to plan, they'd slide down the rope, drop onto the massive animal's back, and then tug and release their ropes so they could gather them back in.

Maggie kept her eyes on the path but spoke out of the side of her mouth. "Hey, what happens if those bird things object to us sharing their ride?"

Michael turned. "If they leave us in peace, we'll do the same for them. If not, we kick them off."

"Here we go." Andy shuffled along a few more feet. "Going to pass a dozen feet out to our left. Move along, everyone."

They did as asked, just as the trees behind them parted and the long neck carried the head through first.

"Good Lord," Jane breathed out.

The head was easily the size of a bus and would pass within just a few feet of them. The massive eyes were made up of thousands of compound lenses that shifted in color from gold to red to emerald green.

Though it had a long snout, the mouth didn't open with jaws, but at the end, it was a mix of cutting and grasping appendages that were constantly moving like a grasshopper. The plates on its neck looked capable of deflecting cannon fire and it was hard to imagine anything being able to worry them in this world.

"Get ready," Michael said with his toes now right on the branch edge.

The body finally emerged from the foliage and was as wide across as half a football field. Massive plates on the broad back were actually covered in some growths that might have been shrubs or something else that had been captured as seeds and taken root on the gargantuan body. Perhaps, a little like a mollusk that hung from the undersides of the great whales.

And then it was directly below them.

"Go." Michael jumped and began to slide down his rope.

They only had to drop a few dozen feet until they landed. Immediately, the insectoid birds squealed and squabbled for a moment, but then they simply shuffled backward toward the rear of the animal and made space for them.

One after the other, the team came down, until they were all secure and winding back in their ropes. Andy looked exhilarated and Michael gave him the thumbs up.

"Good plan."

He grinned. "I'm not just here for my looks, you know."

Michael turned about. "This'll do." Their living platform was stable, and given the slow and ponderous gait, didn't create a threat that they could be shaken off.

Jane walked about for a moment, then stopped and tilted her head. "He-*eeey*, listen."

The group quietened and watched her, perhaps expecting some approaching menace.

Jane smiled. "Hear it? That's breathing."

"So?" Maggie shrugged. "Of course they're breathing."

"No, not with lungs like this." Jane got down on all fours and placed her ear to the thing's back. "Bugs got big during primordial Earth's carboniferous period because there were higher levels of oxygen in the atmosphere." She straightened to her knees. "They needed it because they don't have lungs. Instead, they took in air via a series of openings on their bodies called spiracles, which connect directly to the tissues that need oxygen. But as soon as the oxygen levels of the planet dropped, the giant insects vanished."

"But these guys have grown lungs?" Andy asked. "Or is the oxygen level high down here?"

"Oxygen level seems normal. Otherwise, we'd have blacked out long ago." Jane got to her feet and dusted off her hands. "They must have evolved better breathing mechanisms. It's the only way they could have got so big."

"What else could they have evolved?" Wenton asked.

Jane turned. "Other than gigantism? Maybe longer life spans, intelligence, perhaps things we can't even comprehend."

"And now we're the tiny parasites hitching a ride on the back of them, the giants," Wenton snorted.

"Nice thought. I think I want to go home now." Maggie walked closer to the edge of the joined thorax and abdomen. They were at least 100 feet up from the ground. "Speaking of that, just how do we get down?" she asked.

"Yeah, and *when* do we get down?" Andy added.

Michael chuckled. "We get down when big boy here decides to go in a direction we don't want to go. And as for *how* we get down, I'm thinking it might be the same way we got on—we lasso a branch and swing off and into a tree."

Maggie looked around. "Amazing. If this thing wasn't moving, I'd think we were on the ground."

Michael knew what she meant—there were shrubs, some patches of grass, and even some small pools of water.

"Dust, debris, and leaves fell onto its back and became trapped. Then they broke down to make soil," Jane said. "Add in a few wind-blown seeds, and voila, you have a mini ecology springing up." She smiled. "And a mobile one."

"Well…" Michael sat with his back against a lump of armored shell, "…we've got miles to go, so let's rest while we can."

Wenton did the same and placed a rag over his eyes. He sighed and clasped fingers over his stomach. "This is more like it." In another moment, he was snoring.

CHAPTER 22

Earthquake, he thought, and came immediately awake. Michael sat up, arms out to each side of him, and felt disorientated for a moment. It took him a few seconds to work out where he was.

Then he saw the huge trees moving past and remembered—still on the back of the land leviathan.

Jane, Maggie, and Andy were also awake now, and only Wenton continued to sleep soundly.

"What's going on?" Andy asked and got to his feet. He carefully walked to the edge of the creature's back, arms held like a tightrope walker and knees bent to keep his balance.

"Be careful. This thing has sped up for some reason." Michael also got to his feet.

"Hey, where'd our flying buddies go?" Andy pointed to the now vacant rear of the thing, where the flock of giant bird-like insects had once congregated.

Now, they were alone; while they were sleeping, the avians had taken to the air or the branches close by.

"What do they know that we don't?" Jane asked.

Michael moved as far to the front of the massive insectoid beast as he could, that was just before the trunk of the neck, which was now leaning forward as it gathered speed.

He could see nothing out front and he turned. "Andy, anything behind us?"

Andy jogged to the rear of the beast, and in a few seconds, he was back. "Yeah, danger. A pack of animals that look like a cross between a praying mantis and a *Tyrannosaurus rex* are chasing our ride."

"Can they get up here?" Maggie asked.

"They're big, but not that big. I think we're okay for now," Andy replied.

The creature they were riding smashed into a tree and they were thrown down. It was only through luck that none of them had been close to a side or they'd be thrown off.

"This thing is panicking," Michael said. "Somebody wake Wenton. We need to be ready for anything."

Previously, the huge beast had been moving at around four miles per hour, or walking speed. But now it careened at 20 easily, and though this seemed still insignificant, when you coupled that sort of speed with something that must have weighed a hundred tons, it was terrifying.

"It can't keep this speed up—it must tire soon," Jane said. "Plus, we seem to be moving uphill."

"Then what?" Andy asked. "There was about a dozen of those predator things. I don't think they could bring this big guy down or leap up here, but no one is sure they won't try and take a leap."

"Maybe that's what the flying things were afraid of," Maggie said softly.

The forest started to thin out and Michael could begin to see what was coming up ahead of them. Behind him, Wenton staggered forward.

"Dynamite them," Wenton said groggily.

"Glad you could join us," Michael said. "And if I do, I think that'd give this big guy a heart attack if an explosion went off at its heels." He turned back to the forest. "And we need to save those last few sticks for whatever comes next."

The group threw themselves flat as the massive beast passed underneath a huge limb whose cleaves scraped down its back and threatened to wipe them free as if they were crumbs from a tablecloth.

Slightly to their northeast was a huge cliff that ran toward them. But as the jungle was still thick, it was impossible to tell how far along it went and whether it was directly up ahead.

The cliff only looked to be a few hundred feet high and may or may not have been fatal for the thing they were riding. But it certainly would have been for them.

"There's a drop coming up!" Michael yelled.

"Damn, yeah, of course," Jane said. "This is why the things are nipping at the leviathan, but not attacking it just yet. It's an old hunter's trick—panic the bigger beasts into a stampede and run it into a dead-end...or off a cliff." She turned. "We need to get off, now."

"Good idea." Michael dropped his pack and began pulling out his rope. "Time to leave, people."

All the climbers had snap-hooks that they quickly fitted to the end of the eyelets on their ropes. The stainless-steel hooks were short and strong, and not meant as grappling hooks, but in this case, could be used as a weighted snag to swing around a branch, hook onto an extrusion or itself, and create a sturdy attachment.

"Ready?" Michael had his legs braced. He turned briefly and saw the forest beginning to open out. Soon there'd be no more trees, and then they were screwed.

Time was up.

"Let's go." He began to swing his rope and hook in ever-greater arcs. Michael picked a low-hanging branch and threw it at what he hoped was a suitable place on the limb.

As he hoped, it went over the limb, swung around it, and then hooked onto itself. Michael swung away from the massive beast to slam into the trunk. He clung there and turned back in time to see the others also swinging away.

Only Jane was left and she tossed her rope. He watched it sail toward a branch, but instead of looping around it, she had the misfortune of it hitting the actual limb and bouncing away. As the massive beast disappeared through the last of the trees, Michael saw her frantically reeling her rope back in for another attempt.

The last tree limbs closed around the beast, and Jane and the monstrous thing vanished. With it went the hopping, hissing, and nipping band of creatures that were in pursuit.

As Michael watched, he saw that Jane had been right; they darted forward to nip at the mighty column legs but didn't seek to slow or stop it, only inflict enough torment to keep it moving forward.

The unseen massive leviathan rumbled off, trailing its herd of pursuers. But there had been no sign of Jane leaving the huge thing's back.

"Where is everyone? Speak up!" Michael yelled.

"Yo," Andy replied from about 50 feet along the newly smashed pathway.

"Over here, and with me is Maggie," Wenton said casually from another tree limb.

Michael waited, but there was nothing back from Jane. He saw that the branches touched one another, so he could move through the lower canopy and stay up off the ground.

"Going after Jane," he said.

"I'm coming," Andy replied and quickly joined him on the same limb.

The pair tried to move as quickly as they could along the branches. Some were wide enough that they could run and others meant they had to edge sideways. Even though the forest was thinning, the size of the trees still meant most times the huge limbs overlapped each other, creating a long highway.

The pair crossed from one limb to the next, until they made the very last tree. Michael slowed as they moved out as far as their weight would allow, and it took them out to the precipice of the cliff edge to peer out.

"Shit," Andy said. "It went over."

The huge beast lay like a broken dirigible at the bottom of the cliff. The carnivores being lighter and more agile had scaled down the sheer wall and now swarmed over the prone giant, heading for the places where they could quickly bypass the impossibly thick armor plate, such as the mouth, eyes, and the rear where Michael assumed the anus was.

"Can you see her?" Michael asked.

Andy shook his head. "Don't worry, she got off. She had to."

Michael tried to guess if a person could survive the fall; he doubted it. "We have to get down there," he said softly.

Andy turned to stare at him for a few moments. "Okay, but the carnivores are down there. All of them."

Wenton and Maggie finally caught up. "Any sign?" Wenton asked.

"Nothing." Andy kept his eyes on the huge fallen creature.

"We need to see if she survived. We need to be sure," Michael said. "I'm going down."

"Stupid plan, and suicidal," Wenton declared.

Michael felt his anger rise. "We can wait until the predators leave."

"Really? There's a hundred tons of meat down there. How long do you think that'll take to be eaten—a week? A month?" Wenton's mouth was set in a line. "Forget it, Michael."

"I can't," he said and turned away.

"Fine with me." Wenton rolled his eyes.

Michael ignored him and began to plan a way down, trying to figure a route that was close to the fallen giant but would shield him from the carnivores.

"Wait, she's not down there," Maggie said. "Look."

Michael spun to follow where she was pointing. In the last tree was a hook and rope. And the rope was still swinging.

"She made it out. Told you." Andy grinned.

"*Jane!*" Michael edged toward the rope, followed by Andy, Wenton, and Maggie.

They had to cross firstly to one tree, and then the rope tree, and hurry along the limb.

"*Jane!*" Michael yelled again. He began to search the ground below that was still a considerable 80 feet down—about as high as a seven-story building.

"I can't see her." He began to panic.

Maggie screamed, and Michael spun to her. She was pointing into the branches above, her face a mask of pure terror.

Michael dreaded to look up but had to. He saw Jane, or at least her body from the chest down. The rest of her was being pulled into the mouth of some sort of revolting insect version of a monstrous snake.

Michael's brain was short-circuiting as it tried to process what he was seeing—the thing was a mottled green to blend in with its jungle surroundings, and rings of plates overlapped all the way along its body to a tapering tail that it had coiled around the tree trunk. Its bulging eyes were like slitted glass buttons and moved independently of each other—one was focused on its meal, the other on Michael and the other new arrivals.

Jane's arms were pressed to her sides, but her legs shivered and danced, and her hands flexed and opened as if she was trying to wriggle herself out from being swallowed alive.

Michael screamed and ran at the thing. He leaped, grabbing the snake around the neck, and only barely hanging on, as it was as round as a draft horse. Andy ran beneath it and grabbed Jane's legs and hung on.

In another moment, Michael reached an arm into his bag and grabbed the bolt gun. His was the last they had, and it was preloaded with just two remaining caving bolts. He jammed the gun against the insect serpent's body, careful to keep it away for where he thought Jane was inside its mouth.

The gun's bolt exploded out and punched a hole in the scales and flesh of the creature. It reared up, taking Jane, Andy, and Michael with it.

"*Let go, you bastard.*" Michael had dug his fingers in underneath one of the plates and hung on, and in one smooth motion brought the gun around again and fired his last bolt.

This time, the bolt passed right through the beast, taking a double fist-sized chunk of armor plate and flesh with it.

Either from pain, or shock, the snake vomited. From its mouth came Jane plus a rush of yellow bile. Andy grabbed her and stopped her falling to the ground.

Michael leaped free as the serpent slithered into the upper foliage, rattling branches in its haste to get away. In seconds, it had vanished.

They crowded around as Jane, covered in mucous, burst into tears and shook uncontrollably. She held out her arms to Michael and he took hold of her, wiping the slime from her face and hair and speaking softly to her.

Jane buried her face in the tattered remains of his shirt. He just heard her voice over the sobs.

"I want to go home."

"I'll get you there. I promise." He held her for a while until she stopped shaking.

Michael knew that if there were one promise in this life he would die to keep, it would be this one.

Wenton edged out as far as he could to look down over the precipice. "I think we should go now." He turned. "It's getting a little carnivore-crowded down there."

Michael looked into Jane's face. "Can you walk?"

She nodded and gave him a watery smile. "Just...just stay close."

$$*****$$

The group moved along the highway of enormous branches as they headed north for as far as their wooden highway could take them. But eventually, the boughs became too sparse for the foliage to have linked branches and they finally had to climb back down to the ground.

Even before they exited the trees, they could see the mountainous column rising up to the blood-red ceiling. There was no equivalent on the surface, and this immense geological formation was as alien as it was colossal, with conjured images of a primordial world where everything was on a scale apart from the world above.

Michael had no idea how far around it was, but it could easily have been 10 miles and it dominated everything else surrounding it.

"And that's where your friend said the caves were...that took them home?" Wenton asked.

"Somewhere in that mountain, Katya Babikov said there was probably another gravity well." Michael placed a hand over his eyes to shield them. Touching his forehead made the skin hurt, and for the first time he knew he, like all of them, were burned raw and peeling. He just prayed that the radiation hadn't penetrated too deep.

Katya had been trapped down here a year, and they'd only been here a few months; he just hoped that made a difference. The irony of escaping these horrors to only die from a multitude of cancers on escaping would be too terrible to contemplate.

"Look up toward the middle of the mountain column," Maggie said. "They look like airplanes."

Sure enough, there were strangely formed flying objects landing and taking off from holes in the face of the mountain.

"More like giant bees, maybe?" Andy said.

"I hope so. If they're bees, they'll protect their hive, and if we don't bother them, they'll more than likely leave us alone." Jane exhaled. "But if they're wasps, they're carnivorous, and they'll attack us on sight. Then eat us."

Wenton cursed softly. "And me without my bug spray."

"First, we've got to cross this grassland plane, fast. And I'm betting the slowest thing in this underworld right now is us." Michael looked along

168

the flat landscape. "I don't see anything out there."

The group stared out at the grasslands. The plants looked spindly and only came to about knee height.

"Doesn't look like there's enough cover out there for a large predator," Maggie observed.

"Unless they live in burrows like some sort of trapdoor spider," Michael replied.

Wenton snorted. "Is nothing easy in this world?" He narrowed his eyes. "I estimate it's about a mile, give or take."

"Yup," Michael replied. "And we can't exactly wait for nightfall. Upside is, we can see any predator that comes at us. Downside is, there's probably damn well nothing we could do about it."

"We belly crawl," Jane said. "It'll take a long time, but most predators are triggered by speed and motion. The reduced profile and slower motion will make us less visible."

Andy scoffed. "I did a trial boot camp when I was at high school. We had to do some extreme training and one of the exercises was to crawl over a rough field for about 500 feet. It tore our knees and elbows to shreds."

"Well, what have you got?" Maggie demanded.

Andy looked back at the field bathed in the blaring red light. "I've got nothing better. I just want us to be aware of what some of the risks and drawbacks of our options are."

"Anyone have any other ideas?" Michael asked.

He waited, looking along their faces. After another moment, a few shook their heads slowly. But none of them look convinced.

"Then let's strap our hands and knees with whatever we have left and get started." He grinned at them. "Think of it this way—home stretch."

They sat and began to pull their packs apart and use the pieces to wind the tougher material around their elbows, hands, knees, and if there was any left over, their bellies.

Michael looked back out over the plane. "I can see some sort of rocky outcrop in the center. That'll be our first goal. We make it to that and then assess our plan and progress. Okay?"

They nodded.

Michael crossed to Jane and took her hand. "We can do this."

"I know we can," she said as she wound a piece of canvas strap around her hand. She flexed it and looked up into his face. "Last roll of the dice?"

He chuckled softly. "Well, maybe a few more rolls to go. But I think this might be our last real challenge."

She nodded. "We'll make it."

"One more thing." He motioned her closer.

She leaned in, and he kissed her lips. He felt their dryness and was sure his felt the same. She grabbed his bearded chin and held it to her mouth, prolonging the kiss. It gave him a boost of happiness.

She pulled back, smiled, and shook her head. "Now you damn well better get me home, Mr. Monroe."

"Promise." He hugged her and he kissed her once more on the top of her head.

He smelled her hair and there was something unsettling about it. Then he remembered they had pulled her out of the mouth of some insectoid snake and it had vomited the contents of its stomach on her. His lips felt waxy and he wiped them with his forearm.

Michael took one last look around, searching for any movement anywhere. Other than the things hovering at the mid-point of the mountain, they seemed alone.

He got down on his knees and then belly. "Follow my trail in a line." He began to crawl.

Michael quickly discovered they didn't have the plane to themselves. There was all manner of smaller creatures, either hiding in the clumps of grasses or scuttling back and forth out of their path.

Some were like spiders on stilts, with long tails and bulbous eyes. Others looked like reptiles with extra legs and too many eyes. As one new type of thing shot past, he threw out a hand to grab it.

He examined it, turning it over as it hissed and squirmed. It opened its mouth, displaying a tongue like a pink leaf. Michael rolled on his side and held it up. "Hey, it's a lizard. A *real* lizard."

"Looks like a gecko." Jane had crawled up beside him and took the small lizard from him. "It's like I thought. On the surface world, the amphibians won the evolutionary race and beat the arthropods. The arthropods survived, just didn't evolve as rapidly. Down here, it's the opposite. The arthropods are this world's rulers." She smiled down at it. "Good to see you, and good luck, little guy." She let the thing go.

"So, there could still be mammals?" he asked. "Maybe people do exist down here. In some form or other." He lay back down on his belly. "Onward."

They crawled, and slithered, and pulled themselves forward. Hours went by, and Michael tried to keep focused on their surroundings, trying to ignore the pain already flaring in his hands, hips, and every one of his joints.

His palms began to feel sticky and he knew it'd be either burst blisters or blood.

After four hours of agony, they made it to the rocky outcrop—halfway—and Michael slowly lifted himself up onto it to gaze out over the plane. There was still nothing. He turned to look up at their destination; the column mountain was a towering geological behemoth that filled their

170

vision.

He could see where it punctured the molten core and wondered whether inside it was as hollow as he prayed—*prayed*—because he didn't have the heart to tell the group that he had no idea if it was hollow and would contain another gravity well.

Katya never made it this far. She had turned back with her sister by now. What he was relying on was what she put in her notes from Georgy's study of the ancient alchemist's manuscript. From now on, they were in Arkady Saknussov's long-dead hands.

And one thing he knew—Saknussov didn't make it out either.

"See anything?" Andy crawled up beside him.

"All I see is that big-ass mountain thing," Michael said and turned slowly. "But as for anything else, no."

"That's a good thing, I guess," Andy replied. "Hey, do you think the column's thickness will provide us with enough insulation from the molten heat as we pass through it?"

Michael looked up at the boiling redness of the liquid metal. It made his eyes hurt just looking at it. "Well, if it doesn't, then it'll all be over quickly."

"It will. It did for Katya, right?" Maggie said.

Michael smiled flatly down at her. "She made it home."

"I smell sulfur," Jane said, who was sitting with her back to the rocks. "Might be some volcanic activity going on in there."

"Yeah, I think so too." Up close, Michael saw there were many, many cave openings, some huge and some little more than crawl holes. He had no idea which one they should choose.

"Hey look, a rabbit." Maggie pointed to something watching them from the outside of a burrow about 10 feet from where they rested.

It was covered in fur, had large black liquid eyes, and stared intensely back at them.

"Hello," Maggie said softly.

The thing squeaked and lifted a little more. She wiggled her fingers at it. And it lifted some more, and then some more and more. The front half still looked like a rabbit, but its belly had padded segments, dozens of them, and small furry arms all the way down and along the sides of a long body.

"Oh gross. It's a freaking nightmare," Andy said and stuck his tongue out.

"Yes, this is what a mad scientist would create if he managed to mix rabbit and caterpillar DNA." Wenton's mouth turned down. "However, as the front half looks a little like a rabbit, I might be tempted to eat it if we can catch it."

There came a sound like clicking on the slight breeze, and Michael cocked his head to listen for a moment. "Anyone else hear that? Like knitting needles."

"Like what?" Andy asked.

"Forget it." Michael continued to listen.

They waited, concentrating. Once again, the sound was repeated. This time, they got a direction and all turned back to where they had exited the forest.

Standing at its very edge was a group of about a dozen creatures hunched over with distended abdomens and long, spiked legs like those of a spider.

They must have been eight feet in length and from time to time, they lifted up on their back legs as if to taste the air. Held out in front of them were its front legs but looked like they ended in grasping hands.

"We're being tracked," Michael said softly and began to ease himself down below the spindly plant level. "Let's get behind the rock."

They all moved around the other side and watched as the pack of creatures hesitated, as if unsure of the direction the people had taken. They continued to lift up, looking a little like someone had grafted a human front half to a spider back half. The things clicked and rattled, as they obviously shared some sort of communication.

"I don't think they're herbivores," Jane observed. "Some sort of pack predator."

They noticed that their little rabbit caterpillar friend had vanished.

"The rabbipillar knows it's a threat. Not a good sign," Wenton said.

"No shit. *I know* it's a threat as well," Andy replied.

"What's the plan?" Wenton said.

"We move fast. We can't afford to be caught out in the open by those things."

Andy narrowed his eyes. "I think they know we're in here, but don't know exactly where just yet."

"Good. Stay low and follow me," Michael said. He turned to speak over his shoulder. "This is gonna hurt, but no choice."

He increased his speed. And he was right; it damned hurt as every joint, plus his forearms, knees, and now belly was becoming scraped raw.

Every hundred yards he'd stop and lift his head a little to look back. On the third time he did it, he saw the creatures had entered the grassy plane and were coming quickly—not running, yet, but still moving at around three times the speed the people were moving.

"Are they coming?" Jane asked.

"Don't worry about it. Just keep going." Michael tried to ignore that crawling feeling he was getting on the back of his neck as he knew the pack of predators was bearing down on them.

In another hundred yards, he looked back again—the things had crossed half the grassland between the forest and them already.

From a distance, his imagination had painted them as being centaur-like, but now, closer, he could see the gargoyle faces of creatures, and Jane had been right; they were definitely predatorial. There were multiple forward-facing eyes set high on a polished black forehead, and no nose, but two palps on either side of a mouth carrying vicious-looking fangs.

Michael thought that if you merged a human being with a black widow spider, you might get some idea of the nightmare these things had stepped out of.

There was no doubt they were getting run down and soon they'd need to decide whether they would chance making a run for the caves. The options were to stay low and hope the creatures somehow missed them—which he knew was unlikely—or get to their feet and run. Which he knew would be suicide as well—the long legs of the predators told of an ability to generate huge speeds, and he had once read that if a spider were as big as a person, it would be able to generate speeds of 140 miles per hour.

After another hundred yards, Michael had another quick look back—they were so close, he knew they'd be overtaken in the next few minutes. He turned to the column mountain—it was also close now, and he could see the welcoming darkness of the caves.

Even if the predators followed them there, they might have a chance of defending their position in a cave, instead of being caught out in the open.

Above them, the huge insect things hovered, hanging in the sky or landing and entering their own caves higher up.

They only needed another few hundred yards, but it was still too far.

"We need a diversion," Michael said. "No choice." He began to get to his hands and knees.

Jane launched herself at him and grabbed his arm. "Don't you freaking dare, Michael James Monroe."

"There's no other option," he said. "I can draw them off."

Jane clung on tighter. "No, you will not…"

"Let him go. He's right," Wenton said softly and turned to Michael. "Thank you, Michael. We admire your courage."

"You bastard, Harry," Maggie seethed. "Why don't you do it?"

Wenton shrugged. "I have a sore leg."

"All the more reason it should be you—predators love the old and sick," Andy growled.

Wenton looked up over the top of the grasses. "They're nearly on us." He rummaged in his pocket and pulled out a small object and handed it over. "Last quarter-stick, Michael—I'd been saving it. Perhaps it'll help somehow."

"Thank you." Michael half-smiled and took the tiny stick of dynamite. "Not going to be enough to stop them, or maybe even slow them down. But it might just scare the shit out of them."

"I'm coming," Jane said.

Michael squeezed her hand. "Hey, I have no intention of dying. When I go, you guys continue your quick crawl. Hopefully, you'll have a big enough lead to get in the caves."

"And you?" Andy asked.

Michael chuckled. "I used to be the school sprint champ. I'll be there before you." He looked up and over the grass. The creatures were only a few hundred feet from them and coming fast. They'd be on them in the next few minutes.

Michael sucked in a deep breath. He got to his feet and sprinted hard out to the side.

*****

Michael ran hard, one eye on where he was placing his feet and the other on the predator pack. As soon as he revealed himself and started his run, he saw all their flat faces turn toward him. And then they began to follow. Like all predators, they found a fleeing animal impossible to resist.

They made their odd clicking and rattling sound as they came, the noises growing in amplification as their excitement grew.

In a few more seconds, Michael didn't want to look back and see how close they were, but he only wanted to put as much distance between himself and his team so they wouldn't be noticed as they escaped.

He still gripped the half-stick of dynamite. Truth was, he knew it'd be more an annoyance to them than anything else, but there was no reason for him to die still holding onto it. He reached into his pocket, pulled out one of his last pieces of equipment—his lighter—and steadied himself for a second or two to light it. It flared and fizzed, quickly burning down.

Michael turned to throw it and felt a near electric shock of horror at how close the things were. He tossed the half-stick literally into the face of the lead creature, and then dove.

The explosion was enormously loud and even though only a quarter-stick, the percussive wave slammed Michael's eardrums and threw a wave of heat over him. He immediately turned and sat up.

The lead creature was missing half its head and its spasmodic movements made it look like it was short-circuiting. It finally fell on its side, its legs still running as though trying to carry out the damaged brain's last instructions.

But the other dozen creatures were unharmed and quickly refocused on the main game—Michael.

"*Ah*, shit."

Michael stood stock-still, staring back into their liquid-black eyes, and knew he had nothing left.

Fight or flight? he wondered. He pulled his knife from its scabbard. The thing was, his tank was empty and he was sick of running.

"Fight it is then."

The deep zumm filled the air. It tickled his ears and vibrated right through his body to his bones. The huge spider-like beings crouched and their clicking became rapid and agitated. Collectively, they turned to stare, but not at Michael—at something behind and above him.

He spun, seeing the massive bodies bearing down on them like a squadron of winged torpedoes. The blast, though small, had roused the denizens of the hive above. Michael threw himself to the ground and began to crawl away.

Jane had suggested if they were bees, they would only protect their hive. But if they were something like wasps, then as far as they were concerned, the intrusion was a declaration of war—with the loser being dinner.

The monstrous wasps drew closer and Michael saw they looked more like floating dragons with broad, ribbed wings, powerful arms with long-taloned, finger-like claws on each, and where he had thought the spider-creatures had horrifying faces, these things were another level of terrifying altogether.

The sedan-sized dragon-wasps landed hard on the spiders, crushing them to the ground. Many tried to flee, and fast as they were, they were no match for the ferocity of the flying killers. The clicks and rattling noises became squeals of panic and pain as black spider limbs were cut or torn free and their bodies were efficiently dismembered and then decapitated.

The bulk of the remaining corpse, the fleshy torso and abdomen, was then flown back to the hive to be stored in the larder for later consumption. In another moment, it was over, and the giant wasps had departed, leaving a killing-field stained with ichor and still-twitching limbs.

Michael stayed down, resting his head on his forearms for a moment. "Holy crap," he whispered. He lifted his head, feeling like he had more lives than Felix the Cat.

He looked toward the column mountain and saw his friends climbing up to enter the mouth of the largest cave. One person—Jane, he bet—stood outside, waiting for him.

"I'm coming. *Hell yeah*, I'm coming." He began to crawl.

*****

It took Michael another half-hour to slither to the mouth of the cave, and when he finally arrived, he found he had little energy to even climb to his feet.

Jane came down the rocks to grab him under one arm and help him at least struggle to a crouching position to then hobble into the shade of the massive cave.

Wenton saluted. "You're welcome."

"What?" Michael frowned.

"The dynamite," he said. "Saved your ass."

"Oh yeah, piece of cake." Michael scoffed and shook his head. "Your turn next time, Harry."

Andy came and hugged him. "Thank God. I gotta tell you, I thought you were as good as dead."

"Yeah, me too." Michael finally straightened and began to look around. "Are we in the right place?"

"We don't know." Maggie smiled. "Another good reason that you made it. Now you can help us work that out."

"There's a slight problem." He sighed. "Katya never actually said. She never made it this far." He walked slowly into the cavernous opening, rubbing a bearded chin. He spun back to them. "But Saknussov might have. *Panirovochnyye sukhari*—the Russian words for breadcrumbs. Katya did say that they continued to follow Saknussov's breadcrumbs."

Andy clapped his hands together. "That has to mean his markings, right? He left his marks for us to follow."

"We just have to find them, and we'll be going home." Wenton beamed. "We'll be famous."

"I'll settle for just a cold beer and a hotdog," Jane sighed.

"I'll join you in that," Michael replied.

"Burger and coke. Plus fries…and a hotdog as well." Andy grinned.

"Poached lobster with butternut squash, from Eleven Madison Avenue in New York." Wenton inhaled with his eyes shut as though savoring the aroma of the food. He opened one eye. "They have three Michelin stars this year, you know."

"Maggie?" Andy asked. "What are you going to have first?"

She laughed. "A damn long bath."

"Amen to that." Andy lifted his arm and sniffed loudly. He screwed his nose up.

"Then let's see if we can find if Saknussov left us his *Panirovochnyye sukhari*," Jane said.

The group spread out, and after 20 minutes, they hadn't found anything that remotely looked like a mark made by a human hand. They met again in the center of the cave.

"There are a lot of smaller caves leading off from this cavern. What do we do?" Andy asked. "Split up?"

"Not a chance," Jane said. "I've seen what happens in that movie."

"There's a problem—does anyone have any flashlights? I lost mine on the island," Michael said.

"That's certainly going to make locating any sort of small chisel marks in the dark difficult. Not to mention blundering around in a cave." Wenton raised his eyebrows. "Burning torches?"

"Made from what?" Maggie asked. "Those grasslands we just crossed had nothing remotely looking like a tree branch or even a stick. And I for one am not going back to the forest to gather some wood."

"We burn our shirts, our shoes, and whatever else we need to burn," Wenton replied forcefully.

Michael walked away a few steps, trying to think. "We need more than that. Remember, even if we find the gravity well to take us up through the mantle, we'll still need to climb out through the upper crust, and it took us over a week to scale down. We'll have exhausted all our combustible fuel long before then."

"Somehow, Katya did it," Andy replied.

"I know, but I don't know how." Michael turned. "Anyway, step one, we get some rest, and then we can search as much as we can in these labyrinths. If need be, we can go back to the forest to collect some wood." He shrugged. "It's all I got." He yawned. "And frankly, I'm dead on my feet."

They sat for a while, and Andy and Maggie lay back with arms thrown over their eyes. Wenton went and sat looking out at the plane, and Jane and Michael talked softly, neither able to drop off to sleep.

"What are our chances?" she asked.

"No light, no food, very little water, and we still haven't found the right pathway to the surface. If I was a betting man, I'd say the odds were well against us." He smiled and turned. "But inside, I think we've done the hard yards now. I think what we seek is close by. I just know it. So, I'm feeling pretty good."

"Me too." She reached out to squeeze his forearm.

He continued to watch her. "You know, for someone who was nearly eaten alive by some sort of monster snake-insect, you look damn good."

"Oh yeah." She grinned. "You sure know how to show a girl a good time, Mr. Monroe." She kept her hand on his arm. And she kept it there as he drifted off.

His sleep was absolute, and there were no dreams, just a switching off and switching back on as if he had stepped into a time machine and projected himself two hours into the future.

Michael opened his eyes and felt thirsty, hungry, but enormously better from the rest. Jane's hand was still on his arm, and he carefully sat up.

She sighed, smacked her lips, and then spoke without opening her eyes. "I had the strangest dream. I dreamed you and I were at the center of the Earth."

He leaned closer to her. "Do you want the good or bad news?" He laughed softly.

Jane opened her eyes. "Oh God, it's real." She smiled and sat up with a groan.

He took her hand and got to his feet. "Time to get to work. Besides, I can almost taste that beer and hotdog." He helped her up.

The pair walked toward the rear of the cave and stopped to shut their eyes for a few moments. Being away from the red light from outside meant they needed the light receptors in their eyes to adjust to the darker interior.

They proceeded again, and then when they were around a hundred feet in, the darkness went from twilight, to gloom, and then to them only being able to just make out shapes in the darkness.

"There are more passages." He felt along the wall. "Can't tell which is worthwhile or not." He stood at the entrance of one cave and inhaled, testing the scent and feeling for any air movement on his sweat-slicked cheeks. But there was nothing.

He moved across the rock face to the next cave, a smaller one, and this time he caught a hint of an odor like rising bread. Also, he felt a slight breath of coolness on his cheeks.

"Is it my imagination, or…?" Jane turned to him.

He could make out her face as there was a slight blue glow coming from deep inside the cave. His hands trailed on the cold stone and his fingers fell into three grooves carved in the rock.

"Wait a minute. Feel this." He grabbed her hand and stuck them on the rock. "That's not natural."

She smiled, her teeth shining in both the darkness and a grimy face. "The three marks of Saknussov—his breadcrumbs. This must be it." She turned back to the cave. "And there's light in there." She started to head in.

"Wait." He grabbed her. "Slow down, will you? Jeez, getting eaten by a giant snake thing didn't teach you anything?"

She turned. "Yes, that you'll always come rescue me." She went into the passage.

Michael scoffed and followed her in, down the tunnel that looked like it had once been bigger, but at one point in its history, the roof had collapsed, filling it with debris and partially narrowing the corridor.

She looked up. "Doesn't look all that stable."

"Let's hope for no more tremors while we're down here."

They continued on and in a few more minutes, the narrow tunnel opened out into a huge cathedral-sized cavern.

"It's blue." Jane's mouth dropped open in a wide smile.

"Is that what I think it is?" Michael felt he should be ready to expect anything now, but the sight made him both astounded and relieved. The mushrooms stood about 15 feet in height and their cups were like café sun parasols throwing out at least 10 feet wide. "That's dinner taken care of."

He raced to stand below a smaller one and grabbed at its cup to tear the skin back and grab a handful. He sniffed at it. "Seems okay." He took a bite and turned to her. "High protein, packed with vitamins and minerals, and, delicious. And it'll last for weeks, so we can take some with us."

Jane was tugging at something on one of the walls, and then spun back to him, her hands cupped. "Look."

Michael could already see the blue light escaping from between her fingers. She opened her hand to display a rod-shaped crystal that shone brilliant blue, like it had some sort of stored energy within it.

"Is that...? I have no idea. What is it?" He reached out for it and she placed it in his hands. It was cold, and the luminescence was so intense he had to squint. He held it up and found it threw a glow over 20 feet around him.

Jane reached into his hands to rub the crystal with her finger. "A lot of minerals can reflect light, and usually do. But they do it best under UV radiation. My guess is that the millions of years of being bathed by the radiation of the core has imbued these crystals with significant fluorescing properties."

"They absorb the radiation and release it as light—blue light." He nodded. "I think we now know how Katya and her team were able to navigate the dark labyrinths."

"And I think our odds are improving." She grinned. "Let's go back and tell the others."

They headed back to their group and Andy was waiting for them in the dark rear of the entrance cave.

"Where did you guys go? What happened to the rule of no one wandering off?" he demanded.

"Sorry," Jane said. "We found something. Hold out your hands and close your eyes."

"Is this a joke?" he replied slowly. "Please don't put anything that's alive in my hands."

"No joke, but we have an answer," Michael said. "Come on, hold 'em out."

"Oh boy." Andy held out his hands in a cup and closed his eyes. Jane placed the crystal in them.

"Holy shit," Maggie said from the corner of the cave and raced over.

Jane grinned. "Open your eyes."

Andy did and the blue glow bathed his face. He nodded and laughed. "This. Is. Amazing. It's cold—how's it doing it?"

"We think the crystal has somehow absorbed the radiation down here. But this has got to be how Katya and her team traveled in the darkness," Michael said. "They must have found them in another cave and lit their way home."

"That's not all," Jane enthused. "We found Saknussov's marks."

"And food." Michael held up a chunk of mushroom.

Wenton wandered over and took it from him. "I don't suppose you also found an elevator?" He sniffed at the chunk. "Mushroom?"

Michael nodded.

"Safe?" Wenton raised an eyebrow.

"Looks and tastes like an edible *basidiomycete* mushroom to me," Michael replied.

"You've tried it already?" Wenton looked him up and down, and then pinched off a piece. He tossed it in his mouth, chewed a moment, and then nodded. "Well done."

Andy also took some of the mushroom. "If there's mushrooms, there's moisture, and if there's moisture…"

"There's water as well," Maggie finished.

Michael looked at each of their weary faces in the blue glow. "If we can find our gravity well, then we might have enough to continue on to the surface. Let's gather up some supplies and more of the crystals. I also want some of the skins off the mushrooms as it's like leather. Might come in handy."

Michael and Jane took the group back in through the narrow tunnel to the mushroom cave. On entering, Andy darted forward to leap up onto a boulder.

"Oh my God."

He leaped down and raced to a mushroom as tall as he was. He grabbed at its stalk and shook it, and then grabbed the cup to squeeze. He turned slowly.

"There are hundreds of them." He raced to another stone to leap up on top to survey the cavern.

"Don't go too far," Jane called.

The rest set about gathering the things they needed, plus eating their fill. For the first time in days or even weeks, they felt optimistic about their chances, and Wenton sung in a baritone from somewhere off in the darkness.

Maggie was first to find one wall of the cave running with clear water and pooling in small natural basins. They filled canteens and drank deeply.

As they scouted about, Andy shouted from one side of the cavern. "Here, see this."

They rushed to him and he crouched down on the cave floor. He pushed some debris out of the way and held his crystal out, illuminating what he had found.

"A path made of fitted stone."

They squatted, and Jane pushed rubble out of the way and wiped away a layer of soil. "Not just fitted stones—tiles." She brushed some more. "It's like a mosaic."

They cleaned more tiles and then stood and backed up. It showed an image of people or things that were human-shaped. And some were riding on the backs of stout beasts.

"Magnificent," Maggie said and lifted her crystal. "Do you think this could be where your sea people went?"

"Who knows. I think they went somewhere." Michael looked over the mosaic. "However, this artifact looks just as old or older. Maybe they were contemporaries."

Jane moved some more debris from the tiles. "Where does it lead?"

"Let's find out." Michael turned. "Have we got everything we need?"

The group was ready, with some of them even having made crude sacks out of the mushroom skins to carry more of the fungi and more crystals. They lashed them to their waists or hung them over shoulders.

"Then let's follow the yellow brick road." Michael led them in.

CHAPTER 23

They moved through the narrow cave that soon became a broad passage as wide as a train tunnel. It was strewn with more tumbled debris, evidence of some long-past cataclysm, but it was clear there had once been structures here.

There were thick columns, many fallen to the ground laying in pieces and coated in layers of moss. In some places, the group had to duck under arches carved with faces that may or may not have been human.

Jane pointed. "Only two eyes. That's a good sign."

There were also huge stone doorways that were blocked, and some oddly seemed bricked over. They arrived at a set of steps and ascended them through another carved doorway. Michael was first through and held up his crystal rod in the enormous space.

But he didn't need to. It was already filled with light.

"A city," he breathed out.

Most of the inside of this corner of the mountain seemed hollowed out. Built into the walls and along winding avenues were buildings, all dark now and filled with nothing but shadows and the silence of the tomb.

From some, long strings of mosses hung down over the facades, giving them a hanging garden look, and Michael could almost feel the ghosts of the past crowding the streets and rushing by them.

"They harnessed the crystals," Jane said from beside him.

He nodded and turned his head slowly. At several places around the city, huge columns of the crystals were set on pedestals. Some of the rods were columns 20 feet high and they still threw out a brilliant luminescence that seemed incongruous among the decrepit ruins.

"See here." Andy used his pack to scrub at one of the lichen-covered walls. The debris was wiped away, showing something like glass.

"Crystal," he said. He quickly did the same to another wall. "This too. The entire place is made from crystals." He stood back. "Just imagine what it looked like."

"A crystal city," Maggie whispered. "It must have been beautiful."

"Where did they all go?" Wenton asked. "Was there a plague, a war, or something else?"

"I wish we had more time," Jane asked.

"The craftsmanship is magnificent. I'd love to meet them, even just to talk to them," Maggie added.

"I imagine that perhaps we'd be as alien to them as they are to us." Wenton turned to her. "Perhaps to them, we'd be monsters." He turned back. "Or gods."

"Did they know about us?" Andy asked. "I mean, did they think their world was the only world, or did they have an idea there was something else?"

"Did we think there was another world down here?" Jane asked.

"Saknussov suspected," Michael replied. "And they thought him mad."

"These guys certainly never made it to the surface. We'd know if they did," Andy replied.

"Really? How would we know? I mean, look around. These ruins are thousands of years old. For all we know, they did make it. Back then, even a few thousand years ago, us surface dwellers weren't very advanced." Wenton shrugged.

"I think we would know about it. If they escaped this place, then their own history would have recorded it, somewhere." Jane looked around. "I don't think they made it to the surface, and I'm pretty sure there's no civilization between topside and down here."

"But there is life in the deep caves," Maggie said. "We were hunted by something up in the caves. We only caught sight of them briefly, but they looked more mammalian than insectoid, and super adapted to living in darkness."

"We also encountered some creatures as well, but they were more like giant spiders and could well have come from down here." Michael looked around slowly. "It tells me there was potential food sources in the deep caves. Survival was possible."

The group stood in silence for a few moments before Wenton broke it with a clearing of his throat. "Let's focus. Somewhere around here is our way out. We need to investigate, and it would be a travesty against science not to look around for a while to at least learn a little more about out lost interior folk."

Michael turned slowly. "We can do both. Look for any signs left behind by Mr. Saknussov, or even better, the gravity well. And make sure we all stay in contact or eyesight. Andy with Maggie and Harry—you guys take that side of the city. We'll do our scout in 20-minute bursts. Got it?"

They headed out, and he noticed that Jane had already fashioned her crystal into a necklace to hang at her chest and illuminate her way. She turned to him.

"How long do you think we've been down here? I've lost track of the days with no night."

"In our surface days or center of the Earth days? They're two different things." He smiled as her brows came together.

"What I mean is, the inner wheel turns slower than the outer wheel. In my research, I found that mathematical simulations suggested that the gravity from the Earth's center causes a slight distortion in time, so time is actually moving slower down here." He stopped to look up, as if seeing through the cave ceiling. "Months have passed down here, but a lot less up there."

"So, Katya might have been trapped down here for longer and not known it?" she asked. "Poor woman. No wonder she lost her mind."

"Yeah, maybe, but I think she got torn up a lot through grief. And also because no one believed her." Michael pointed with his chin. "Come on, let's check over there."

There was a large doorway with the remains of long-petrified wooden doors seeming to be only held together with thick mosses. As Michael gently pushed one, the steel hinges showered to the ground in a rain of red dust, and the once-mighty wooden beams broke off in his hands like paper.

Inside, the blue glow of their crystals cast a ball of illumination around the pair but still left the darker corners to deep shadow.

The room was large and dust was still suspended in a deathly still air. At the room's center was some sort of stone table or altar.

"A place of worship?" Jane asked.

"Maybe. I wonder what sort of god they prayed to." Michael lifted his crystal to the wall. "Looks like writing."

Jane joined him. "Where's a good linguist when you need one." She looked along the lettering. "I can't make out anything resembling any sort of character set from the surface. I know there are about 101 different alphabets in the world, from English to Arabic, Greek, Latin, Cyrillic, Kanji, and the list goes on. But there's nothing of them I see in this. It looks more like code."

"At least we can say it probably isn't a derivative of one of them, and more than likely an entirely new language. I wonder what it sounded like?" he asked.

"This is better." Jane had moved along the wall a little further. "Picture writing."

There were carved images that appeared in a fresco style running along the wall. "They *were* people." Michael squinted. "But their faces look different."

The image showed a figure standing on a pedestal with arms outstretched, and a group of men and women kneeling around it.

"Their leader maybe? Or some sort of divinity figure?" Jane asked.

The next figure showed an image of a massed group of people, but now they seemed armed with spears and shields. Some of them rode on the back of huge beasts, like elephants except with six legs.

"This is an army," she said.

"And this is why." Michael held his crystal closer to the wall's fresco.

The army of people faced another force. The small, carved figures were shown facing another massed group of a different sort of creature.

Michael brought his light and face closer. These new figures looked to be either wearing armor, or they themselves were armor-plated. He rummaged in his woven bag for the small statue of the figure he had found. It was similar to those in the picture—human-shaped, but armored.

"The arthropod army. Looks like they *did* evolve," she said. "Remember when I said that on the surface the amphibians won the race to colonize the land? And eventually, we humans evolved from those first limbed fish? Seems the arthropods were the ones who were highly evolved here and continued to make war on the mammals."

The next image was one of carnage—with the bigger, armored people killing, impaling, and burying their faces into the bodies of the fallen mammalian people.

"They were getting massacred," Jane said softly. "And feasted on."

Michael looked around. "Yes, and it looks like the bigger guys eventually won."

"Or this race was chased off or escaped." Jane was at the last few images. It showed columns of people being led out of the city by the divine figure. But some were heading into the deeper labyrinths of the cave.

"Maybe they're still in here, or out there in the jungle somewhere." She stepped back. "But they never came back here."

"Some that escaped took to the sea in boats." Michael traced the outlines of the fleet of small craft. "And some chose the endless darkness of the deeper caves. Which ones survived?"

The pair continued walking around, examining the walls, but they showed little else.

"They left perhaps tens of thousands of years ago. If some went further into the caves, they would have found the gravity wells and surely would have traveled in them," Jane said.

"Maybe they only planned to stay in hiding for a few years, and then come back. Maybe something happened and they got trapped." Michael sighed. "So many theories, and no one to ask."

"Hey, Jane, Michael."

"That was Andy. He must have found something," Michael said. "Come on."

They headed out of the gallery and stood on the stone steps for a moment, trying to locate their friends. A few hundred yards in the distance, a small blue glow rose up on the end of a waving arm.

"There he is." Jane grinned.

They moved through the tumbled stone columns and around large, cracked pathways. Michael wondered if at one chaotic time, these roads ran red with the blood of the former occupants.

They leaped up onto a fallen wall and kept climbing a hill of rubble to the top. Andy was waiting, a grin splitting his face. He stood aside and pointed.

"Arkady Saknussov, I presume?"

In a shallow basin was a skeleton, human, and still in the remains of tattered clothing. A leather belt was around its waist with the scabbard and hilt of an ancient blade still in the sheath. Plus, there looked to be a desiccated satchel tucked under one of its hips. The bones of one of his legs were horribly broken, and he had obviously dragged himself here, but no further.

Close to the body was a metal hammer and several spikes, the ancient tools of a caver from over 500 years ago. But this time, they had been used for other purposes.

"The last thing he did was to leave us a message," Wenton said. "In Russian."

There were lines of Cyrillic lettering close to him, and Michael crouched and held the crystal over them. He began to read the words.

"I'm too late and have missed the gentle people of the interior by perhaps a thousand, thousand years. It seems their choices were hard ones: to fight, die, and be feasted upon. To flee to other lands perhaps across their red sea. Or maybe some ascended to their own idea of heaven in the caves above." Michael looked up at Jane. "Just as we thought."

He looked back down at the last few sentences. He frowned. *"The others know I'm here. And they are always watching."*

Michael looked up slowly. "That's all he wrote."

"Well, that's certainly comforting," Wenton lamented. "To be feasted upon by the attackers, and also, they were watching him. *Who* was watching him?"

"I assume he meant the same group that attacked this city." Michael

186

looked up.

"Makes no sense," Wenton huffed. "The events would be thousands of years apart."

"Why? Even topside, we have some groups that have clan or religious wars carrying on centuries," Jane replied.

"Are we safe here?" Maggie asked.

"I think we'll be okay. Whatever massacre happened here, happened many millennia ago," Michael said. "It'd be like us finding the remains of Troy and worrying about invading Greeks in wooden horses."

Wenton waved it away. "But Saknussov was alive only a few hundred years ago."

Jane kneeled by the skeleton that was propped up against a column of stone. One hand was lying palm up next to the fallen hammer and chisel, and the other rested on a rock. She stared at the hand.

"I can see the poor guy has some badly broken fingers, but look at this—is he pointing?"

The group stared at the hand and then in the direction the single finger was indicating. Carved into the far wall was a single doorway.

"You don't think...?" She stood slowly.

"The way out." Maggie turned, her fists balled. "He's showing us the way out."

"Maybe," Michael said. "Or maybe the path the last occupants had taken. And they never made it to the surface."

"We don't know that," Maggie replied. "Maybe they didn't want to."

"There's one way to find out." Andy leaped up on a boulder and rock-hopped across the debris to the doorway.

The group followed as the young caver held his crystal inside the entrance—all except Michael, who pulled free the satchel under Saknussov's hip and searched inside. As he hoped, there was a book, wrapped in oilcloth, and he quickly opened the cloth to examine it.

"Michael," Jane yelled. "Come see."

"Coming." He quickly rewrapped the book and tucked it inside the ragged remains of his shirt. He then turned to leap up over the debris to his friends.

"Shit. I knew it was too good to be true." Andy lowered his arm. "Blocked."

They caught up with him, and Michael stepped inside. He saw that there were huge blocks across the entranceway, totally sealing it off. He ran his hand over a few of them.

"You know what I see here?" He stepped back. "This was no cave-in—this entrance was bricked up on purpose. Either the people that escaped into this opening sealed it from the inside, or the people who remained sealed it from out here."

"That's a scary thought," Jane said. "That maybe the invaders sealed it up to stop anyone else getting away."

A horn sounded long and deep, and they turned slowly to look back at the entrance.

"What. Was. That?" Maggie asked with round eyes.

The horn sounded again and Michael slowly turned away. "That didn't sound like an animal's bellow. More like some sort of instrument."

"A war trumpet," Wenton lamented. "Usually carried at the head of an advancing army." He snorted softly, his mouth turning up on one side. "Remember what dear old Saknussov said? *They are watching.* Well, my dear friends, looks like they still are."

"Crap on crap." Andy's eyes were wide. "Hey, guys, I really do not want to be here if that's the thing that killed and ate the people from this city."

"None of us do." Michael looked about. "Harry, go and do a quick reconnoitre and tell me what you see."

"Are you kidding me?" Wenton frowned.

"No, I'm not." Michael held his ground.

"And what are you going to be doing?" Wenton's frown deepened.

Michael pulled the very last stick of dynamite from the tattered remains of his kit. "Try and open this doorway."

"Andy, come with me, if you please." Wenton clicked his fingers.

"No." Michael shook his head. "If I manage to open this hole, I expect there will be debris to be moved, and damn quickly. I'll need him. Come on, Harry, get to it. We need to know what's coming and how much time we have."

Wenton grumbled and turned away. He then jogged awkwardly down over the fallen ruins back out to the mouth of the cave.

Michael turned back to the blockage. In his caving expeditions, he was loath to use explosives. But he knew there were many times when it was necessary—if a caver was trapped and they needed to get some medical equipment in to them because of spinal injuries, then caves needed to be widened. And every expert caver had experience in targeted demolitions on a small scale.

Michael immediately saw that the pivot point was probably the larger slab mid doorway that had smaller stones beneath it and some larger boulders above. Theoretically, blowing the mid-slab should cause the rest to tumble out. Theoretically, anyway.

He jammed the dynamite stick in under the center of the slab, packing another stone in over it, and then turned to Jane and exhaled through pressed lips as he crossed himself.

"Here goes nothing. Everyone take cover." He lit the fuse, noticing his lighter was just about dead. The fuse sputtered and went out.

"Goddamn."

He calmed himself and also waited until his hands stopped shaking and tried to light it again—the tiny striking wheel didn't spark. It didn't spark the second or third time.

"Come on, you little bastard, you can do it."

It took three more spins of the striker wheel before a tiny, weak flame erupted. This time, the fuse lit and burned.

He sprinted away and got behind an ancient wall. He put his hands over his ears and as soon as he did, the concussive blast rushed past them in a flurry of dust and ejected stone. He said a quick prayer and sprinted back to the doorway.

"*Yes.*"

The huge slab had split and fallen out, releasing a lot of the other rocks. It wasn't totally cleared, but there was an opening now big enough for them to fit inside.

Michael wiped his hands together. "Andy, check it out. I'm going to go down and see what's keeping…"

"*Go, go, go*…" Wenton came sprinting back up the ancient path toward them. Even in the muted blue glow from his crystal, they could see his face was bleached from fear.

Michael jogged down a few paces to meet him. "What is it?"

"They're coming. So many." Wenton puffed. "Big, too big. Monsters." He grabbed Michael's shoulders and began to push him backward. "We need to go, *now!*"

Michael grabbed him. "We don't even know if this is the right cave."

"Saknussov thought it was." Wenton continued to push Michael toward the cave.

"You mean Saknussov that never even went inside it?" Jane said.

Andy poked his head out. "It's big, deep, and keeps on going."

Wenton closed his eyes and stood rod straight for a moment. "Listen, Michael, please, everyone. We do not want to be here when those abominations arrive. Do you understand?"

"I vote we go for it," Maggie said. "Our freaking backs are to the wall anyway."

Michael nodded. "Okay, but we seal it once we're in. That way if it's not the right path, we have a chance of coming back out without them following."

"*Yes, yes, good plan, go*, go." Wenton pushed him in the back.

Maggie went over the top of the rocks as Andy helped her in. Jane was next, followed by a near-panicking Wenton.

Michael hesitated. His curiosity screamed at him to at least see the creatures, these intelligent arthropods that seemed to have dominated this world.

But they had butchered or scattered this entire ancient race and he had no doubt they would do the same to them if they caught them. *Another time,* he thought, as Jane called to him from over the lip of stone.

He clambered up and over, and already Andy, Wenton, and Maggie were moving a stone to the top of the opening and piling it up to close the hole. Michael and Jane assisted, and bigger stones went first, and as the opening shrank, they wedged in smaller and smaller stones.

Though it wouldn't hold up to a concentrated push, it might just mask where they had gone.

Michael looked out through the last small hole in the wall and caught sight of the long-dead Russian's skeleton.

"I hope you're right, Arkady. We're in your hands now."

He wedged the last piece of stone into the hole and used another rock to hammer it in. The entrance was sealed once again.

*****

"Hurry, let's get the hell out of here." Wenton backed up.

"It's okay, Harry, we're safe for now. Tell us, what did you see?" Michael asked.

Wenton stared straight ahead. He laughed, but the sound was almost a sob. "Lovecraft," he said.

"What? The author?" Michael frowned as they moved through the dark labyrinth.

"Yes." He licked his lips. "I remember reading HP Lovecraft in my youthful years. And the thing that struck me was the way he had of describing these horrible creatures in his stories that were a mix of humans that were blended with either arthropod or sea creature characteristics." He dry swallowed. "They were like that—big, seven feet tall at least, and immensely powerful looking. Six arms, or legs, I don't know. They carried weapons." He turned and stopped for a moment. "And they had cages ready... for us."

"Jesus," Jane whispered.

"I suddenly wish we had more dynamite," Andy said.

"You and me both," Michael replied. He just hoped they didn't find their cave, or they at least had enough of a head-start on their pursuers to stay in front of them.

But what if they hit a dead end? he wondered darkly. *Cross that bridge if we ever come to it,* he thought.

The tunnel they passed through was ornately carved, with smooth brickwork over its façade and no natural stone showing. Some alcoves had small bowls inside them; perhaps once they held food or other things the fleeing humanoids had once stored here that had long rotted or dried away.

There were also discarded weapons, but of these only some of the handles and hilts of swords remained as the steel spikes of spears, heads of axes, and once formidable sword blades were now just discolored mineral marks on the stone.

Their path gradually tilted upward and Michael took that as a good sign—up was where they needed to be. Just that they needed to be up by about another 6,000 miles.

It was after only another few minutes that they found the first body. An age-browned skeleton was lying in one of the alcoves. It had probably had sheets laid over it at one time and also some jewelry of colored stones that were lying loosely on the ribs, as the string holding them together had long vanished.

Jane crouched. "They were small. Not more than four and a half feet."

"Could it be a child?" Maggie asked.

"No, the teeth are adult teeth. It was a male as well, looking at the pelvic structure," Jane replied.

"We would have been giants to them," Andy added.

"Imagine what the arthropod people must have been like then? Absolute monsters," Wenton said.

"Who came to catch and eat them. The arthropod people might have just seen them as another herd of food creatures to take back for their pot." Maggie shivered. "Can we get moving now?"

Far back the way they came, the sound of a bouncing rock was heard as it fell to the ground.

Everyone froze for a few seconds as they stared back into the darkness.

"Yeah, okay, and let's pick up the pace." Michael held out his crystal and led them on.

EPISODE 05

"As long as a man's heart beats, as long as a man's flesh quivers— while there is life there is hope." — Jules Verne

CHAPTER 24

Jane sucked in a thick breath of the rapidly warming air and wiped an arm across her brow. The tunnel had begun to incline sharply at least a mile back and the going was more arduous. Along the way, they saw that the ancient caravan of people had begun to discard clothing and other possessions.

Perhaps the heat was getting to them or maybe the fatigue. But soon, it was more than just their possessions they left behind—more skeletons were found, some laying in groups as though entire families had simply lain down to die, and others with broken bones and signs of trauma.

"Did they start fighting among themselves?" Maggie asked.

"Maybe resources were becoming scarce. Maybe they started to panic," Michael said.

"Maybe there was something else in here that caused them to panic," Wenton said softly.

"No, I don't think so," Jane said. "They knew these caves, and I think that there was a lot of scared and depressed people. They'd just been attacked and had to flee into these catacombs. More likely depression, psychosis, and who knows how many other psychological traumas they were suffering."

"But they got away. There was no sign that tunnel blockage had been breached before us," Andy said. "Those things didn't go after them, so they should have been relieved by that."

Wenton chuckled softly from behind them. "You're making an assumption based on what you hope happened." His eyes glinted blue from the light of the crystals. "For all we know, those arthropod humanoids were the ones who sealed the entrance. Maybe to stop them ever getting back out. Or perhaps they chased them in and sealed it up so they could keep them alive. Like keeping them as stock on hand." He wiped his mouth. "These things were huge, and I'm sure moving the stones would not have been a problem for them."

"That's a shitty thought," Jane said and then exhaled. "But it's a possibility."

The bricked tunnel finally became raw cave, and then they were beginning to navigate the rough, ancient stone of the mountain. Signs of the people fleeing became less distinct.

Wenton puffed hard and then stopped for a moment, leaning one hand against the wall and drawing in deep draughts of the warm air. "Want another shitty thought?"

Maggie groaned. "Not really."

"How do we know this is the right way back? I mean, we're certainly committed now so there are no other options for us. But what if we're wrong?" Wenton agonized.

"All we have is Saknussov's dying advice. Besides, we didn't really have time for a committee decision, did we?" Michael replied.

"But like Jane said, he never actually tried it, did he?" Wenton lifted his chin.

Michael stopped and turned. "You were the one that urged us on. What do you want from us, Harry?"

"And here's another thought—neither did your little Russian friend. After all, the wall was intact and would have been 50 years ago, when Katya escaped." Wenton straightened.

Jane knew he was right and hated him for it. "Forget it, this is just navel-gazing—we had no choice. We can't go back now."

"We could. We could wait those creatures out if need be. Maybe we shouldn't go too much further. We reach a point of no return due to no more supplies, and we're screwed." Wenton put his hands on his hips and stretched his back. "The main cave has food, water, and light. We're leaving that long behind us now."

Michael looked at the raw tunnel before them, and then looked back into the unfathomable darkness behind. They had traveled many miles, and though there was no evidence other than Saknussov's pointing finger that this was the right way, there was also no evidence it was the wrong choice.

"Harry, right about now, we don't need you sowing seeds of doubt. We're moving ahead," Michael said resolutely. "Happy for anyone who wishes to go back and wait to do so."

Wenton threw his hands up. "For God's sake, Monroe, I'm not trying to lead a damned revolt. But look…" He motioned to more skeletons tucked into alcoves. "These poor saps were fleeing for their lives. And looks like most of them died doing it. We can afford to make decisions with a little more measure."

The projectile came out of the dark and pierced Wenton's shoulder—

it went right through the meat with the barbed tip coming out the front. He gagged and gripped it with both hands.

"What the hell?" Andy rushed to him, just as another of the projectiles smacked into the wall over his head.

"Get down!" Michael shouted.

To everyone's horror, Wenton started to be dragged backward as he howled in pain. The projectile that had pierced him was attached to a tether. And now it was being reeled in.

Andy hung onto his legs, and Maggie crawled to him. Jane reached into the bag hanging on her hip and drew forth another shard of glowing crystal and tossed it back down into the darkness where the spear had come from.

The crystal flew 40 feet, struck rock, and exploded into dozens of glowing shards. The entire cave was illuminated and in that glow was a vision from Hell.

"Oh God no." Maggie let go of Wenton and crawled backward.

"Don't let me go!" Wenton screamed.

The cave tunnel was crowded with carapace-covered creatures that stood on multiple back legs. In their clawed hands, they held spears, weapons like crossbows with tethers attached, and worst of all, nets.

Their faces were a mix of insect and lobster with black eyes on quivering tendrils that were never still and moving mouthparts that seemed to be shivering with excitement at the prospect of a human's capture.

One of the creatures in front began to pull the rope, eliciting another howl of pain and panic from Wenton. Michael leaped on him and pulled out his blade, trying to cut through the tether and the projectile. But whatever the spear tip was, bone or some sort of hardened material, he wasn't even making a mark on it. And unfortunately, his knife had long ago lost its edge and sawed uselessly against the toughened rope fibers.

Another of the barbs flew at Michael, but this one only pierced the sack on his shoulder. The monstrous creatures then began to advance on them.

Jane crouch-ran at Michael and pulled him and Andy backward. "We have to go," she whispered into his ear.

"Don't leave me. *Please*," Wenton cried.

"I'm sorry. I'm so sorry." Jane dragged Michael back and Andy scuttled away.

Without the added weight of Michael and Andy holding him, Wenton was then pulled roughly down the cave, as the crystal shards dimmed only because the crush of huge arthropod bodies moved over them.

Michael grimaced, as he watched Harry Wenton be dragged toward the waiting horde. "I'm sorry, Harry."

They turned and ran.

*****

Michael's eyes welled up as they heard Wenton's screams continuing on for many minutes. But then they abruptly shut off with a strangled gurgle. Michael hated himself for the thought, but he just hoped the man was dead and wouldn't be taken prisoner.

From time to time, they still heard sounds of pursuit, whether it was the scrape of hard shell against stone, or the click and squeak of their language.

Andy led them up the ever-steepening cave tunnel, and the tethered spears had stopped being flung at them long back. The advantage they had was smaller human bodies were faster in the tight spaces than the bulkier bodies of the arthropods could ever hope to be.

Michael prayed that they had entered a choke point that wouldn't allow the creatures to follow at all, or...

Andy was first into the open chamber, followed by Maggie who had tear streaks in the dirt on her cheeks. Jane then, and also Michael, piled in. He expected that they had a huge lead on their pursuers, but just not enough time to rest.

The room was large, and on the floor at its center were rock debris, bones all piled up, plus all manner of strange items.

"Look," Andy said.

Hanging mid-air was a rock, levitating.

Michael lifted his crystal and in the cave's ceiling was an opening, about 30-feet wide. He immediately reached into the woven pouch at his waist and drew forth one of his own spare crystals and tossed it upward.

They watched as the blue, glowing speck kept going up and away until it vanished.

He exhaled with relief. "The gravity well. Saknussov was right, thank God."

Jane looked back down the dark passage they had exited from. "I think they're still coming."

"Will they even know what the gravity well is for?" Maggie asked.

Michael quickly looked around the chamber. There were multiple tunnels leading into it. He crossed to one and grabbed another of his crystals. He rolled it far and hard. Luckily, it didn't shatter but bounced away end over end into the darkness, eliciting a blue glow from deep inside the space.

"Just in case. Let's hope they follow that, instead of us."

Jane stood beneath the well and held up her crystal. "Time to fly, little birds." She crossed herself, and then leaped.

Maggie next, Andy, and then Michael took one last glance back before doing the same.

CHAPTER 25

The remaining ragged humans slumbered as they flew upward. Without knowing it, they attained speeds of nearly 250 miles per hour, but in the center of the gravity well, there was no friction, no weight, and not even dreams of pursuing monsters.

The fatigue meant there was no way any of them could have withstood the desire to rest in the cocoon of warmth, weightlessness, and what they hoped was relative safety.

It was the well itself that slowed them down as they came to their final junction. After traveling for nearly 25 hours, they decelerated, and then stopped to hang in space over the dark hole like some sort of conjurer's trick to levitate a human body.

Jane was first to open her eyes. Disorientation and fear jerked her to full wakefulness.

"What?" She pinwheeled her arms. "*Michael.*"

She swam toward him and tugged at his long hair. He spun in the air and smacked his flaking lips as his eyes opened to slits.

"What is it, honey?" His eyes widened. "*Shit.*"

"We're here," Jane said. "Andy, Maggie, wake up, hurry."

The two groggily came to their senses and the four swam awkwardly to the side of the pit. Once over the solid land, they dropped, feeling gravity take hold again and weighing their bodies down once more.

Maggie stayed down on all fours and coughed. "Oh God. Jet lag."

Andy lay on his back, breathing hard. He began to laugh. "We made it."

Jane got carefully to her feet. "By made it, you mean we're still many miles beneath the surface and have no idea whether these caves even lead to the surface."

"Oh yeah, that." Andy sat up. "But I still feel better."

Michael also got to his feet and stretched his back and then shook himself out. He then began to walk around the outside of the chamber, looking into each of the caves that fed into it. He spat on his hand and held it up in front of each cave mouth, feeling for the slightest breath of air movement.

"Nothing."

Jane exhaled. "Okay, step one, let's see what supplies we have."

They checked their woven bags they had over their shoulders and wrapped around their waists. They all had several of the blue crystals that were like lanterns in the darkness. Plus, large chunks of raw mushroom left. In the dry atmosphere of the caves, it would last for weeks. Also, it was light to carry, so that was a plus. Their water bottles had been filled before they left so if they rationed them and didn't find any more water sources, they could stretch it out for more than a week as well.

The downside was they expected to be miles underground and climbing for a full day was as arduous as it got; they'd be burning more energy than they were replacing. Losing what little weight they had left wasn't the problem; what was a problem was the loss of muscle mass, and that would doom them.

Michael did his best to boost everyone's spirits. "A good haul. We can make this." He also knew that a positive outlook could drive a human being for days. And the corollary was a depressive mood could roll you into a ball to die alone in the darkness.

"Where did they all go?" Andy asked. "Of all of the fleeing people, some must have made it up here. So what happened?"

"Everyone spread out," Maggie said. "Look at the ground, look at the walls, look for any clue or indication of where they went."

They spread out, holding the crystals close to the walls and then the cave floor.

"Ground's churned up," Andy observed. "But in a deep cave that could have happened yesterday, or 50,000 years ago."

Michael straightened. "The ground is also disturbed over here, but not in the exit cave. How about yours?"

"Not mine," Jane replied.

"These are also undisturbed." Maggie turned back to the group.

"Yep, yep, got something. There's disturbance that goes all the way into the cave," Andy said. "Someone or something went this way."

Michael looked at each of them. "It's all we've got. Any objections?"

"All we've got is all we need. Let's do it," Jane said.

Michael held up his crystal and walked into the cave.

*****

They hiked for a few hours with the caves narrowing and then opening out dozens of times. So far, the going was easy and only on a gentle incline.

Jane hurried to walk beside Michael. "Where do you think we are? Geographically, I mean?"

"I've been wondering that as well." He glanced at her. "We traveled for many miles at the center, and a mile down there could be the equivalent of hundreds up here. We could be anywhere by now."

"As long as it's not under an ocean then I don't care where we surface," Jane replied.

He looked down at her. "Remember sunlight? Used to be pretty cool, I recollect."

"You're tired of nightclub blue already?" She grinned.

"Oh yeah." He sniffed, and his brows came together. "Hey, you smell something?"

Jane did the same. "I do." She lifted her chin and sniffed again.

Michael turned. "Hey, anyone taking a piss back there?"

Both Maggie and Andy had stopped and both shook their heads.

"I can smell it though," Maggie said. "Uric acid—definitely piss."

"Got to be fresh then," Jane said. "Animal urine with its associated oils and minerals breaks down in only a few weeks."

"Do you think it's the people from below?" Andy asked.

"I don't know. But I've smelled tiger's urine at the zoo, and it has the same ammoniac scent. This is a carnivore waste," Jane said.

"That's not good," Michael said.

They entered a larger cave and Michael stopped the group. "I think we just found what happened to our long-lost inner Earth tribe."

The floor of the cave was littered with ancient bones. There were dozens, if not hundreds, of bodies.

"Notice something?" Jane asked as she walked into the center of their small group and then squatted down. She waved her arm over the skeletal remains. "The skeletons aren't intact."

"So, what does that mean?" Andy's voice was small.

"It means they've been moved," Michael said.

Jane reached out to lift a long bone. She held her blue crystal closer to it.

"Look here."

The group crowded closer.

"See these marks? They look like tooth marks," she said.

"Tooth marks? You think they were attacked by a freaking predator?" Maggie demanded.

"Maybe. Or maybe they attacked each other." She dropped the age-browned bone and waved her light slowly around. "Yes, see, the thick bones are grouped together, same as the arm bones. I think this was a feast."

"Oh...God," Maggie stammered.

"So this is where that proud race ended their journey." Michael kicked a bone out of the way.

"I don't think all of them," Jane said. "I think some became predator and some became prey—the strong preyed on the weak." She moved from skeleton to skeleton. "Male, male, male, male, female, male...." she stopped. "This is like what happens when one tribe takes over another. They kill all the able-bodied men and take their women and children."

"They became cannibals?" Andy shook his head. "That's insane."

"We don't know how long they were trapped in this mid-world," Michael sighed. "But it doesn't bode well for a way to the surface."

"I don't know. Maybe they preferred it here. Maybe they thought that even worse things awaited them at the surface. Maybe they enjoyed the dark. I have a million maybes, and it's all just theory." Jane shrugged.

"So where are they now?" Andy asked.

"Do we really want to find them?" Maggie cast an arm around. "After this?"

"No, but I think we need to stop following them and we need to climb the hell out of here right now." Andy lifted his blue crystal and raised his face. He quickly jerked back down. "*Shit.*"

The thing was hanging in the crevice above them and sped away when it knew it was seen.

"*That's them! That's them!*" Maggie screamed. "They're the things we saw on the way down."

"Don't panic!" Michael barked. "It's gone now."

"We've got to stay together. Anyone that runs off in the dark is going to find nothing but trouble," Jane said.

Andy wiped his face and kept his eyes closed for a moment. He pushed his long, stringy hair back off his face, and his voice trembled. "Sorry, I've just about had it. I've got to get out of here."

"We will. But I think you're right." Michael also held his crystal upward. "We've been following these horizontal passages long enough. It's time we headed up."

Andy grinned and shook his head. "Yeah. Go vertical and go home."

CHAPTER 26

They climbed upward for a day, navigating chimneys so tight they had to flex shoulders and then worm their way upward inches at a time. There were cracks in rift walls that scraped their chests and the tips of their fingers quickly became abraded. And they perched on ledges overhanging cliffs into voids that seemed to fall all the way back down to the center of the Earth.

The small group had to stop often and they ate their ever-dwindling supplies of mushrooms. They could only sip at their water even though their throats screamed out for more, and their tongues dried in their mouths.

The thing in the darkness had been ghosting them, staying close, but not coming within sight now. It meant that someone always had to stay awake, at a time when sleep wasn't just needed, but without it, could prove deadly.

Like Jane, they all had their crystal lights tied around their necks, and in the blue light, Michael noticed that Jane's face looked thin and haunted, with deep rings underneath glassy eyes as she chewed her food like an automaton. He bet he looked the same, or worse.

Michael saw that Maggie half-dozed, and when he looked to Andy, he saw that the young man was almost in darkness.

"Andy, your crystal," Michael said softly.

The caver nodded and opened the pouch at his hip. The other crystals were also fading.

"It'll probably happen to all of them soon," Jane said hoarsely. "The further we move away from the core's radiation, the less the crystals have to absorb and then emit."

Her eyes slid to his, and Michael knew what question it held—how much longer would they be in the caves, verse how much longer the crystals would continue to glow with their comforting cobalt blue light? It was now a race.

Michael sighed. "Don't worry, we only need one to get us to the top."

He felt their eyes on him. He'd been in caves before when the lights went out. The total absence of light was enough to freak out even the hardiest of cavers. In that black nothingness, having your eyes open or closed made no difference.

Compounding the dread for them was that there was a creature down here that was able to locate them with senses beyond eyesight. And that creature was most likely a carnivore.

He suddenly had a horrible thought—maybe that was why the things were staying out of reach for now; they might know that the crystals would fade, and then the big, dumb, and blind humans would be at their mercy.

"Well then." He slapped his thighs. "Let's not wait until we're all sitting around singing songs in the dark. We climb until we have nothing left in the tank." Michael got to his feet and ignored his screaming muscles and joints. He flexed his fingers, trying to get the blood flow back into them.

He held one hand out flat. "Until there's nothing left."

"Until there's nothing left in the tank," Maggie repeated as she placed her hand over his.

Jane and Andy did the same. Michael walked to the edge of their small ledge and looked upward. The good news was that it was a large rift cliff and continued up for as far as his illumination allowed him to see. The downside was it was a sheer face, and it meant most of it would have to be done as a free climb.

One of the things they taught you in basic speleological training was to never climb when drunk, sick, or tired. You made mistakes. And a single mistake on a sheer face meant death.

"Michael." Andy lifted his chin.

"Yeah?" Michael turned.

"Do you think we'll still win that award?" He grinned.

They laughed, hard, and all of them sounded a little mad. But it felt good.

"They damn well better give it to us." He pounded the meat of his fist against the rock face as he took one last look upward. His smile fell away. "Okay, boys and girls, last lap."

Michael closed his eyes for a moment, and a line from an old classic story crept into his mind: *long is the way and hard, that out of Hell leads up to light.*

It was from Milton's *Paradise Lost*, written over 400 years ago. About the same time Arkady Saknussov was writing his manuscript. One man wrote of an inner Earth paradise that was lost, and another theorized about a hidden paradise to be found.

He opened his eyes.

Out of Hell leads up to light. Michael used the tips of his fingers to hang onto a half-inch extrusion of stone. He lifted his leg to rest the side on a small jutting rock and then levered himself up another few feet—the fingers, arms, and shoulders were important, but the powerful legs did a lot of the work. And by now, they screamed at every inch he stole up the dark rock face. He lifted his hand to the next hold.

Their world shrunk to only being the next few feet, as what was going on hundreds of feet above didn't matter, because unless you climbed the next two, you were never going to get to the next two hundred. Inch after inch, foot after foot, and every fraction was fought for and was agony.

Michael found a small ledge and rested his elbows on it. "How we all doin'?"

The team had spread out a little. Andy was the lowest, down and to his left, and Maggie and Jane were just to his right, with Jane slightly up front.

"Good, but gonna need one hellova manicure," Maggie shouted back.

"Amen to that," Jane replied.

"Hurtin', but still tracking okay," Andy yelled up at them.

Michael liked that they still had a few ounces of good spirits left. It all helped. He looked upward but there was nothing to see but blackness. His halo of blue light was shrinking, but he had to fight the urge to try and rush. One slip, and it was over. He took a deep breath and continued.

Tock.

Michael frowned and paused.

Tock.

"You hear that?" he asked.

"Water dripping?" Jane turned her head.

Tock.

"Yeah, I hear it. Coming from below us, I think," Andy said. He tried to look over his shoulder but was constrained by the angle of his shoulders.

"Weird." The hair on the back of Michael's neck prickled.

He levered himself up onto his little ledge a fraction more and carefully reached into his pouch for one of his last shards of glowing crystal. They were only a pale blue now and distressingly, all seemed to be giving up at once.

He let the crystal fall, and it plummeted down the rock face, past Andy, and threw a small ball of blue light as it dropped.

As he watched, the breath caught in his throat—about 50 feet below his friend he saw a pale body clinging to the wall. Michael only saw it for a second or two but it was as big as a man and hanging on with strong claws on each hand.

Michael swallowed down his fear. "Andy, *ah*, keep coming to me, buddy."

Tock, tock.

"What's up?" Andy tried to look over his shoulder again. "That damn sound is still here."

"Just. Come. To me." Michael urged in the calmest voice he could muster.

"O-ooka-aay." Andy's brows knitted, and he tried to turn again.

"*Don't*. Just keep coming." Michael started to see the thing enter Andy's halo of light and he heard Jane suck in her breath out to his side.

The thing literally walked up the stone, hanging onto cracks and crevices that even the best caver couldn't possibly hope to do. Closer now, Michael could only stare in horrified fascination at the face—vestigial slits for a nose, eyes that were totally white bulging orbs that quivered in a backward-sloping brow.

The mouth hung open and large, strong, yellow tusk-like incisors were displayed. This thing was mammalian, a carnivore, and perfectly dark-adapted. The body was longer than that of a person, and the back hind legs were shorter than normal, meaning it probably moved on all fours, and its long body meant it could slither through the tightest of openings in the rock faces.

It was right behind Andy and its nose flaps opened and closed wetly as it inhaled his scent.

Andy grimaced, obviously sensing the thing. "Stinks." He made a whining noise in his throat and tried to increase his speed.

The young guy was still 15 feet down from Michael, but he had no idea what he'd do when Andy got to him. Being stuck to a cliff face wasn't exactly the best place to start a fight.

"Keep coming. You got this, Andy. Don't look back. Just keep coming to me." Michael tried to sound calm but heard the edge creeping into his own voice.

Then it had him.

The thing reached out a clawed hand and gripped his ankle. Andy screamed and hung on tight. He was lucky he had made it to a larger lip of stone; otherwise, he would have easily been plucked off the wall.

The thing lifted itself closer, bringing its grotesque face near to Andy's ankle to sniff at it. A pointed tongue snuck out to lick at the sweat-drenched skin. It shivered in pleasure.

"Oh God, it's got me." Andy's teeth were bared and his eyes like saucers as he clung on.

I got them into this nightmare, Michael thought as a strange calm came over him.

He had very few tools left, but still nestled in his pocket was Georgy's penknife. He carefully reached for it and closed his eyes as he concentrated on opening the blade with one hand.

"Help." Andy started to be pulled backward, his arms straightening to the elbow from where he hung on.

Michael had the blade open now and briefly glanced down. He turned to look at Jane once, and then turned back. He lined up the thing below Andy. Then let go of the rock face.

He sailed close to the wall, and at the exact moment he was beside the creature, he grabbed it and plunged the four-inch blade deep into the center of its muscled back.

It shrieked like the creature from Hell it was and let go of Andy to slide down the cliff face. Michael hung on to the blade and also momentarily to the slick, rank-smelling skin of the creature.

He swung as the creature tried to throw him off. Michael's weight dragged the blade down its back, opening the slick skin and muscle like a zipper.

The pain and damage were too much and the monster let go of the wall. Michael used its motion to swing himself back at the rock face, finding a small edge of stone and clinging there. The knife had been dragged from his hand as the colorless thing fell backward into the void.

Michael kept his forehead against the cool stone and only then felt the nausea and giddiness kick in.

Don't throw up, don't throw up, he begged as he breathed in and out and tried to calm his breathing and heart rate.

"Michael!" Jane yelled.

"I'm...okay." He looked up, and his eyes were blurred with tears. "Just, keep, going. Find a pitch ledge to take a break."

"Thank you," Andy said softly. And then: "You idiot."

"Always was." Michael chuckled. "Now keep going."

Michael hung on the wall for a moment more, straining his ears. It didn't matter, he guessed. If there were more following him, he didn't have anything more to fight with.

And this is where luck is supposed to kick in, he thought. With all his remaining strength, he levered himself up to the next handhold.

CHAPTER 27

Andy and Jane pulled Michael over the lip of the rock shelf, and he rolled a few feet away from the edge and just lay there on his back, panting.

Jane came and kissed his forehead and brushed his long hair back from his sweat-streaked face.

"That was the bravest and dumbest thing I've ever seen in my life." She kissed him again.

He snorted softly. "I can't think about it. Because when I do, I want to throw up." He groaned and shut his eyes. "And if I had thought about it, I would never have done it."

Andy came and rested his hand on Michael's shoulder. "Well, I'm glad you didn't think about it and just did it, or I'd be monster food by now." He grinned. "I feel like kissing you as well, and bear in mind, I haven't cleaned my teeth in months."

"Rain check." Michael chuckled.

Andy turned. "Maggie, was that one of those...?"

"Yeah, yeah, that was one of the things we saw on the way down. Like a cross between a bat and an ape, I think." She shook her head. "Freaking horrible."

Michael groaned as he sat upright. "Some sort of mammal that has evolved to live down here."

"It was a true cavernicolous species, a troglobite. But for a mammalian species, it shouldn't exist," Jane said. "And for a creature that big, there'll be more, a breeding population somewhere."

"It gives me the creeps knowing there could be a pack of these horrors down here somewhere." Maggie shook her head and grimaced.

"The people from the core—the skeletons," Andy replied, turning to Jane.

"You think these could be the things that killed them? Oh God, that's horrible. Those poor people." Maggie rubbed her face and stood. "Climbing all this way to escape the shell people—all those women, children, whole families—only to be picked off in the dark by these nightmares."

Michael looked into Jane's half-lidded eyes. "Yeah, maybe," he replied softly.

Jane got to her feet and walked slowly to the lip of the ledge and looked down for a few moments. "Those who descend into the void find monsters. Or become them." She exhaled and walked away to the rear of the shelf.

"I don't think Jules Verne could ever have imagined what the truth really was." Michael pushed the hair up off his face. "Sometimes, the comfort of fiction is better for us."

Maggie began to laugh and then sob as she clung to something on the wall at the rear of their ledge. "Thank you." They all turned to her.

"What is it?" Andy asked.

Maggie faced them, grinning from ear to ear. "The most beautiful thing I've seen in my entire life." She dropped her hand and held her waning crystal close to the rock.

Hammered into the wall was a rusting climbing pin; many decades old, but there it was.

Michael and Andy leaped to their feet and rushed to her.

"Oh my God, oh my God...people were here." Jane clasped her hands together like a child. She spun, her eyes luminous. "We can't be that far from the surface."

"Find more. Find where they came from or where they went." Michael went to one side of the ledge and Andy to the other, while Maggie and Jane searched the rear of the small alcove.

"Got a squeeze hole." Maggie was on her belly. "This must be where they went." She stuck a hand in and raked at it. "Sealed up though."

Andy threw himself down and slid forward. He grabbed at some of the rocks blocking the tiny hole. "Not a natural blockage." He grunted and tugged. A small rock popped free into his hands. He tossed it aside and kept digging.

In another 20 minutes, there was a pile of different-sized stones around him. Then he held the pale, glowing crystal before him and slid forward on his belly. In a moment, he pulled himself out backward and sat up.

"We can get in there."

Maggie exhaled with relief. "If it means no climbing for a while, then let's go."

Who sealed it, and why? Michael wondered. The last cave they encountered that was blocked was done to keep out the arthropod creatures. So what was this one blocked for? To keep those cave things trapped down here, or to stop people finding this place?

He looked at his friends who were now little more than ghostly shadows of themselves. Plus, the luminescent crystals were on the verge of dying, just like they were. They had no choice.

"Then what are we waiting for? Take us in, Andy."

Michael wiped his hands and noticed there was blood on his forearms from the creature he'd stabbed. He tore a strip off the rags he wore, wiped his arms, and went to throw it over the edge.

He paused, looking at the rag. Then he tore it in half and jammed one piece of the bloody material in his pocket and tossed the rest where it fluttered down into the darkness until it vanished.

Andy held his crystal out and immediately slithered into the tiny hole. Maggie didn't waste a second in following him.

Jane reached up and kissed his bearded cheek. "I have my fingers and toes crossed."

"You and me both." He watched as she slithered into the small hole, and he got down on his hands and knees to follow.

Tock.

Michael looked back over his shoulder.

Tock.

"Go to Hell." He slithered in after her.

*****

In a line, they wormed their way along the narrow hole, now glad that they had all lost so much weight. As they came out, Andy was first to stand and lowered his waning crystal to the remains of a small fire pit, and the piles of burst-open food tins accompanied by a scrawled note.

Michael joined the group and had to crouch to get really close to see the words in the growing darkness. "Can anyone read that? Doesn't look like Russian."

"It's not; it's Romanian. I can read a little." Maggie squinted. "Basically, it says: clean up your shit." She turned and laughed. "Trash— welcome back to the modern world."

"Romania?" Andy asked.

"If that's where we are, then we've traveled all the way under the Black Sea; over 1,000 miles," Jane said.

Michael stood. "Come on, we're running out of light. Minutes count now."

They climbed, slid, and scraped for several more hours. But the thought that they were heading home gave them the extra energy they needed. In another hour, they began to find guide ropes already set into the stone. And then some formal notices.

"It *is* Romania," Michael said. "I recognize this; it's the V5-Cave in Fața Muncelului, the deepest cave in Romania. We must be close to the surface now."

"I feel sick," Maggie said. "I'm scared that I'll close my eyes and then wake up and find it's a dream, and I'm still stuck way down below."

"It's real," Michael said. "Jane? Where are...?"

"Here," she said from behind him. "My crystal is dead."

"It's okay, we just follow the ropes now." Michael reached out to draw her closer to him.

For the most part, they now had to use their outstretched hands to feel their way. But in another hour, an illumination up ahead drew them on. And in a few more moments, they came to a final chimney. Looking up, they saw stars.

Jane sighed. "Never have I seen something so wonderful in all my life."

Andy inhaled. "I can smell grass, and pine needles, and...*freedom.*" He grinned, his eyes near glowing as he stared upward at the celestial bodies.

There was an iron ladder set into the wall, and climbing it, even after the fatigue, physical torture, and lack of food and water, would be the easiest thing they had done in their lives. Even Michael bet he could have flown up the last few hundred feet if he had wings.

He watched as the others started to climb, and he turned back to the dark labyrinths of the cave.

"Goodbye Angela, Jamison, Bruno, Ronnie, and even you, Harry. We'll miss you all." He turned back and began to climb.

At the top, they crawled out of the hole in the earth and immediately ran to an open patch of soft grass. It was some time in the night, and the evening's warmth made it feel like late spring. There were the tiny bells of white wild flowers dotted around them that were almost glowing in the darkness.

Their crystals were nothing but shards of inert quartz now, just decorations hanging from their necks as mementos of a world hidden thousands of miles below them.

They lay on the grass, arms and legs outstretched, all holding hands. Andy turned to them.

"Coolest. Adventure. Ever." He grinned.

"Never. Ever. Again," Maggie replied. "My caving days are *over.*"

"Mine too," Jane said. "I think I'll take up surfing."

Michael just lay there staring up at the sky, his mind working. "Was it real?" He turned his head. "Already, I don't believe it."

"It was real," Jane said. "And the center of the Earth is a nightmare."

*****

Thousands of feet below them, the creatures sniffed at the blood-covered rag that had floated down to them. It carried the blood scent of their kin, but also of something else.

They began climbing up the sheer wall, tracking the scent, until they arrived at the small cave with rubble pulled free. One eased closer and its nostril flaps flared open as it inhaled the intoxicating smells of the strange warm-blooded animals.

It squeezed in to follow.

EPILOGUE

"How many things have been denied one day, only to become realities the next?" — **Jules Verne**

A full year had now gone by and Michael Monroe sat at his desk making notes. He, Jane, Andy, and Maggie had undergone bleach scrubs and iodine treatments to minimize the effects of the radiation they suffered for months. It seemed to be working, as none of them had yet suffered Katya's tumorous fate.

The calendar had said they were gone 43 days in surface world time. But he knew they had been down at the center of the Earth for over twice that. *The wheel within the wheel*, he thought.

They had all agreed for now that they would keep their expedition secret, at least until Michael finished with all his notes.

Though his friends seemed to want to just forget about it, Michael couldn't let it go. However, the work was proving difficult.

He stared down at the page he had just finished. He was creating an illustration based on his recollection of the pictoglyphs he and Jane had seen on the wall of the gallery ruins in what he thought of as the crystal city.

In his illustration, he displayed a fleet of small ships sailing off into the distance on a blood-red, endless sea.

He sat back, letting his eyes travel to the small broken statue of the humanoid figure on his desk. He still had so many questions that they interrupted his sleep and curiosity still burned within him like at the heart of a furnace.

There was intelligent life down there. *Still* down there. He knew it as keenly as he knew his own name. And there were so many other darker questions—what exactly were those things they encountered on the climb back to the light? He had his suspicions, horrible ones, and he had sent off the rag containing the blood sample of the creature to zoological hematologists and was awaiting the results.

He sat back, his imagination still working. And what of the group that sailed away? Were they like us? Did they find another place to start again? Could they be found?

He had also been examining all the stories he could find, whether just hearsay or not, about cavers disappearing in deep caves, and of new caves in remote places that were considered taboo for containing evil spirits. One thing he had found during his research was that all legends had a kernel of truth at their heart.

He sat brooding for a moment and then slid open his desk drawer and removed the small book wrapped in oilcloth. He carefully opened the leather cover and glanced at the words again.

Saknussov had kept a diary of his time at the center of the Earth, and the things he said he had witnessed made Michael tremble with both excitement and fear at the book's revelations.

Could they all be true? he wondered. Or was sickness, and madness guiding his hand by then?

Michael sighed, closed the diary, and sat back as he knew there were only so many answers to be had on the Earth's surface.

He smiled. Jane had seen the look in his eye and simply held up a finger in front of his face. *Don't*, she had warned.

He folded his arms, ruminating. Explorers enter caves, new caves, in the hope of finding something undiscovered and extraordinary. He had found something so extraordinary that it would change everything they knew about the evolution of the species, their world, and mankind's place in it.

Michael closed his eyes for a moment. *"Don't,"* he whispered.

He slowly opened his eyes and they immediately moved to the picture he had been drawing of the vast pellucid sea and a sky glowing blood red.

Its pull was irresistible.

END

CHECK OUT OTHER GREAT DINOSAUR BOOKS

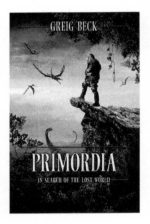

PRIMORDIA
by **Greig Beck**

Ben Cartwright, former soldier, home to mourn the loss of his father stumbles upon cryptic letters from the past between the author, Arthur Conan Doyle and his great, great grandfather who vanished while exploring the Amazon jungle in 1908.

Amazingly, these letters lead Ben to believe that his ancestor's expedition was the basis for Doyle's fantastical tale of a lost world inhabited by long extinct creatures. As Ben digs some more he finds clues to the whereabouts of a lost notebook that might contain a map to a place that is home to creatures that would rewrite everything known about history, biology and evolution.

But other parties now know about the notebook, and will do anything to obtain it. For Ben and his friends, it becomes a race against time and against ruthless rivals.

In the remotest corners of Venezuela, along winding river trails known only to lost tribes, and through near impenetrable jungle, Ben and his novice team find a forbidden place more terrifying and dangerous than anything they could ever have imagined.

PANGAEA EXILES
by **Jeff Brackett**

Tried and convicted for his crimes, Sean Barrow is sent into temporal exile—banished to a time so far before recorded history that there is no chance that he, or any other criminal sent back, has any chance of altering history.

Now Sean must find a way to survive more than 200 million years in the past, in a world populated by monstrous creatures that would rend him limb from limb if they got the chance. And that's just his fellow prisoners.

The dinosaurs are almost as bad.

CHECK OUT OTHER GREAT DINOSAUR BOOKS

FLIPSIDE
by JAKE BIBLE

The year is 2046 and dinosaurs are real.

Time bubbles across the world, many as large as one hundred square miles, turn like clockwork, revealing prehistoric landscapes from the Cretaceous Period.

They reveal the Flipside.

Now, thirty years after the first Turn, the clockwork is breaking down as one of the world's powers has decided to exploit the phenomenon for their own gain, possibly destroying everything then and now in the process.

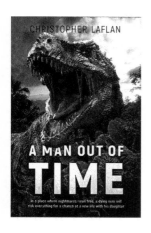

A MAN OUT OF TIME
by Christopher Laflan

Five years after the Chinese Axis detonated an unknown weapon of mass destruction off the southern coast of the United States, Special Ops Sergeant John Crider and the members of Shadow Company have finally captured what they all hope will lead to the end of the war. Unfortunately, the population within the United States is no longer sustainable. In an effort to stabilize the economy, the government enacts the Cryonics Act. One hundred years in suspended animation, all debt forgiven, and a chance at a less crowded future are too good to pass up for John and his young daughter.

Except not everything always goes as planned as Sergeant John Crider finds himself pitted against a land of prehistoric monsters genetically resurrected from the fossil record, murderous inhabitants, and a future he never wanted.

CHECK OUT OTHER GREAT DINOSAUR BOOKS

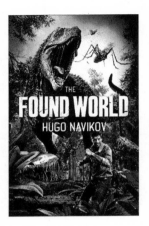

THE FOUND WORLD
by **Hugo Navikov**

A powerful global cabal wants adventurer Brett Russell to retrieve a superweapon stolen by the scientist who built it. To entice him to travel underneath one of the most dangerous volcanoes on Earth to find the scientist, this shadowy organization will pay him the only thing he cares about: information that will allow him to avenge his family's murder.

But before he can get paid, he and his team must enter an underground hellscape of killer plants, giant insects, terrifying dinosaurs, and an army of other predators never previously seen by man.

At the end of this journey awaits a revelation that could alter the fate of mankind ... if they can make it back from this horrifying found world.

HOUSE OF THE GODS
by **Davide Mana**

High above the steamy jungle of the Amazon basin, rise the flat plateaus known as the Tepui, the House of the Gods. Lost worlds of unknown beauty, a naturalistic wonder, each an ecology onto itself, shunned by the local tribes for centuries. The House of the Gods was not made for men.

But now, the crew and passengers of a small charter plane are about to find what was hidden for sixty million years.

Lost on an island in the clouds 10.000 feet above the jungle, surrounded by dinosaurs, hunted by mysterious mercenaries, the survivors of Sligo Air flight 001 will quickly learn the only rule of life on Earth: Extinction.

Made in the USA
Monee, IL
26 October 2022

16593516R00132